THE
DESERT VALLEY

I0617622

JACKSON GREGORY

1st WORLD
LIBRARY
Literary Society

The Desert Valley

Jackson Gregory

© 1st World Library, 2007
PO Box 2211
Fairfield, IA 52556
www.1stworldlibrary.com
First Edition

LCCN: 2007924140

Softcover ISBN: 978-1-4218-4279-0
Hardcover ISBN: 978-1-4218-4181-6
eBook ISBN: 978-1-4218-4377-3

Purchase *"The Desert Valley"*
as a traditional bound book at:
www.1stWorldLibrary.com/purchase.asp?ISBN=978-1-4218-4279-0

1st World Library is a literary, educational organization
dedicated to:

- Creating a free internet library of downloadable ebooks

- Hosting writing competitions and offering book
publishing scholarships.

Interested in more 1st World Library books?
contact: literacy@1stworldlibrary.com
Check us out at: www.1stworldlibrary.com

1st World Library Literary Society

Giving Back to the World

"If you want to work on the core problem, it's early school literacy."

- James Barksdale, former CEO of Netscape

"No skill is more crucial to the future of a child, or to a democratic and prosperous society, than literacy."

- Los Angeles Times

Literacy... means far more than learning how to read and write... The aim is to transmit... knowledge and promote social participation."

- UNESCO

"Literacy is not a luxury, it is a right and a responsibility. If our world is to meet the challenges of the twenty-first century we must harness the energy and creativity of all our citizens."

- President Bill Clinton

"Parents should be encouraged to read to their children, and teachers should be equipped with all available techniques for teaching literacy, so the varying needs and capacities of individual kids can be taken into account."

- Hugh Mackay

CONTENTS

THE DESERT

Over many wide regions of the south-western desert country of Arizona and New Mexico lies an eternal spell of silence and mystery. Across the sand-ridges come many foreign things, both animate and inanimate, which are engulfed in its immensity, which frequently disappear for all time from the sight of men, blotted out like a bird which flies free from a lighted room into the outside darkness. As though in compensation for that which it has taken, the desert from time to time allows new marvels, riven from its vitals, to emerge.

Though death-still, it has a voice which calls ceaselessly to those human hearts tuned to its messages: hostile and harsh, it draws and urges; repellent, it profligately awards health and wealth; inviting, it kills. And always it keeps its own counsel; it is without peer in its lonesomeness, and without confidants; it heaps its sand over its secrets to hide them from its flashing stars.

You see the bobbing ears of a pack-animal and the dusty hat and stoop shoulders of a man. They are symbols of mystery. They rise briefly against the skyline, they are gone into the grey distance. Something beckons or something drives. They are lost to human sight, perhaps to human memory, like a couple of chips drifting out into the ocean. Patient time may witness their return; it is still likely that soon another incarnation will have closed for man and beast, that they will have left to mark their passing a few glisteningly white bones, polished untiringly by tiny sand-chisels in the grip of the desert winds.

They may find gold, but they may not come in time to water. The desert is equally conversant with the actions of men mad with gold and mad with thirst.

To push out along into this immensity is to evince the heart of a brave man or the brain of a fool. The endeavour to traverse the forbidden garden of silence implies on the part of the agent an adventurous nature. Hence it would seem no great task to catalogue those human beings who set their backs to the gentler world and press forward into the naked embrace of this merciless land. Yet as many sorts and conditions come here each year as are to be found outside.

Silence, ruthlessness, mystery—these are the attributes of the desert. True, it has its softer phases—veiled dawns and dusks, rainbow hues, moon and stars. But these are but tender blossoms from a spiked, poisonous stalk, like the flowers of the cactus. They are brief and evanescent; the iron parent is everlasting.

Jackson Gregory

CHAPTER I

A BLUEBIRD'S FEATHER

In the dusk a pack-horse crested a low-lying sand-ridge, put up its head and sniffed, pushed forward eagerly, its nostrils twitching as it turned a little more toward the north, going straight toward the water-hole. The pack was slipping as far to one side as it had listed to the other half an hour ago; in the restraining rope there were a dozen intricate knots where one would have amply sufficed. The horse broke into a trot, blazing its own trail through the mesquite; a parcel slipped; the slack rope grew slacker because of the subsequent readjust-ment; half a dozen bundles dropped after the first. A voice, thin and irritable, shouted 'Whoa!' and the man in turn was briefly outlined against the pale sky as he scrambled up the ridge. He was a little man and plainly weary; he walked as though his boots hurt him; he carried a wide, new hat in one hand; the skin was peeling from his blistered face. From his other hand trailed a big handkerchief. He was perhaps fifty or sixty. He called 'Whoa!' again, and made what haste he could after his horse.

A moment later a second horse appeared against the sky, following the man, topping the ridge, passing on. In silhouette it appeared no normal animal but some weird monstrosity, a misshapen body covered everywhere with odd wart-like excres-cences. Close by, these unique growths resolved them-selves into at least a score of canteens and water-bottles of many shapes and sizes, strung together with bits of rope.

Undoubtedly the hand which had tied the other knots had constructed these. This horse in turn sniffed and went forward with a quickened pace.

Finally came the fourth figure of the procession. This was a girl. Like the man, she was booted; like him, she carried a broad hat in her hand. Here the similarity ended. She wore an outdoor costume, a little thing appropriate enough for her environment. And yet it was peculiarly appropriate to femininity. It disclosed the pleasing lines of a pretty figure. Her fatigue seemed less than the man's. Her youth was pronounced, assertive. She alone of the four paused more than an instant upon the slight eminence; she put back her head and looked up at the few stars that were shining; she listened to the hushed voice of the desert. She drew a scarf away from her neck and let the cooling air breathe upon her throat. The throat was round; no doubt it was soft and white, and, like her whole small self, seductively feminine.

Having communed with the night, the girl withdrew her gaze from the sky and hearkened to her companion. His voice, now remarkably eager and young for a man of his years, came to her clearly through the clumps of bushes.

'It is amazing, my dear! Positively. You never heard of such a thing. The horse, the tall, slender one, ran away, from me. I hastened in pursuit, calling to him to wait for me. It appeared that he had become suddenly refractory: they do that sometimes. I was going to reprimand him; I thought that it might be necessary to chastise him, as sometimes a man must do to retain the mastery. But I stayed my hand. The animal had not run away at all! He actually knew what he was doing. He came straight here. And what do you think he discovered? What do you imagine brought him? You would never guess.'

'Water?' suggested the girl, coming on.

Something of the man's excitement had gone from his voice when he answered. He was like a child who has propounded a riddle that has been too readily guessed.

'How did you know?'

'I didn't know. But the horses must be thirsty. Of course they would go straight to water. Animals can smell it, can't they?'

'Can they?' He looked to her inquiringly when she stood at his side. 'It is amazing, nevertheless. Positively, my dear,' he added with a touch of dignity.

The two horses, side by side, were drinking noisily from a small depression into which the water oozed slowly. The girl watched them a moment abstractedly, sighed and sat down in the sand, her hands in her lap.

'Tired, Helen?' asked the man solicitously.

'Aren't you?' she returned. 'It has been a hard day, papa.'

'I am afraid it has been hard on you, my dear,' he admitted, as his eyes took stock of the drooping figure. 'But,' he added more cheerfully, 'we are getting somewhere, my girl; we are getting somewhere.'

'Are we?' she murmured to herself rather than for his ears. And when he demanded 'Eh?' she said hastily: 'Anyway, we are doing something. That is more fun than growing moss, even if we never succeed.'

'I tell you,' he declared forensically, lifting his hand for a gesture, 'I know! Haven't I demonstrated the infallibility of my line of action? If a man wants to—to gather cherries, let him go to a cherry tree; if he seeks pearls, let him find out the favourite habitat of the pearl oyster; if he desires a—a hat, let him go to the hatter's. It is the simplest thing in the world, though fools have woven mystery and difficulty about it. Now—'

'Yes, pops.' Helen sighed again and saw wisdom in rising to her feet. 'If you will begin unpacking I'll make our beds. And I'll get the fire started.'

'We can dispense with the fire,' he told her, setting to work with the first knot to come under his fingers. 'There is coffee in the thermos bottle and we can open a tin of potted chicken.'

'The fire makes it cosier,' Helen said, beginning to gather twigs. Last night coyotes had howled fearsomely, and even dwellers of the cities know that the surest safeguard against a ravening beast is a camp-fire. For a little while the man strove with his tangled rope; she was lost to him through the mesquite. Suddenly she came running back.

'Papa,' she whispered excitedly. 'There's some one already here.'

She led him a few paces and pointed, making him stoop to see. Under the tangle of a thin brush patch he made out what she had seen. But a short distance from the spot they had elected for their camp site was a tiny fire blazing merrily.

'Ahem,' said Helen's father, shifting nervously and looking at his daughter as though for an explanation of this oddity. 'This is peculiar. It has an air of—of—'

'Why, it is the most natural thing in the world,' she said swiftly. 'Where would you expect to find a camp-fire if not near a spring?'

'Yes, yes, that part of it is all right,' he admitted grudgingly. 'But why does he hold back and thereby give one an impression of a desire on his part for secrecy? Why does he not come forward and make himself known? I do not mean to alarm you, my dear, but this is not the way an honest fellow-wayfarer should behave. Wait here for me; I shall investigate.' Intrepidly he walked toward the fire. Helen kept close to his side.

Jackson Gregory

'Hello!' he called, when they had taken a dozen steps. They paused and listened. There was no reply, and Helen's fingers tightened on his arm. Again he looked to her as though once more he asked the explanation of her; the look hinted that upon occasion the father leaned on the daughter more than she on him. He called again. His voice died away echoless, the silence seeming heavier than before. When one of the horses behind them, turning from the water, trod upon a dry twig, both man and girl started. Then Helen laughed and went forward again.

Since the fire had not lighted itself, it merely bespoke the presence of a man. Men had no terror to her. In the ripe fullness of her something less than twenty years she had encountered many of them. While with due modesty she admitted that there was much in the world that she did not know, she considered that she 'knew' men.

The two pressed on together. Before they had gone far they were greeted by the familiar and vaguely comforting odours of boiling coffee and frying bacon. Still they saw no one. They pushed through the last clump of bushes and stood by the fire. On the coals was the black coffee-pot. Cunningly placed upon two stones over a bed of coals was the frying-pan. Helen stooped instinctively and lifted it aside; the half-dozen slices of bacon were burned black.

'Hello!' shouted the man a third time, for nothing in the world was more clear than that whoever had made the fire and begun his supper preparations must be within call. But no answer came. Meantime the night had deepened; there was no moon; the taller shrubs, aspiring to tree proportions, made a tangle of shadow.

'He has probably gone off to picket his horse,' said Helen's father. 'Nothing could be more natural.'

Helen, more matter-of-fact and less given to theorizing, looked about her curiously. She found a tin cup; there was no bed, no pack, no other sign to tell who their neighbour might be. Close by the spot where she had set down the frying-pan she noted a second spring. Through an open space in the stunted desert growth the trail came in from the north. Glancing northward she saw for the first time the outline of a low hill. She stepped quickly to her father's side and once more laid her hand on his arm.

'What is it?' he asked, his voice sharpening at her sudden grip.

'It's—it's spooky out here,' she said.

He scoffed. 'That's a silly word. In a natural world there is no place for the supernatural.' He grew testy. 'Can I ever teach you, Helen, not to employ words utterly meaningless?'

But Helen was not to be shaken.

'Just the same, it is spooky. I can feel it. Look there.' She pointed. 'There is a hill. There will be a little ring of hills. In the centre of the basin they make would be the pool. And you know what we heard about it before we left San Juan. This whole country is strange, somehow.'

'Strange?' he queried challengingly. 'What do you mean?'

She had not relaxed her hand on his arm. Instead, her fingers tightened as she suddenly put her face forward and whispered defiantly:

'I mean *spooky*!'

'Helen,' he expostulated, 'where did you get such ideas?'

'You heard the old Indian legends,' she insisted, not more than half frightened but conscious of an eerie influence of the still loneliness and experiencing the first shiver of excitement as she stirred her own fancy. 'Who knows but there is some foundation for them?'

Jackson Gregory

He snorted his disdain and scholarly contempt.

'Then,' said Helen, resorting to argument, 'where did that fire come from? Who made it? Why has he disappeared like this?'

'Even you,' said her father, quick as always to join issue where sound argument offered itself as a weapon, 'will hardly suppose that a spook eats bacon and drinks coffee,'

'The—the ghost,' said Helen, with a humorous glance in her eyes, 'might have whisked him away by the hair of the head!'

He shook her hand off and strode forward impatiently. Again and again he shouted 'Hello!' and 'Ho, there! Ho, I say!' There came no answer. The bacon was growing cold; the fire burning down. He turned a perplexed face towards Helen's eager one.

'It is odd,' he said irritably. He was not a man to relish being baffled.

Helen had picked up something which she had found near the spring, and was studying it intently. He came to her side to see what it was. The thing was a freshly-peeled willow wand, left upright where one end had been thrust down into the soft earth. The other end had been split; into the cleft was thrust a single feather from a bluebird's wing.

Helen's eyes looked unusually large and bright. She turned her head, glancing over her shoulder.

'Some one was here just a minute ago,' she cried softly. 'He was camping for the night. Something frightened him away. It might have been the noise we made. Or—what do you think, papa?'

'I never attempt to solve a problem until the necessary data are given me,' he announced academically.

'Or,' went on Helen, at whose age one does not bother about

such trifles as necessary data, 'he may not have run away at all. He may be hiding in the bushes, listening to us. There are all kinds of people in the desert. Don't you remember how the sheriff came to San Juan just before we left? He was looking for a man who had killed a miner for his gold dust.'

'You must curb a proclivity for such fanciful trash.' He cleared his throat for the utterance. He put out his hand and Helen hastily slipped her own into it. Silently they returned to their own camp site, the girl carrying in her free hand the wand tipped with the bluebird feather. Several times they paused and looked back. There was nothing but the glow of the dwindling fire and the sweep of sand, covered sparsely with ragged bushes. New stars flared out; the spirit of the night descended upon the desert. As the world seemed to draw further and further away from them, these two beings, strange to the vastness engulfing them, huddled closer together. They spoke little, always in lowered voices. Between words they were listening, awaiting that which did not come.

CHAPTER II

SUPERSTITION POOL

Physically tired as they were, the night was a restless one for both Helen and her father. They ate their meal in silence for the most part, made their beds close together, picketed their horses near by and said their listless 'good nights' early. Each heard the other turn and fidget many times before both went to sleep. Helen saw how her father, with a fine assumption of careless habit, laid a big new revolver close to his head.

The girl dozed and woke when the pallid moon shone upon her face. She lifted herself upon her elbow. The moonlight touched upon the willow stick she had thrust into the sand at her bedside; the feather was upright and like a plume. She considered it gravely; it became the starting-point of many romantic imaginings. Somehow it was a token; of just exactly what, to be sure, she could not decide. Not definitely, that is; it was always indisputable that the message of the bluebird is one of good fortune.

A less vivid imagination than Helen's would have found a tang of ghostliness in the night. The crest of the ridge over which they had come through the dusk now showed silvery white; white also were some dead branches of desert growth—they looked like bones. Always through the intense silence stirred an indistinguishable breath like a shiver. Individual bushes assumed grotesque shapes; when she looked long and intently at one she began to fancy that it moved. She scoffed at herself, knowing that she was lending aid to tricking her own senses, yet her heart beat a wee bit faster. She gave her mind to large considerations: those of infinity, as her eyes were lifted heavenward and dwelt upon the brightest star; those of life and death, and all of the mystery of mysteries. She went to sleep struggling with the ancient problem: 'Do the dead return? Are there, flowing about us, weird, supernatural influences as potent and intangible as electric currents?' In her sleep she continued her interesting investigations, but her dreaming vision explained the evening's problem by showing her the camp-fire made, the bacon and coffee set thereon, by a very nice young man with splendid eyes.

She stirred, smiled sleepily, and lay again without moving; after the fashion of one awakening she clung to the misty frontiers of a fading dream-country. She breathed deeply, inhaling the freshness of the new dawn. Then suddenly her eyes flew open, and she sat up with a little cry; a man who would have fitted well enough into any fancy-free maiden's dreams was standing close to her side, looking down at her. Helen's hands flew to her hair.

Plainly—she read that in the first flashing look—he was no less astounded than she. At the moment he made a picture to fill the eye and remain in the memory of a girl fresh from an Eastern City. The tall, rangy form was garbed in the picturesque way of the country; she took him in from the heels of the black boots with their silver spurs to the top of his head with its amazingly wide black hat. He stood against a sky rapidly filling to the warm glow of the morning. His horse, a rarely perfect creation even in the eyes of one who knew little of fine breeding in animals, stood just at its master's heels, with ears pricked forward curiously.

Helen wondered swiftly if he intended to stand there until the sun came up, just looking at her. Though it was scarcely more than a moment that he stood thus, in Helen's confusion the time seemed much longer. She began to grow ill at ease; she felt a quick spurt of irritation. No doubt she looked a perfect

Jackson Gregory

fright, taken all unawares like this, and equally indisputably he was forming an extremely uncomplimentary opinion of her. It required less than three seconds for Miss Helen to decide emphatically that the man was a horrible creature.

But he did not look any such thing. He was healthy and brown and boyish. He had had a shave and haircut no longer ago than yesterday and looked neat and clean. His mouth was quite as large as a man's should be and now was suddenly smiling. At the same instant his hat came off in his big brown hand and a gleam of downright joyousness shone in his eyes.

'Impudent beast!' was Helen's quick thought. She had given her mind last night a great deal less to matters of toilet than to mystic imaginings; it lay entirely in the field of absurd likelihood that there was a smear of black across her face.

'My mistake,' grinned the stranger. 'Guess I'll step out while the stepping's good and the road open. If there's one sure thing a man ought to be shot for, it's stampeding in on another fellow's honeymoon. *Adios, senora.*'

'Honeymoon!' gasped Helen. 'The big fool.'

Her father wakened abruptly, sat up, grasping his big revolver in both hands, and blinked about him; he, too, had had his dreams. In the night-cap which he had purchased in San Juan, his wide, grave eyes and sun-blistered face turned up inquiringly; he was worthy of a second glance as he sat prepared to defend himself and his daughter. The stranger had just set the toe of his boot into the stirrup; in this posture he remained, forgetful of his intention to mount, while his mare began to circle and he had to hop along to keep pace with her, his eyes upon the startled occupant of the bed beyond Helen's. He had had barely more than time to note the evident discrepancy in ages which naturally should have started his mind down a new channel for the explanation of the true relationship, when the revolver clutched tightly in unaccustomed fingers went off with an unexpected roar. Dust spouted up a yard beyond the feet of the man who held it. The horse plunged, the stranger went up into the saddle like a flash, and the man dropped his gun to his blanket and muttered in the natural bewilderment of the moment:

'It—it went off by itself! The most amazing—'

The rider brought his prancing horse back and fought with his facial muscles for gravity; the light in his eyes was utterly beyond his control.

'I'd better be going off by myself somewhere,' he remarked as gravely as he could manage, 'if you're going to start shooting a man up just because he calls before breakfast.'

With a face grown a sick white, the man in bed looked helplessly from the stranger to his daughter and then to the gun.

'I didn't do a thing to it,' he began haltingly.

'You won't do a thing to yourself one of these fine days.' remarked the horseman with evident relish, 'if you don't quit carrying that sort of life-saver. Come over to the ranch and I'll swap you a hand-axe for it.'

Helen sniffed audibly and distastefully. Her first impression of the stranger had been more correct than are first impressions nine times out of ten; he was as full of impudence as a city sparrow. She had sat up 'looking like a fright'; her father had made himself ridiculous; the stranger was mirthfully concerned with the amusing possibilities of both of them.

Suddenly the tall man, smitten by inspiration, slapped his thigh with one hand, while with the other he curbed rebellion in his mare and offered the explosive wager:

'I'll bet a man a dollar I've got your number, friends. You are Professor James Edward Longstreet and his little daughter

Helen! Am I right?'

'You are correct, sir,' acknowledged the professor a trifle stiffly. His eye did not rise, but clung in a fascinated, faintly accusing way to the gun which had betrayed him.

The stranger nodded and then lifted his hat for the ceremony while he presented himself.

'Name of Howard,' he announced breezily. 'Alan Howard of the old Diaz Rancho. Glad to know you both.'

'It is a pleasure, I am sure, Mr. Howard,' said the professor. 'But, if you will pardon me, at this particular time of day—'

Alan Howard laughed his understanding.

'I'll chase up to the pool and give Helen a drink of real water,' he said lightly. 'Funny my mare's name should be Helen, too, isn't it?' This directly into a pair of eyes which the growing light showed to be grey and attractive, but just now hostile. 'Then, if you say the word, I'll romp back and take you up on a cup of coffee. And we'll talk things over.'

He stooped forward in the saddle a fraction of an inch; his mare caught the familiar signal and leaped; they were gone, racing away across the sand which was flung up after them like spray.

'Of all the fresh propositions!' gasped Helen.

But she knew that he would not long delay his return, and so slipped quickly from under her blanket and hurried down to the water-hole to bathe her hands and face and set herself in order. Her flying fingers found her little mirror; there wasn't any smudge on her face, after all, and her hair wasn't so terribly unbecoming that way; tousled, to be sure, but then, nice, curly hair can be tousled and still not make one a perfect hag. It *was* odd about his mare being named Helen. He must have thought the name pretty, for obviously he and his horse were both intimate and affectionate. 'Alan Howard.' Here, too, was rather a nice name for a man met by chance out in the desert. She paused in the act of brushing her hair. Was she to get an explanation of last night's puzzle? Was Mr. Howard the man who had lighted the other fire?

The professor's taciturnity was of a pronounced order this morning. Now and then as he made his own brief and customarily untidy toilet, he turned a look of accusation upon the big Colt lying on his bed. Before drawing on his boots he bestowed upon his toe a long glance of affection; the bullet that had passed within a very few inches of this adjunct of his anatomy had emphasized a toe's importance. He had never realized how pleasant it was to have two big toes, all one's own and unmarred. By the time the foot had been coaxed and jammed down into his new boot the professor's good humour was on the way to being restored; a man of one thought at the time, due to his long habit of concentration, his emotion was now one of a subdued rejoicing. It needed but the morning cup of coffee to set him beaming upon the world.

Alan Howard's sudden call: 'Can I come in now, folks?' from across a brief space of sand and brush, found Professor Longstreet on his knees feeding twigs to a tiny blaze, and hastened Helen through the final touches of her dressing. Helen was humming softly to herself, her back to him, her mind obviously concentrated upon the bread she was slicing, when the stranger swung down from his saddle and came forward. He stood a moment just behind her, looking at her with very evident interest in his eyes.

'How do you like our part of the world?' he asked friendliwise.

Helen ignored him briefly. Had Mr. Alan Howard been a bashful young man of the type that reddens and twists its hat in big nervous hands and looks guilty in general. Miss Helen Longstreet would have been swiftly all that was sweet and kind to him. Now, however, from some vague reason or clouded instinct, she was prepared to be as stiff as the fanged stalk of a cactus. Having ignored him the proper length of time, she replied coolly:

'Father and I are very much pleased with the desert country. But, may I ask just why you speak of it as your part of the world rather than ours? Are we trespassing, pray?' The after-thought was accompanied by an upflashing look that was little less than outright challenge.

'Trespassing? Lord, no,' conceded Howard heartily. 'The land is wide, the trail open at both ends. But you know what I meant.'

Helen shrugged and laid aside the half-loaf. Since she gave him no answer, Howard went on serenely:

'I mean a man sort of acquires a feeling of ownership in the place in which he has lived a long time. You and your father are Eastern, not Western. If I came tramping into your neck of the woods—you see I call it *yours*. Right enough, too, don't you think, professor?'

'In a way of speaking, yes,' answered the professor. 'In another way, no. We have given up the old haunts and the old way of living. We are rather inclined, my dear young sir, to look upon this as our country, too.'

'Bully for you!' cried Howard warmly. 'You're sure welcome.' His eyes came back from the father to rest upon the daughter's bronze tresses. 'Welcome as a water-hole in a hot land,' he added emphatically.

'Speaking of water-holes,' suggested Longstreet, sitting back upon his boot heels in a manner to suggest the favourite squatting position of the cowboys of whom he and his daughter had seen much during these last few weeks, 'was it you who made camp right over yonder?' He pointed.

Helen looked up curiously for Howard's answer and thus met the eyes he had not withdrawn from her. He smiled at her, a frank, open sort of smile, and thereafter turned to his questioner.

'When?' he asked briefly.

'Last night. Just before we came.'

'What makes you think some one made camp there?'

'There was a fire; bacon was frying, coffee boiling.'

'And you didn't step across to take a squint at your next-door neighbour?'

'We did,' said the professor. 'But he had gone, leaving his fire burning, his meal cooking.'

Howard's eyes travelled swiftly to Helen, then back to her father.

'And he didn't come back?'

'He did not,' said Longstreet. 'Otherwise I should not have asked if you were he.'

Even yet Howard gave no direct answer. Instead he turned his back and strode away to the deserted camp site. Helen watched him through the bushes and noted how he made a quick but evidently thorough examination of the spot. She saw him stoop, pick up frying-pan and cup, drop them and pass around the spring, his eyes on the ground. Abruptly he turned away and pushed through a clump of bushes, disappearing. In five minutes he returned, his face thoughtful.

'What time did you get here?' he asked. And when he had his answer he pondered it a moment before he went on: 'The gent didn't leave his card. But he broke camp in a regular blue-blazes hurry; saddled his horse over yonder and struck out the shortest way toward King Canon. He went as if the devil himself and his one best bet in hell hounds was running at his stirrups.'

'How do you know?' queried Longstreet's insatiable curiosity. 'You didn't see him?'

'You saw the fire and the things he left stewing,' countered Howard. 'They spelled hurry, didn't they? Didn't they shout into your ears that he was on the lively scamper for some otherwhere?'

'Not necessarily,' maintained Longstreet eagerly. 'Reasoning from the scant evidence before us, a man would say that while the stranger may have left his camp to hurry on, he may on the other hand have just dodged back when he heard us coming and hidden somewhere close by.'

Again Howard pondered briefly.

'There are other signs you did not see,' he said in a moment. 'The soil where he had his horse staked out shows tracks, and they are the tracks of a horse going some from the first jump. Horse and man took the straightest trail and went ripping through a patch of mesquite that a man would generally go round. Then there's something else. Want to see?'

They went with him, the professor with alacrity, Helen with a studied pretence at indifference. By the spring where Helen had found the willow rod and the bluebird feather, Howard stopped and pointed down.

'There's a set of tracks for you,' he announced triumphantly. 'Suppose you spell 'em out, professor; what do you make of them?'

The professor studied them gravely. In the end he shook his head.

'Coyote?' he suggested.

Howard shook his head.

'No coyote,' he said with positiveness. 'That track shows a foot four times as big as any coyote's that ever scratched fleas. Wolf? Maybe. It would be a whopper of a wolf at that. Look at the size of it, man! Why, the ugly brute would be big enough to scare my prize shorthorn bull into taking out life insurance. And that isn't all. That's just the front foot. Now look at the hind foot. Smaller, longer, and leaving a lighter imprint. All belonging to the same animal.' He scratched his head in frank bewilderment. 'It's a new one on me,' he confessed frankly. Then he chuckled. 'I'd bet a man that the gent who left on the hasty foot just got one squint at this little beastie and at that had all sorts of good reasons for streaking out.'

A big lizard went rustling through a pile of dead leaves and all three of them started. Howard laughed.

'We're right near Superstition Pool!' he informed them with suddenly assumed gravity. 'Down in Poco Poco they tell some great tales about the old Indian gods going man-hunting by moonlight. *Quien sabe*, huh?'

Professor Longstreet snorted. Helen cast a quick, interested look at the stranger and one of near triumph upon her father.

'I smell somebody's coffee boiling,' said the cattleman abruptly. 'Am I invited in for a cup? Or shall I mosey on? Don't be bashful in saying I'm not wanted if I'm not.'

'Of course you are welcome,' said Longstreet heartily. But Howard turned to Helen and waited for her to speak.

'Of course.' said Helen carelessly.

CHAPTER III

PAYMENT IN RAW GOLD

'You were merely speaking by way of jest, I take it, Mr. Howard,' remarked Longstreet, after he had interestedly watched the rancher put a third and fourth heaping spoonful of sugar in his tin cup of coffee. 'I refer, you understand, to your hinting a moment ago at there being any truth in the old Indian superstitions. I am not to suppose, am I, that you actually give any credence to tales of supernatural influences manifested hereabouts?'

Alan Howard stirred his coffee meditatively, and after so leisurely a fashion that Longstreet began to fidget. The reply, when finally it came, was sufficiently non-committal.

'I said "*Quien sabe?*" to the question just now,' he said, a twinkle in the regard bestowed upon the scientist. 'They are two pretty good little old words and fit in first-rate lots of times.'

'Spanish for "Who knows?" aren't they?'

Howard nodded. 'They used to be Spanish; I guess they're Mex by now.'

Longstreet frowned and returned to the issue.

'If you were merely jesting, as I supposed—'

'But was I?' demanded Howard. 'What do I know about it? I know horses and cows; that's my business. I know a thing or two about men, since that's my business at times, too; also something like half of that about half-breeds and mules; I meet up with them sometimes in the run of the day's work. You know something of what I think you call auriferous geology. But what does either of us know of the nightly custom of dead Indians and Indian gods?'

Helen wondered with her father whether there were a vein of seriousness in the man's thought. Howard squatted on his heels, from which he had removed his spurs; they were very high heels, but none the less he seemed comfortably at home rocking on them. Longstreet noted with his keen eyes, altered his own squatting position a fraction, and opened his mouth for another question. But Howard forestalled him, saying casually:

'I have known queer things to happen here, within a few hundred yards of this place. I haven't had time to go finding out the why of them; they didn't come into my day's work. I have listened to some interesting yarns; truth or lies it didn't matter to me. They say that ghosts haunt the Pool just yonder. I have never seen a ghost; there's nothing in raising ghosts for market, and I'm the busiest man I know trying to chew a chunk that I have bitten off. They tell you down at San Juan and in Poco Poco, and all the way up to Tecolote, that if you will come here a certain moonlight night of the year and will watch the water of the pool, you'll see a vision sent up by the gods of the Underworld. They'll even tell you how a nice little old god by the name of Pookhonghoya appears now and then by night, hunting souls of enemies—and running by the side of the biggest, strangest wolf that human eyes ever saw.'

Helen looked at him swiftly. He had added the last item almost as an afterthought. She imagined that he had embellished the old tale from his own recent experience, and, further, that Mr. Alan Howard was making fun of them and was no adept in the science of fabrication.

Jackson Gregory

'They go further,' Howard spun out his tale. 'Somewhere in the desert country to the north there is, I believe, a tribe of Hidden People that the white man has never seen. The interesting thing about them is that they are governed by a young and altogether maddeningly pretty goddess who is white and whose name is Yahoya. When they come right down to the matter of giving names,' he added gravely, 'how is a man to go any further than just say, "*Quien sabe?*"'

'That is stupid.' said Longstreet irascibly. 'It's a man's chief affair in life to *know*. These absurd legends—'

'Don't you think, papa,' said Helen coolly, 'that instead of taxing Mr. Howard's memory and—and imagination, it would be better if you asked him about our way from here on?'

Howard chuckled. Professor Longstreet set aside his cup, cleared his throat and agreed with his daughter.

'I am prospecting,' he announced, 'for gold. We are headed for what is known as the Last Ridge country. I have a map here.'

He drew it from his pocket, neatly folded, and spread it out. It was a map such as is to be purchased for fifty cents at the store in San Juan, showing the main roads, towns, waterholes and trails. With a blue pencil he had marked out the way they planned to go. Howard bent forward and took the paper.

'We are going the same way, friend,' he said as he looked up. 'What is more, we are going over a trail I know by heart. There is a good chance I can save you time and trouble by making it a party of three. Am I wanted?'

'It is extremely kind of you,' said Longstreet appreciatively. 'But you are on horseback and we travel slowly.'

'I can spare the time,' was the even rejoinder. 'And I'll be glad to do it.'

During the half-hour required to break camp and pack the two horses, Alan Howard gave signs of an interest which now and then mounted almost to high delight. He made no remark concerning the elaborate system of water-bottles and canteens, but his eyes brightened as he aided the professor in making them fast. When the procession was ready to start he strode on ahead, leading his own horse and hiding from his new friends the widening grin upon his face.

The sun was up; already the still heat of the desert was in the air. Behind the tall rancher and his glossy mare came Professor Longstreet driving his two pack animals. Just behind him, with much grave speculation in her eyes, came Helen. A new man had swum all unexpectedly into her ken and she was busy cataloguing him. He looked the native in this environment, but for all that he was plainly a man of her own class. No illiteracy, no wild shy awkwardness marked his demeanour. He was as free and easy as the north wind; he might, after all, be likeable. Certainly it was *courtois* of him to set himself on foot to be one of them. The mare looked gentle despite her high life; Helen wondered if Alan Howard had thought of offering her his mount?

They had come to the first of the low-lying hills.

'Miss Longstreet,' called Howard, stopping and turning, 'wouldn't you like to swing up on Sanchia? She is dying to be ridden.'

The trail here was wide and clearly defined; hence Longstreet and his two horses went by and Helen came up with Howard. Hers was the trick of level, searching eyes. She looked steadily at him as she said evenly:

'So her name is Sanchia?'

For an instant the man did not appear to understand. Then suddenly Helen was treated to the sight of the warm red seeping up under his tan. And then he slapped his thigh and

Jackson Gregory

laughed; his laughter seeming unaffected and joyous.

'Talk about getting absent-minded in my old age,' he declared. 'Her name did use to be Sanchia; I changed it to Helen. Think of my sliding back to the old name.'

Helen's candid look did not shift for the moment that she paused. Then she went on by him, following her father, saying merely:

'Thank you, I'll walk. And if she were mine I'd keep the old name; Sanchia suits her exactly.'

But as she hurried on after her father she had time for reflection; plainly the easy-mannered Mr. Alan Howard had renamed his mare only this very morning; as plainly as had he in the first place called her Sanchia in honour of some other friend or chance acquaintance. Helen wondered vaguely who the original Sanchia was. To her imagination the name suggested a slim, big-eyed Mexican girl. She found time to wonder further how many times Mr. Howard had named his horse.

They skirted a hill, dipped into the hollow which gave passageway between this hill and its twin neighbour, mounted briefly, and within twenty minutes came to the pool about which legends flocked. From their vantage point they looked down upon it. The sun searched it out almost at the instant that their eyes caught the glint of it. Fed by many hidden springs it was a still, smooth body of water in the bowl of the hills; it looked cool and deep and had its own air of mystery; in its ancient bosom it may have hidden bones or gold. Some devotee had planted a weeping willow here long ago; the great tree now flourished and cast its reflection across its own fallen leaves.

Helen's eyes dreamed and sought visions; the spot touched her with its romance, and she, after the true style of youth, lent aid to the still influences. Alan Howard, to whom this was scarcely other than an everyday matter, turned naturally to the new and was content to watch the girl. As for Longstreet, his regard was busied with the stones at his feet, and thereafter with a washout upon a hill-side where the formation of the hills themselves was laid bare to a scientific eye.

'There's gold everywhere about here,' he announced placidly. 'But not in the quantities I have promised you, Helen. We'll go on to the Last Ridge country before we stop.'

Howard turned from the daughter to consider the father long and searchingly, after the way of one man seeking another's measure.

'As a rule I go kind of slow when it comes to cutting in on another fellow's play,' he said bluntly. 'But I'm going to chip in now with this: I know that Last Ridge country from horn to tail, and all the gold that's in it or has ever been in it wouldn't buy a drink of bad whisky in Poco Poco.'

The light of forensic battle leaped up bright and eager in Longstreet's eyes. But Howard saw it, and before the professor's unshaken positiveness could pour itself forth in a forensic flood the rancher cut the whole matter short by saying crisply:

'I know. And it's up to you. I've shot my volley to give you the right slant and you can play out your string your own way. Right now we'd better be moseying on; the sun's climbing, partner.'

He passed by them, leading his mare toward a crease in the hills which gave ready passage out of the bowl and again to the sweep of the desert. Longstreet dropped in behind him, driving his two horses, while Helen stood a little alone by the pool, looking at it with eyes which still brooded. In her hatband was a bluebird feather; her fingers rose to it reminiscently. A faint, dying breeze just barely stirred the drooping branches of the willow; in one place the graceful pendant leaves merged with their own reflections below, faintly blurring them with the slightest of ripples. Here, in the sunlight, was a languid place of dreams; by mellow, magic moonlight what wonder if there came hither certain of the last remnants and relics of an old superstitious people, seeking visions? And an old saw hath it, 'What ye seek for ye shall find.'

Helen looked up; already Howard had passed out of sight; already her father's two pack horses had followed the rancher's mare beyond the brushy flank of the hill and Longstreet himself would be out of her sight in another moment. She turned a last look upon the still pond and hurried on.

Now again, as upon yesterday and the day before, the desert seemed without limit about them. The hot sun mounted; the earth sweltered and baked and blistered. Heat waves shimmered in the distances; the distances themselves were withdrawn into the veil of ultimate distances over which the blazing heat lay in what seemed palpable strata; crunching rock and gravel in the dry water-courses burned through thick sole-leather; burning particles of sand got into boots and irritated the skin; humans and horses toiled on, hour after hour, from early listlessness to weariness and, before noon, to parched misery. Even Howard, who confessed that he was little used to walking, admitted that this sort of thing made no great hit with him. During the forenoon he again offered his mount to Helen; when she sought to demur and hoped to be persuaded, he suggested a compromise; they would take turns, she, her father and himself. By noon, when they camped for lunch and a two hours' rest, all three had ridden.

Barely perceptibly the sweeps about them had altered during the last hour before midday. Here and there were low hills dotted occasionally by trees, covered with sparse dry grass. Here, said Howard, were the outer fringes of the grazing land; his cattle sometimes strayed as far as this. The spot chosen for nooning was a suspicion less breathlessly hot; there was a sluggish spring ringed about with wiry green grass and shaded by a clump of mongrel trees.

Helen ate little and then lay down and slept. Longstreet, his knees gathered in his arms, his back to a tree, sat staring thoughtfully across the billowing country before them; Howard smoked a cigarette, stood a moment looking curiously down at the weary figure of the girl, and then strode off to the next shade for his own siesta.

'Rode pretty well all night,' he explained half apologetically to Longstreet as he went. 'And haven't walked this much since last time.'

Between two and three they started on again. It grew cooler; constantly as they went forward the earth showed growing signs of fertility and, here and there, of moisture guarded and treasured under a shaggy coat of herbage. Within the first hour they glimpsed a number of scattered cattle and mules; once Helen cried out at the discovery of a small herd of deer browsing in a shaded draw. Then came a low divide; upon its crest was an outcropping of rock. Here Howard waited until his two companions came up with him; from here he pointed, sweeping his arm widely from north to east and south of east.

'The Last Ridge country, yonder,' he said.

They saw it against the north-eastern horizon. From the base of the hills on which they stood a broad valley spread out generously. Marking the valley's northern boundary some half-dozen miles away, thrown up against the sky like a bulwark, was a long broken ridge like a wall of cliff, an embankment stained the many colours of the south-west; red it looked in streaks and yellow and orange and even lavender and pale elusive green. It swept in a broad, irregular curve about the further level lands; it was carved and notched along its crest into strange shapes, here thrusting upward in a single needle-like tower, there offering to the clear sky a growth like a monster toadstool, again notched into saw-tooth edges.

'And here,' said Howard, his voice eloquent of his pride of ownership, 'my valley lands. From Last Ridge to the hills across yonder, from those hills as far as you can see to the south, mile after mile of it, it's mine, by the Lord! That is,' he amended with a slow smile under Helen's amazed eyes, 'when I get it all paid for! And there,' he continued, pointing this time to something white showing through the green of a grove upon a meadow land far off toward the southern rim of the valley, 'there is home. You'll know the way; I'm only twelve or fifteen miles from the Ridge, and so, you see, we're next-door neighbours.'

To Helen, as she gazed whither his finger led, came a strange, unaccustomed thrill. For the first time she felt the glory, and forgot the discomfort, of the hot sun and the hot land. There was a man's home; set apart from the world and yet sufficient unto itself; here was a man's holding, one man's, and it was as big and wide as a king's estate. She looked swiftly at the tall man at her side; it was his or would be his. And he need not have told her; what she had read in the timbre of his voice she saw written large in his eyes; they were bright with the joy of possession.

'Neighbours, folks,' he was saying. 'So let's begin things in neighbourly style. Come on home with me now; stick over a day or so resting up. Then I'll send a wagon and a couple of the boys over to the ridge with you and they'll lend you a hand at digging in for the length of your stay. It's the sensible thing,' he insisted argumentatively as he saw how Longstreet's gaze grew eager for the Ridge. 'And I'd consider it an honour, a high honour.'

'You are extremely kind, sir,' said Longstreet hesitatingly. 'But—'

'Come on,' cut in Howard warmly, his hand on the older man's shoulder. 'Just as a favour to me, neighbour. Every-thing's plain out our way; nothing fancy. But I've got clean beds to sleep in and the kitchen store-room's full and—Why, man, I've even got a bathtub! Come ahead; be a sport and take a chance.'

Longstreet smiled; Helen watched him questioningly. Suddenly she realized that she was a trifle curious about Alan Howard; bath and clean beds did tempt her weary body, and besides there would be a certain interest in looking in upon the stranger's establishment. She wondered for the first time if there were a young Mrs. Howard awaiting him?

'How about it, Helen?' asked her father. 'Shall we accept further of this gentleman's kindness?'

'If we were sure,' hesitated Helen, 'that we would not be imposing—'

So it was settled, and Howard, highly pleased, led the way down into the valley. Making the gradual descent their trail, well marked now by the shod hoofs of horses, wound into a shady hollow. In the heart of this where there was a thin trickle of water Howard stopped abruptly. Helen, who was close to him, heard him mutter something under his breath and in a new tone of wrath. She looked at him wondering. He strode across the stream and stopped again; he stooped and she saw what he had seen; he straightened up and she saw blazing anger in his eyes.

Here, no longer ago than yesterday, a yearling beef had been slaughtered; the carcass lay half hidden by the bushes.

'Now who the hell did that for me?' cried out the man angrily. 'Look here; he's killed a beef for a couple of steaks. He's taken that and left the rest for the buzzards. The low-down, hog-hearted son of a scurvy coyote.'

Helen held back, frightened at what she read in his face. Her father came up with her and demanded:

'What is it? What's wrong?'

'Some one has killed one of his cows,' she whispered, catching hold of his arm. 'I believe he would kill the man who did it.'

Howard was looking about him for signs to tell whence the marauder had come, whither gone. He picked up a fresh rib bone, that had been hacked from its place with a heavy knife and then gnawed and broken as by a wolf's savage teeth. He noted something else; he went to it hurriedly. Upon a conspicuous rock, held in place by a smaller stone, was a small rawhide pouch. It was heavy in his palm; he opened it and poured its contents into his palm. And these contents showed to Longstreet and Helen, looking at them wonderingly.

'The gent took what he wanted, but he paid for it,' he said slowly, 'in enough raw gold to buy half a dozen young beeves! That's fair enough, isn't it? The chances are he was in a hurry.'

'Maybe,' suggested Helen quickly, 'he was the same man whose camp fire we found. *He* was in a hurry.'

Howard pondered but finally shook his head. 'No; that man had bacon and coffee to leave behind him. It was some other jasper.'

Longstreet was absorbed in another interest. He took the unminted gold into his own hands, fingering it and studying it.

'It is around here everywhere, my dear,' he told Helen with his old placid assurance. 'It is quite as I have said; if you want fish, look for them in the sea; if you seek gold, not in insignificant quantities, but in a great, thick, rich ledge, come out toward the Last Ridge country.'

He returned the raw metal to Howard, who dropped it into its bag and the bag into his pocket. Silent now as each one found company in his own thoughts, they moved down the slope and into the valley.

CHAPTER IV

IN DESERT VALLEY

The world is an abiding-place of glory. He who cannot see it dyed and steeped in colourful hues owes it to his own happiness to gird up his loins and move on into another of the splendid chambers of the vast house God has given us; if the daily view before him no longer offers delight, it is merely and simply because his eyes have grown accustomed to what lies just before them and are wearied with it. For, after all, one but requires a complete change of environment to quicken eye and interest, to fill again the world with colour. Thus, put the man of the sea in the heart of the mountains and he stares about him at a thousand little things which pass unnoted under the calm eyes of the mountaineer. Or take up the dweller of the heights and set him aboard a wind-jammer bucking around the Horn and he will marvel at a sailor's song or the wide arc of a dizzy mast. So Helen Longstreet now, lifted from a college city of the East and set down upon the level floor of the West; so, in the less nervous way of greater years, her father.

The three were full two hours in walking from the base of the hills to Howard's ranch headquarters. Continuously the girl found fresh interests leaping into her quick consciousness. They waded knee-deep in lush grass of a meadow into which Howard had brought water from the hills; among the grass were strange flowers, red and yellow and blue, rising on tall stalks to lift their heads to the golden sun. From the grass rose birds, startled by their approach, one whirring away voicelessly

Jackson Gregory

from a hidden nest, another, a yellow and black-throated lark, singing joyously. They crossed the meadow and came up the swelling slope of a gentle hill; upon its flatfish top were oaks; in the shade of the oaks three black-and-white cows looked with mild, approving eyes upon their three tiny black-and-white calves. With the pictured memory unfading, Helen's eyes were momentarily held by an eagle balancing against the sky; the great bird, as though he were conscious that he held briefly centre stage, folded his wings and dropped like a falling stone; a ground squirrel shrilled its terror through the still afternoon and went racing with jerking tail toward safety; the great bird saw the frantic animal scuttle down a hole and unfolded its wings; again it balanced briefly, close to the ground; then in a wide spiral reascended the sky.

Came then wide fields with cattle browsing and drowsing; it was the first time Helen had harkened to a bellowing bull, the first time she had seen one of his breed with bent head pawing up grass and earth and flinging them over the straight line of his perfect back; she sensed his lusty challenge and listened breathlessly to the answering trumpet call from a distant, hidden corral. She saw a herd of young horses, twenty of them perhaps, racing wildly with flying manes and tails and flaring nostrils; a strangely garbed man on horseback raced after them, shot by them, heading them off, a wide loop of rope hissing above his head. She saw the rope leap out, seeming to the last alive and endowed with the will of the horseman; she heard the man laugh softly as the noose tightened about the slender neck of one of the fleeing horses.

'That's Gaucho,' said Howard. 'He's my horse breaker.'

But already the girl's interests had winged another way. Within ten steps they had come to a new view from a new vantage point. From some trick of sweep and slope the valley seemed more spacious than before; through a natural avenue in an oak grove they saw distinctly the still distant walls of the ranch house; the sun touched them and they gleamed back a spotless white. Helen was all eagerness to come to the main building;

from afar, here of late having seen others of its type, she knew that it would be adobe and massive, old and cloaked with the romance of another time; that even doors and windows, let into the thick walls, would be of another period; that somewhere there would be a trellis with a sprawling grape-vine over it; that no doubt in the yard or along the fence would be the yellow Spanish roses.

Below the house they came to the stable. Here Howard paused to tie the three horses, but not to unpack or unsaddle.

'I haven't anybody just hanging around to do things like this for me,' he said lightly as he rejoined his guests. 'Not until I get the whole thing paid off. What men I've got are jumping on the job from sun-up to dark. I'll turn you loose in the house and then look after the stock myself.'

They passed several smaller outbuildings, some squat and ancient-looking adobes, others newer frame buildings, all neatly whitewashed. And then the home itself. Quite as Helen had provisioned, there was a low wooden fence about the garden; over the gateway were tangled rose vines disputing possession with a gnarled grape; the walk from the gate was outlined with the protruding ends of white earthen bottles, so in vogue in the southland a few years ago; a wide, coolly-dark veranda ran the length of the building; through three-feet-thick walls the doorways invited to further coolness. Howard stood aside for them to enter. They found underfoot a bare floor; it had been sprinkled from a watering pot earlier in the afternoon. The room was big and dusky; a few rawhide-bottomed chairs, a long rough table painted moss-green, some shelves with books, furnished the apartment. At one end was a fireplace.

Howard tossed his hat to the table and opened a door at one end of the room. Before them was a hallway; a few steps down were two doors, one on each hand, heavy old doors of thick slabs of oak, hand-hewn and with rough iron bands across them, top and bottom, the big nail heads showing. Howard threw one open, then the other.

'Your rooms,' he said. 'Yours, Miss Helen, opens upon the bath. You'll have to go down the hall to wash, professor. Make yourselves free with the whole house. I'll feed the horses and be with you in three shakes.'

Before his boot heels had done echoing through the living-room it was an adventure to Helen to peep into her room. She wondered what she was going to find. Thus far she had had no evidence of a woman upon the ranch. She knew the sort of housekeeper her father had demonstrated himself upon occasions when she had been away visiting; she fully counted upon seeing the traces of a man's hand here. But she was delightfully surprised. There was a big, old-fashioned walnut bed neatly made, covered in smooth whiteness by an ironed spread. There was a washstand with white pitcher like a ptarmigan in the white nest of a bowl, several towels with red bands towards their ends flanking it. There was a little rocking-chair, a table with some books. The window, because of the thickness of the wall, offered an inviting seat whence one could look into the tangle of roses of the *patio*.

'It is like a dream,' cried Helen. 'A dream come true.'

She glanced into her father's room. It was like hers in its neatness and appointments, but did not have her charming outlook. She was turning again into her own room when she heard Howard's voice outside.

'Angela,' he was calling, 'I have brought home friends. You will see that they have everything. There is a young lady. I am going to the stable.'

She heard Angela's mumbled answer. So there was, after all, at least one woman at the ranch. Helen awaited her expectantly, wondering who and what she might be. Then through her window she saw Angela come shuffling into the *patio*. She was an old woman, Mexican or Indian, her hair grey and black in streaks, her body bent over her thumping stick and wrapped in a heavy shawl. Never had Helen seen such night-black, fathomless, inscrutable eyes; never had she looked upon a face so creased and lined or skin so like dry, wrinkled parchment.

Angela pounded across the floor looking like a witch with her great stick, and waved a bony hand to indicate the bathroom. Catching her first glimpse of Longstreet, who came to his daughter's door, she demanded:

'Your papa?'

'Yes,' Helen answered her.

'You frien's Senor Alan?' And when Helen, hesitating briefly, said 'Yes,' Angela asked:

'You come from Santa Rita, *no*?'

'No,' said Helen. 'From San Juan and beyond.'

'You come far,' mumbled Angela. She scrutinized the girl keenly. Then abruptly, 'Senor Alan got *muchos amigos* to-day. Senor Juan Carr comes; El Joven with him.'

Helen asked politely who these two were Juan Carr and El Joven. But the old woman merely shook her head and relapsed into silence frankly studying her. The girl was glad of the interruption when Howard rapped at the door. His arms were full of bundles.

'I've brought everything I could find that looked like your and your father's personal traps,' he informed her as he came in and put the things down on the floor. 'I looked in at the kitchen and figure it out we've got about twenty or thirty minutes before dinner. Come on, Angela; give Miss Longstreet a chance to get ready.'

Angela transferred her scrutiny to him; Howard laughed at her

Jackson Gregory

good-humouredly, laid his hand gently on her shrunken shoulder and side by side they went out.

Helen went singing into her bath, her weary body rested by the thought of coolness and cleanliness and a change of clothing. Little enough did she have in the way of clothing, especially for an evening when she was to meet still other strangers. But certain feminine trinkets had come with her journeying across the desert, and a freshly laundered wash dress and a bit of bright ribbon work wonders. When she heard voices in the *patio*, that of Alan Howard and of another man, this a sonorous bass, she was ready. She went to her father's door; Longstreet was in the final stages of his own toilet-making, his face red and shiny from his towelling, his sparse hair on end, his whole being in that condition of bewildering untidiness which comes just before the ultimate desired orderliness quite as the thick darkness before the dawn. In this case the rose fingers of Aurora were Helen's own, patting, pulling and readjusting. Within three minutes she slipped her hand through the arm of a quiet scholarly looking gentleman and together they paced sedately into the *patio*.

Howard jumped up from a bench and dragged forward his friend John Carr, introducing him to his new friends. And in employing the word friend and repeating it, he spoke it as though he meant it. Here was a characteristic of the man; he was ready from dawn until dark to put out his big square hand to the world and bring the world home to his home for supper and bed and all that both connote.

But Helen's interest, at least for the flitting moment, was less for him than for his friend; Howard she had known since dawn, hence hers had been ample time to assign him his proper place in her human catalogue. Now she turned her level eyes upon the new man. Immediately she knew that if Alan Howard were an interesting type, then no less so, though in his own way, was John Carr. A bigger man, though not so tall; an older man by something like half a dozen years, but still young in the eyes and about the clean-shaven mouth; a man with clear, unwinking bluish-grey eyes and a fine head carried erect upon a massive brown throat. Carr was dressed well in a loose serge suit; he wore high-topped tan boots; his soft shirt was of good silk; his personality exuded both means and importance. He glanced at Longstreet and looked twice or three times as long at Longstreet's daughter. Helen was quite used to that, and it was for no particular reason that she felt her colour heighten a little. She slipped her hand through her father's arm again and they went in to supper. Howard, having indicated the way, clapped Carr upon the thick shoulders and the two friends brought up the rear.

Helen was still wondering where was the second guest; Angela had distinctly mentioned Juan Carr and another she termed El Joven. Yet as they passed from the *patio* into the big cool dining-room with its white cloth and plain service and stiff chairs, she saw no one here. Nor did she find any answer in the number of places set, but rather a confused wonder; the table was the length of the long room, and, at least in so far as number of plates went, suggested a banquet.

Howard drew out chairs at one end of the table so that the four sat together.

'The boys will be rolling in for supper in half an hour,' he explained. 'But you folks are hungry and will want to get to bed early, so we are not waiting for them.'

The 'boys' were, supposedly, the men he had working for him; there must be close to a score of them. And they all ate at one table, master and men and guests when he had them.

'Who is El Joven?' asked Helen.

Howard looked puzzled; then his face cleared.

'Angela told you El Joven was here, too?' And to Carr: 'He came with you, John?'

Jackson Gregory

Carr nodded. Howard then answered Helen.

'That's Angela's pet name for him; it means The Youngster. It is Barbee, Yellow Barbee the boys call him. He's one of John's men. They say he's a regular devil-of-a-fellow with the ladies, Miss Helen. Look out he doesn't break your heart.'

Angela peered in from the kitchen and withdrew. They heard her guttural utterance, and thereafter a young Indian boy, black of eyes, slick of plastered hair and snow-white of apron, came in bringing the soup. Howard nodded at him, saying a pleasant '*Que hay, Juanito?*' The boy uncovered the rare whiteness of his splendid teeth in a quick smile. He began placing the soup. Helen looked at him; he blushed and withdrew hastily to the kitchen.

Throughout the meal the four talked unconstrainedly; it was as though they had known one another for a dozen years and intimately. Longstreet, having pushed aside his soup plate, engaged his host in an ardent discussion of the undeveloped possibilities of the Last Ridge country; true, he had never set foot upon it, but he knew the last word of this land's formation and geological construction, its life history as it were. All of his life, he admitted freely, he had been a man of scholarship and theory; the simplest thing imaginable, he held blandly, was the demonstration of the correctness of his theories. Meantime Helen talked brightly with John Carr and listened to Carr's voice.

And a voice well worth listening to it was. Its depth was at once remarkable and pleasing. At first one hearkened to the music of the rich tone itself rather than to the man's words, just as one may thrill to the profound cadences of a deep voice singing without heeding the words of the song. But presently she found herself giving her rapt attention to Carr's remarks. Here again was one of her own class, a man of quiet assurance and culture and distinction; he knew Boston and he knew the desert. For the first time since her father had dragged her across the continent on his hopelessly mad escapade, Helen felt that after all the East was not entirely remote from the West. Men like Howard and his friend John Carr, types she had never looked to find here, linked East and West.

Juanito, with lowered, bashful eyes, brought coffee, ripe olives from the can, potato salad, and thick, hot steaks. Soon thereafter the boys began to straggle in. Helen heard them at the gate, noisy and eager; for them the supper hour was diurnally a time of a joyous lift of spirit. They clattered along the porch like a crowd of schoolboys just dismissed; they washed outside by the kitchen door with much splashing; they plastered their hair with the common combs and brushes and entered the shortest way, by the kitchen. They called to each other back and forth; there was the sound of a tremendous clap as some big open hand fell resoundingly upon some tempting back and a roar from the stricken and a gale of booming laughter from the smiter and the scuffle of boots and the crashing of two big bodies falling. Then they came trooping in until fifteen or twenty had entered.

One by one Howard introduced them. Plainly none of them knew of Helen's presence; all of their eyes showed that. Among them were some few who grew abashed; for the most part they ducked their heads in acknowledgment and said stiffly, 'Pleased to meet you,' in wooden manner to both Longstreet and his daughter. But their noisiness departed from them and they sat down and ate in business-like style.

Never had Helen sat down with so rough a crowd. They were in shirt sleeves; some wore leathern wrist guards; their vests were open, their shirts dingy, they were unshaven and their hair grew long and ragged; they brought with them a smell of horses. There was one man among them who must have been sixty at the least, a wiry, stoop, white-haired, white-moustached Mexican. There were boys between seventeen and nineteen. There were Americans; at least one Swede; a Scotchman; several who might have been any sort of mixture of southern bloods. And among them all Helen knew at once, upon the instant that he swaggered in, El Joven,

Yellow Barbee.

The two names fitted him as his two gloves may fit a man's hands; among the young he was The Youngster, as among blondes he was Yellow Barbee. His dress was extravagantly youthful; his boots bore the tallest heels, he was full-panoplied as to ornate wristbands and belt and chaps as though in full holiday attire; one might wager on the fact of his hat on a nail outside being the tallest crowned, the widest brimmed. His face was like a girl's for its smoothness and its prettiness; his eyes were like blue flowers of sweet innocence; on his forehead his hair was a cluster of little yellow ringlets. And yet he managed full well to convey the impression that he was less innocent than insolent, a somewhat true impression; for from high heels to finger-tips he was a downright, simon-pure rascal.

Yellow Barbee's eyes fairly invaded Helen's as he jerked her his bow. They were two youngsters, and in at least, and perhaps in at most, one matter they were alike: she prided herself that she 'knew' men, and to Barbee all women were an open, oft-read book.

Plainly Barbee was something of a favourite here; further, being a visitor, he was potentially of interest to the men who had not been off the ranch for matters of weeks and months. When Alan Howard and the professor picked up their conversation, and again Helen found herself monopolized by John Carr, from here and there about the table came pointed remarks to Yellow Barbee. Helen, though she listened to Carr and was never unconscious of her father and Howard, understood, after the strange fashion of women, all that was being said about her. Early she gathered that there was, somewhere in the world, a dashing young woman styled the 'Widow.' Further, she had the quick eyes to see that Barbee blushed when an old cattle-man with a roguish eye cleared his throat and made aloud some remark about Mrs. Murray. Yes; Barbee the insolent, the swaggering, the worldly-wise and conceited Barbee, actually blushed.

Though the hour was late it was not yet dark when the meal was done. Somehow Howard was at Helen's side when they went to the living-room and out to the front porch; Carr started with them, hesitated and held back, finally stepping over for a word with an old Mexican. Helen noted that Barbee had moved around the table and was talking with her father. As she and Howard found chairs on the porch, Longstreet and Barbee passed them and went out, talking together.

CHAPTER V

THE GOOD OLD SPORT

The Longstreets remained several days upon Desert Valley Ranch, as the wide holding had been known for half a century. Also John Carr and his young retainer, Yellow Barbee, prolonged their stay. It appeared that Carr had come over from some vague place still further toward the east upon some matter of business connected with the sale of this broad acreage; Carr had owned the outfit and managed it personally for a dozen years, and now was selling to Alan Howard. It further devolved that Barbee had long been one of Carr's best horsemen, hence a favourite of Carr, who loved good horses, and that he had accompanied his employer merely to help drive over to the ranch a small herd of colts which had been included in the sale but had not until now been delivered. Carr was a great deal with Howard, and Howard managed to see a great deal of the Longstreets; as for Barbee, Helen met his insolent young eyes only at mealtimes.

'My business is over,' Carr confessed to Helen in the *patio* the next morning. 'There's no red tape and legal nonsense between Al and me. To sell a ranch like this, when you know the other chap, is like selling a horse. But,' and his eyes roved from his cigar to a glimpse through an open door of wide rolling meadows and grazing stock, 'I guess I'm sort of home-sick for it. If it was to do over I don't know that I'd sell it this morning.'

Helen had rested well last night; this morning she had thrilled anew to the world about her. She thought that she had never seen such a sunrise; the day appeared almost to come leaping and shouting up out of the desert; the air of the morning, before the heat came, was nothing less than glorious. Her eyes were bright; there was the flush of joyousness in her cheeks.

'How a man could own this,' she said slowly, 'and then could sell it—' She shook her head and looked at him half wonderingly. 'I don't see how you could do it.'

'You feel that way about it, too?' He brought his eyes back soberly to his cigar.

Howard, whose swinging stride Helen had learned to know already, came out from the living-room, hat in hand, carrying a pair of spurs he had been tinkering with.

'What are you talking about?' he laughed. 'Somebody dead?'

'Miss Longstreet was saying,' Carr said quietly, his eyes still grave, 'that she couldn't understand a man selling an outfit like this, once he had called it his own.'

'Good for you, Miss Helen,' cried Howard heartily. 'I am with you on that. John, there, must have been out of his senses when he let me talk him out of Desert Valley.'

'I don't know but that I was,' said Carr.

Howard looked at him swiftly, and swiftly the light in his eyes altered. For Carr had spoken thoughtfully and soberly, and there was no hint of jest in the man.

'You don't mean, John,' said Alan, a trifle uncertainly, 'that you are sorry you let go? That you are not satisfied—'

Carr appeared to be considering the matter as though it were enwrapped in his cigar. He took ample time in replying, so much time, in fact, that Helen found herself growing impatient for his reply.

'Suppose I were sorry?' he said finally. 'Suppose I were not satisfied? Then what? The deal is made, and a bargain, old-timer, is a bargain.'

Now it was Howard's turn for silence and sober eyes. He looked intently into his friend's face; then with a lingering affection across his broad lands.

'Not between friends,' he said. 'Not between friends like you and me, John. I've hardly got my hooks into it; you had it long enough for it to get to be a part of you. If you made a mistake in selling, if you know it now—' He shrugged and smiled. 'Why, of course it doesn't mean as much to me as to you, and anyway, it's yours until I get all my payments made, and if you say the word—'

'Well?' asked Carr steadily.

'Why,' cried Howard, 'we'll frame a new deal this very minute and you can take it over again!'

'You'd do that for me, Al?'

'You're damned well right, I would!' cried Howard heartily. And Helen understood that for the moment at least he had forgotten that she was present.

A slow smile came into Carr's eyes.

'That's square shooting, Long Boy.'—he spoke more impe-tuously than Helen had thought the man could—'but I never went back on a play yet, did I? I'm just sort of homesick for the old place, that's all. Forget it.' He slapped Howard upon the shoulder, the two friends' eyes met for a moment of utter understanding and he went on down to the stable, calling back, 'I'm going to take the best horse you've got—that would be Bel and no other—and ride. So long.'

'So long,' answered Howard.

Carr gone from sight, Howard stood musing a moment, unconscious of Helen's wondering eyes upon him. Then he turned to her and began speaking of his friend: big and generous and manly was Carr; a man to tie to, and, though he did not say it in so many words, a man to die for. He explained how Carr had taken the old Diaz ranch that had been Spanish and then Mexican in its time and had made it over into what it was, the greatest stock run north of the Rio Grande and west of the Mississippi. Helen's interest was ready and sympathetic, and Howard passed from one point to another until he had sketched the way in which the ranch had been sold to him. And the girl, though she knew little enough about business methods, was startled to learn how these two men trusted each other. She recalled what Carr had said; between him and Howard a deal involving many thousands of dollars was as simple a matter as the sale of a horse. The two, riding together, had in a few words agreed upon price and terms. They had returned to the house and Howard had written a cheque for seven thousand dollars as first payment; all of his ready cash, he admitted freely, saving what he must keep on hand for ranch manipulation. There was no deed given, no deed of trust, no mortgage. It was understood that Howard should pay certain sums at certain specified dates; each man had jotted down his memoranda in his own hand; the deal was made.

'But,' gasped Helen, 'if anything unforeseen should happen? If—if he should die? Or you? If—'

'In any case there would be one of us left, wouldn't there?' he countered in his off-hand way. 'Unless we both went out, and then what difference? He has no one to look out for; neither have I. Besides,' he laughed carelessly, 'John and I both plan on being on the job a good fifty years from now. Come out here and I'll show you a real horse.'

She went with him to the porch. Carr was leaving the stable, riding Bel. Helen knew little enough of horseflesh and yet she understood that here was an animal to catch anyone's eye; yes, and Carr, sitting massive and stalwart in the saddle, was a man to hold any woman's. The horse was a big, bright bay; mane and tail were like fine gold; the sun winked back from them and from the glorious reddish hide. Carr saw them and waved his hat; Bel danced sideways and whirled, and for an instant stood upon his rear legs, his thin, aristocratic forelegs flaying the air. Then came Carr's deep bass laugh; the polished hoofs struck the ground and they were off, flashing away across the meadowlands.

'Some day,' said Helen, her eyes sparkling, 'I want to ride a horse like that!' She turned to him, asking eagerly, 'Could I learn?'

'If with all my heart I wanted to be a first-rate Philadelphia lawyer or a third-rate San Francisco politician,' he announced with that sweeping positiveness which was one of his characteristics, 'I'd consider the job done to start with! All you've got to do is to want a thing, want it hard, and it's as good as yours. Now, to begin with, you love a horse. The rest is easy.'

Helen saw her father, accompanied by young Barbee, emerge from behind the stable, and sighed.

'I don't believe you know what failure means,' she said.

'There isn't any such bird,' he laughed at her.

'Not really.'

'Then,' her eyes still upon the pair talking together by the stable door, 'dear old dad should find his gold-mine. He wants it with all his heart, Heaven knows. And he has the faith that is supposed to move mountains.'

Howard scratched his head. Within the few hours he had come

to like the old professor, for Longstreet, though academic, was a straight-from-the-shoulder type of man, one of no subterfuges. And yet he did not greatly inspire confidence; he was not the type that breathes efficiency.

'Tell me about him,' Howard urged. 'What makes him so dead certain he can nail his Golconda out here? I take it he has never been out this way before, and that he doesn't know a whole lot of our part of the country.'

Confidence inspires confidence. Howard had hardly finished sketching for her his own plans and hopes; he had gone succinctly and openly into detail concerning his deal with John Carr. Now Helen, glad to talk with some one, answered in kind.

'The University elected a young president, a New Broom,' she said bitterly. 'He is a man of more ambition than brains. His slogan is "Young Men." He ousted father together with a dozen other men of his age. I thought father's heart would be broken; he had devoted all of the years of his life, all of his best work, to his University. But instead he was simply enraged! Can you imagine him in a perfectly towering rage?'

Howard grinned. 'Go ahead,' he chuckled. 'He's a good old sport and I like him.'

'Well,' said Helen, without meeting his smile, 'father and I went into business session right away. We had never had much money; father had never cared for wealth measured in money; had always been richly content with his professor's salary; had never saved or asked me to save. When the thing happened, all we had in the world was a little over seven hundred dollars. I was right away for economizing, for managing, for turning to some other position. But father, I tell you, was in a perfect rage. When I mentioned finances to him he got up and shouted. "Money!" he yelled at me. "What's money? Who wants money? It's a fool's game to get money; anybody can do it." When he saw that I doubted he told me to pack up that very day and he'd show me; he'd show the world. The new University man named him an old fogy, did he? He'd show him. Didn't he know more than any other man living about geology? About the making of the earth and the minerals of the earth? Was it any trick to find gold? Not in the dribbles, but such a mine as never a miner drove a pick into yet?'

She sighed again and grew silent. Howard, toying idly with the spurs in his hands, could at the moment find nothing to say.

'Dear old pops,' she said more softly in a moment. 'I am afraid that his heart-breaking time is coming now—when he learns that it isn't so easy to find gold, after all.'

'No,' said Howard slowly. 'No. It doesn't break a man's heart, for he is always sure that it is coming the next day and the next and the next. I've known them to go on that way until they died, and then know in their hearts that they'd make a strike the next day—if only the Lord would spare them twenty-four hours more.'

'I wanted father to bank our money,' went on Helen, her eyes darkening. 'I wanted to go to work, to earn something. I can teach. But he wouldn't hear of it. He said—he said that if the time had come when he couldn't support his own daughter it was high time he was dead.'

Howard nodded his understanding. 'He's a good sport, I tell you,' he maintained warmly. 'And I like him. Who knows but that he may make his ten-strike here after all? Or,' as he marked the droop of the girl's mouth and understood how she must be thinking of how little was left of their pittance, he added briskly, 'this is a better place than the East any day; there are more chances. If a man is the right sort there is always a chance for him. If you want to teach— Well, we've got schools out here, haven't we?'

Helen's eyes rounded at him. 'Have you? Where?'

'And bully good schools,' he insisted. 'There's the Big Springs school not over ten miles off, over that way. You could have a job there to-morrow, if you said the word.'

Her eyes brightened. 'There is a vacancy, then?'

'Well,' he admitted, 'I'm not so sure about that. There's a teacher there, I believe. But,' and now it was his eyes that brightened, 'it could be fixed somehow. Just leave it to John and me.'

She laughed at him and all her gaiety came surging back.

'Here I've been drawing a face a mile long,' she cried lightly, 'when everything's all right as far as I can see in all directions. I am going down to see what father is up to; he and Mr. Barbee look to me like a couple of youngsters plotting trouble.'

A look of understanding flashed between Yellow Barbee and Professor Longstreet as the two came down from the ranch-house. Thereafter Longstreet beamed upon his daughter while Yellow Barbee, his hat far back upon the blonde cluster of curls, turned his insolent eyes upon her. Helen, deeming him overbold, sought to 'squelch' him with a look. Instead she saw both mirth and admiration shining in the baby-blue eyes. She turned her back upon El Joven, who retaliated by turning his back upon her and swaggering away into the stable, whistling through his teeth as he went. Howard went with him for his horse.

'Papa,' said Helen after the stern fashion which in time comes natural to the girl with a wayward father, 'what are you two up to?'

'My darling,' said Longstreet hurriedly, 'what do you mean?'

'I mean you and that young scamp. He's bad, papa; bad all the way through. And you, you dear old innocent—'

Longstreet glanced hastily over his shoulder and then frowned at her.

'You mustn't talk that way. He is a remarkably fine young fellow. We are in a new environment, you and I, Helen. We are in Rome and must learn something of the Romans. Now, Mr. Barbee—'

'Is Roman all the way through!' sniffed Helen. 'You just look out that he doesn't lead you into mischief.'

In the stable Howard was saddling two horses, meaning to invite Helen to begin her serious study now. He, too, was interested in the odd friendship which seemed to be growing up so swiftly between two men so utterly unlike. He turned to Barbee to ask a question and saw the young fellow stoop and sweep up something that had fallen into the straw underfoot. Howard's eyes were quick and keen; it was only a flash, but he recognized a ten of spades. He turned back to the latigo he was drawing tight. But before they left the stable he offered carelessly:

'What do you think of the professor, Barbee?'

And Barbee answered joyously:

'He's a reg'lar ring-tailed old he-devil, Al.' He winked brightly. 'One of these days him and me is going to drift down to Tres Pinos. And, say, won't the town know about us?'

'What do you mean?' demanded Howard sharply.

Barbee considered him a thoughtful moment. Then he shrugged.

'Oh, nothing,' he said.

CHAPTER VI

THE YOUTHFUL HEART

To both Helen and her father, tarrying at Desert Valley Ranch, the long, still, hot days were fraught with much new interest. Life was new and golden, viewed from this fresh viewpoint. Helen had come hitherward from her city haunts with trepidation; even Longstreet, serenely optimistic regarding the ultimate crown of success to his labour, was genuinely delighted. The days passed all too swiftly.

As can in no way be held reprehensible in one of her age and maidenly beauty and charm, Helen's interest had to do primarily with men, two men. They, quite as should be in this land of novelty, were unlike the men she had known. With each passing hour Helen came to see this more clearly. She was a bright young woman, alert and with at least a modicum of scientific mental attitude inherited from the machinery of her father's brain. Like any other healthy young animal, she wanted to know whys and wherefores and the like.

The evening of their first day, alone in her room for an hour before bed, she settled for herself the first difference between these men of the desert fringes and the men she had known at home. To begin with, she reviewed in mind her old acquaintances: there were a half-dozen professors, instructors, assistants who called infrequently on her father and whom she had come to know with a degree of familiarity. The youngest of them had been twenty years older than Helen, and, whereas

Jackson Gregory

her father was always an old dear, sometimes a hopeless and helpless old dear, they were simply old fogies. They constituted, however, an important department in her male friends; the rest were as easily catalogued. They were the young college men—men in name only, boys in actuality. They were of her own age or two or four years older or a year younger. They danced and made mysterious references to the beer they had wickedly drunk; they motored in their fathers' cars and played tennis in their fathers' flannels when they fitted; no doubt they were men in the making, but to judge them as men already was like looking prematurely into the oven to see how the bread was doing; they were still under-baked. So far they were playing with the game of life; life, herself, had not yet taken them seriously, had not reached out the iron hand that eventually would seize them by the back of the neck, the slack of the trousers, and pitch them out into the open arena.

Helen was considerably pleased with the result of her meditations: her father's academic friends had held back behind college walls and thus had never come out into the scrimmage that makes men; her own young friends had not yet reached the time when they would buckle on their armour and mount and talk lance in hand. Alan Howard and John Carr were men who for a number of years had done man's work out in the open, no doubt giving and receiving doughty blows. She considered Carr: he had taken a monster outfit like Desert Valley and had made it over, in his own image, like a god working. There were thousands of acres, she had no idea how many. There were cattle and horses and mules; again she thought of them only vaguely as countless. There were many men obeying his orders, taking his daily wage. Carr had mastered a big job and the job had made a masterly man of him. Then had come Alan Howard with vision and determination and courage. He had expended almost his last cent for a first payment upon the huge property; he was risking all that he had gathered of the world's goods, he was out in the open waging his battle like a young king claiming his heritage. Helen clothed the act in the purple and gold of romance and thrilled at her own picture.

'After all,' she discovered, 'there *are* different kinds of men and I never knew men like these two.'

Then, when she thought of Yellow Barbee, she sniffed. Barbee was about her own age; she considered him a mere child and transparent.

She had said good night to her father, but now suddenly in a mood for conversation went out into the hall and tiptoed to his door. When there came no response to her gentle tapping she opened the door and discovered only darkness and emptiness. She was mildly surprised; distinctly she had heard him go into his room and close his door and she had not heard him go out again.

There are men who, though they may live to be a hundred years old, keep always the fresh heart of twenty. James Edward Longstreet was one of them. He was a man of considerable erudition; he had always supposed that the choice had lain entirely with him. He had always been amply content with his existence, had genially considered that the whole of the bright stream of life, gently deflected, had flowed through his college halls and under his calm eyes. Now his youthful soul was in a delightful turmoil; adventures had come to him, more adventures were coming. Men like Barbee had given him the staunch hand of friendship; they had welcomed him as an equal. And something until now untouched, unguessed, that had lived on in his boy's heart, stirred and awoke and thrilled. To-night, with a vague sense of guilt which made the escapade but the more electric, while his daughter had imagined that he was getting himself sedately into his long-tailed, sedate nightgown, he was beaming warmly upon the highly entertained group of ranch hands down in the men's bunk-house, whither, by the way, he had been led by Barbee.

There comes now and then to such an isolation as Desert Valley a boon from the gods in the guise of a tenderfoot. But never tenderfoot, agreed the oldest Mexican with the youngest Texan, like this one. They sat lined in back-tilted chairs about the four walls and studied him with eyes that were at all times appreciative, often downright grave. His ignorance was astounding, his hunger for information amazing. He was a man from Mars who knew all that was to be known in his own world but brought into this strange planet a frank and burning curiosity. Barbee's chaps delighted him; a hair rope awoke in his soul an avaricious hunger for a hair rope of his own; commonplace ranch matters, like branding and marking and breeding and weaning and breaking, evoked countless eager questions. For so academic a man, the strange thing about him was his attitude toward these day labourers; he looked upon them as brothers; not only that, but as older brothers. He forgot his own wisdom in his thirst to partake of theirs. He gave the full of his admiration to a man whom he had seen that day cast a wide loop of rope about the horns of a running steer.

He was making discoveries hand over fist; perhaps therein lay a sufficient reason why the man of science in him was fascinated. True, those discoveries which he made were new only to him; yet one might say the same of America and Columbus. For one thing, it dawned on him that here was a new and excellent technical vocabulary; he stored away in his brain strange words as a squirrel sticks nuts and acorns into a hole. Hondo, tapaderos, bad hombre, tecolote, bronco, maverick, side-winder—rapaciously he seized upon them as bits of the argot of fairyland. He watched the expert roll the brown tube of a cigarette and yearned for the skill; he observed tricks in riding, and there was within him the compelling urge to ride like that; not a trifle escaped his shark-eyes, be it the way the men combed their hair, mounted their horses, or dragged their spurs. To-night and with unhidden elation he accepted Barbee's invitation to 'set in and roll the bones' with them. 'Roll the bones!' When some day he went back home, the owner of the 'greatest little mine this side of the Rockies,' he'd work that off on his old chum, Professor Anstruther. He drew up his chair to the table, piled a jumble of coins in front of him and took into his hands the enticing cubes.

He did not think of it as gambling; he had never gambled, had never wanted to. But he was all alive to join in the amusements of his new friends, to be like them. After all, he was putting up as sorts of markers a few five and ten-cent pieces with an occasional quarter or half-dollar, and to him money had never had much significance. The game was the thing and he found in it from the first a keen mathematical interest. There were five dice; each dice with its six surfaces had six different numbers. While he beamed into the veiled eyes of the old Mexican he was figuring upon the various combinations possible and the likelihood, the theory of chances, of a six or an ace upon the second throw. From the jump the game fascinated him; it is to be questioned, however, if ever before a man knew just the sort of fascination which enthralled him. No matter who won or lost, when the rolling cubes behaved in conformity with the mathematical laws, he fairly sparkled. And in the end he lost only six or seven dollars and did not in the least realize that he had lost a cent. When at last he left to go to bed, all of the eyes in the room followed him. They were puzzled eyes.

'The old boy's all right,' said one man. It was Tod Barstow, an old hand. And he added, nodding, 'He's a damn good loser.'

Barbee chuckled and pocketed his small winnings.

'That's what I'm playing him for, Toddy,' he admitted with his cheerful grin.

In the end the Longstreets went from Desert Valley straight on to the nearest town, that of Big Run, only a dozen miles still east of the ranch. The suggestion came from Longstreet himself, who had had a picturesque account of the settlement from Barbee.

'I estimate,' the professor announced at breakfast, 'that we shall be the matter of two or three months at Last Ridge. What comforts we have there will be the results of our own efforts. Now, though we have brought with us certain of the absolute necessities, there is much in the way of provision and sundries that we should have. Mr. Howard has been so very considerate as to offer us a wagon and horses and even a driver. I think, my dear, that we would do well to drive into Big Run, which I understand is a progressive community with an excellent store. We can get what we require there and the next day return to the Last Ridge.'

Only approval greeted his words. Howard, it appeared, had business in Big Run and would make the trip with them; Carr judged that it was time for him to be clearing out, and his way led through Big Run. So they hurried through breakfast and started.

Tod Barstow handled the reins of the four mules; beside him on the high, rocking seat, sat Longstreet. During his sojourn on the ranch he had acquired a big bright-red bandana hand-kerchief which now was knotted loosely about his sun-reddened throat; the former crease in his big hat had given place to a tall peak: he wore a pair of leather wrist-cuffs which he had purchased from Barbee. Barstow grunted and turned the grunt into a shrill yell directed at his mules; they knew his voice and jammed their necks deep into their collars, taking the road at a run. Longstreet, taken unawares, bounced and came dangerously near toppling off the seat. Then with both hands he clung to the iron guard-rod at the back of the seat and took his joy out of a new mode of travel.

Helen had elected to go on horseback. Howard had brought out for her a pretty little mare, coal-black and slender-limbed, but sufficiently gentle. Barbee, who had been watching, suddenly set his toe in his own stirrup and went up into the saddle, racing on to overtake and pass the wagon. Howard and Carr glanced swiftly at each other; then their eyes went to the girl. Howard helped her to mount and reined in at her right, Carr dropped into place at her left, and so, the three abreast, they followed Barbee.

They rode slowly, and now Howard, now Carr, told her of the points of interest along the trail. When they crossed the lower end of the valley and came to the top of the gentle slope extending along its eastern edge, Helen made a discovery. All these latter days she had thought of the desert as behind her, lying all to the westward. Now she understood how the ranch was aptly named Desert Valley; it was a freak, an oasis, a fertile valley with desert lands to east as well as west, and to north and south. When they had ridden down the far slope of the hills they were once more upon the edges of the solitudes of sand-sweep and sand-ridge and cactus and mesquite and utter drought. Every step their horses took carried them further into a land of arid menace; at the end of the first hour it was difficult to imagine green water-fields only a handful of miles away.

'It's just the water that makes the difference,' Howard told her. 'Isn't it, John?' Carr nodded. 'If a man could get water to put on this land that is burning our horses' fetlocks off right now, he'd have all the crops and stock range he wanted. Why, the bigger part of Desert Valley was like this before John took hold of it; he developed the water, and I've gone on with his work, and look what we've got now!'

'That makes your ranch all the more wonderful!' cried Helen.

Howard's eyes glowed; she noted that they always did when he spoke thus of Desert Valley or when she bespoke her hearty approval of his choice. Something prompted her to turn swiftly to Carr; his head was down; he was frowning at the horn of his saddle; Helen, not devoid of either intuition or tact, changed the conversation. But not before she noted that Howard, too, had looked toward his friend.

Big Run huddled among tall cottonwoods in a shallow hollow. It was blessed with several clear, pure springs, its only blessing. It was self-sufficient, impudent. About it on all sides was the sweep of grey desert; in the shade of its cottonwoods, along its thicket of willows, was a modicum of greenness and coolness; its ugly houses like toads squatting in the shade had an air of jeering at the wastes of sand and scrub. The place was old in years and iniquity. The amazing thing connected with it was that its water could remain pure; one would have thought that through the years even the deathless springs would have been contaminated. Long ago it had been a Hopi camp; in their tongue it was called the 'Half-Way between Here and There.' Later a handful of treacherous devils from below the border had swooped down into the cottonwood hollow. They had dissipated the Indian group, for the sake of robbery and murder. They had squatted by the water-holes, prototypes of the crooked buildings which now recalled them; they had builded the town by the simple device of driving Indian labourers to the task. White men subsequently had come, men of the restless foot, lone prospectors, cattlemen. They had lodged briefly at the hotel which necessity had called into being, had played cards in the adobe of 'Tonio Moraga, had quarrelled with the surly southerners, had now and then shot their way out into the clear starlit night or had known the cruel bite of steel, and in any case had left Big Run as they had found it—a town oddly American in nothing whatever save its name, which had come whence and how no man knew.

First into town that morning rode Yellow Barbee; with no urge to linger and a definite destination ahead, he always rode hard, his hat far back, his blue eyes shining. He sent his lean roan on the run down the crooked street among the crooked houses; he scattered a handful of dirty ducks flopping and scuttling out of his way; he drew after him a noisy barking of dogs, startled out of their sleep in the shade; he brought his horse up with a sharp jerk of the reins before the blue-and-white sign of the saloon; he was half out of the saddle when a glimpse of something down the street altered his intention in a flash; he wheeled his horse, and, with one stirrup flying wildly, his big hat in his hand, his eyes on fire, he went racing back down the street and again stopped with a jerk. This time the sign before him spelled hotel. Leaving his horse to pant and fight flies, Yellow Barbee strode in at the open door.

Next came in due time Tod Barstow and the mule team and Longstreet. They clattered along in clouds of high-puffed dust, harness jingling. Barstow swung his leaders skilfully and narrowly around the broken corners of old adobes and slammed on his brake before the store, that is to say, half-way between saloon and hotel. He climbed down, Longstreet after him.

Finally came the loiterers, Helen and Carr and Howard. They noted Barbee's roan at its hitching-rail; further they glimpsed through a thirsty-looking dusty vine—that which Barbee had glimpsed before them. Some one wearing cool, laundered white was out upon the side porch; Barbee's voice, young and eager, low yet vibrant, bespoke Barbee's proximity to the Someone.

'The widow.' said Carr. He looked at Howard. 'I'll bet you a hat it's Mrs. Murray, Al.'

It was vaguely impressed upon Helen that a significance less casual than the light words themselves lay in Carr's remark. She, too, looked at Howard. There was a frown in his eyes. Slowly, as his look met hers, a flush spread in his cheeks. Carr saw it and laughed amusedly.

'Look out, Al,' he chuckled. 'She'll get you yet.'

Now Howard laughed with him and the flush subsided.

'John thinks he's a great little josher, Miss Helen,' he said lightly. 'No doubt you'll meet Mrs. Murray at lunch; you just watch the way she looks at John Carr!—there's the professor waiting for us. John, I'll lay you a bet of another hat!'

'Well?' asked Carr.

'I'll bet you Jim Courtot has turned up again.'

But Longstreet had sighted them and was out in the road calling to them, and Carr made no answer.

CHAPTER VII

WAITING FOR MOONRISE

For upward of two hours Longstreet and Helen were at the store, making their purchases. Carr said good-bye, promising to look them up at their camp at the ridge by the time they should be ready for callers; he shook hands warmly with the professor, and for a moment stood over Helen, looking steadily into her eyes. She returned his regard frankly and friendlily, but in the end flushed a little. When Carr went out, Howard, saying that he would be back presently, went out with him.

'Two bang-up, square-shooting gents!' cried Longstreet warmly. Helen turned upon him in amazement.

'Papa!' she gasped. 'Where on earth did you get that sort of talk?'

Longstreet smiled brightly.

'Haven't I told you, my dear.' he explained, 'that when in Rome one should learn from the Romans?'

He led the way to the counter. It was heaped high with all sorts of merchandise, dry goods and groceries, and hardware— anything the purchaser might desire from ham and bacon and tinned goods to shirts and overalls, spurs and guns. Behind it stood the proprietor, a slant-eyed, thievish-looking Mexican, while behind him were his untidy shelves—a further jumble of commodities. He looked his approval at the girl, his professional interest at the father.

Longstreet frankly turned out the contents of his purse upon the counter, his ready way of computing their resources and judging the proper cash outlay for the present. The slant eyes grew narrower with speculation.

'One hundred and eighty-odd dollars,' he computed approximately. 'We'll spend about a hundred with you to-day, my friend.'

'*Bueno, senor*,' agreed the Mexican. And he waved to his shelves.

Helen, who knew only too well her father's carelessness in money matters, was not satisfied with an approximate estimate of their resources. She counted carefully.

'You should have had nearer two hundred dollars, pops,' she told him gently. 'Have you felt in all your pockets? I am afraid that you have lost a five or ten-dollar piece.'

He evaded. 'It's of no moment.' he said hastily. 'A few bucks one way or the other won't plug a hole in a 'dobe wall. And this *hombre* is waiting.'

This time Helen did not even gasp. Something had occurred to work havoc with her father's accustomed fine academic speech. This smacked, she thought, of the influence of Barbee.

But soon she forgot this and with it the discrepancy in cash; she had begun to purchase, to barter with the storekeeper, to fairly revel in delights of camp preparations. For, after all, life was not all seriousness, and here, offering itself for the morrow, was a rare lark. A spice of recklessness entered the moment; the dollars went skipping across the counter, and packages and boxes came heaped up in their places.

Jackson Gregory

Howard looked in on them once; they did not see him. He went his way, and still Longstreet made new suggestions and Helen and the Mexican bargained. The first coolness of the late afternoon was stirring, the broad sun had gone down, leaving the land in soft, grateful shadow, something over a hundred dollars had been spent, when with a sigh Helen put the residue of the family fortune into the old purse, and the purse, though reluctantly, into her father's pocket. She did not want to hurt his feelings now; but she really thought that once they were settled in their new home, she ought to employ some tactful method of acquiring custody.

They went down the dusty street arm in arm and in gay spirits. Tod Barstow had driven off to a stable somewhere; the goods were to be called for to-morrow morning; now they could go down to the hotel, to the chairs on the shady porch, and then to dinner. And, thought Helen, with more than a flicker of interest, she would see the 'widow.'

As though she were awaiting them, Mrs. Murray was on the porch. With her was Barbee, who rose promptly and elaborately performed the ceremony of introduction.

'Mr. Longstreet,' he said formally, 'shake hands with my friend, Mrs. Murray. Miss Longstreet, make you acquainted with my friend, Mrs. Murray.'

Mrs. Murray shook hands with them both, exclaiming brightly at her delight. Then, as they all sat down, she and Helen considered each other. Oddly, Helen had known all along that she would not like Mrs. Murray; now, and after the first probing glance, she was prepared for downright dislike. Longstreet, on the other hand, was obviously very favourably impressed. Nor without more than a little to be said on his side of the question. The woman was young, petite, dark and unusually pretty. Her teeth flashed in engaging smiles, her eyes were large and quick and bright; she was all vivacity; her glance could be at one moment limpid, humid, haunting, and at the moment hold a gleam and sparkle of mirth. Even Helen could find no fault with her little travelling suit.

Plain to be read by anyone with a claim to eyesight was Yellow Barbee's devotion; equally plainly decipherable, thought Helen, was the fact of Mrs. Murray's amusement at Barbee's infatuation. It meant nothing to her; she was playing with him as, no doubt, she had played with many another susceptible youngster. Helen was sure she read that in the eyes which the young woman turned now and then upon the languishing young cowboy.

Presently Alan Howard put in his appearance, freshly shaven and shorn, and they all went in together to supper. Helen was unaffectedly glad to see him; she had seen all that she cared to see of Mrs. Murray and something more than that of Barbee. Howard greeted Mrs. Murray casually; she cried a friendly, 'Oh, hello, Al!' and he stepped to Helen's side. Barbee hastened to place his big palm under Mrs. Murray's elbow and steered her, after the approved fashion of the community, in to the table. She allowed him the liberty; but while Barbee's eyes devoured her face, Helen managed to mark that the 'widow' was studying Alan Howard.

At table Alan and Helen found a variety of subjects to interest them; Mrs. Murray stared at them a moment, then shrugged her plump shoulders and made Barbee transcendently happy and miserable by turns; Longstreet ate his dried beef stew abstractedly. Barbee and Mrs. Murray, who finished first, excused themselves and went back to the gathering dusk of the porch, whence her light laughter came now and then trilling back into the dining-room.

'Who is she?' asked Helen, her eyes full upon Howard's.

'Mrs. Murray?' He shrugged. 'That is all I know of her; or that anyone I know knows of her. I don't fancy,' he added coolly, 'that you will like her.'

'I don't,' the girl announced briefly.

'Mind you,' he hurried to continue, 'I don't know a blessed thing against her. I just meant that I didn't think her your kind.'

'Thank you,' Helen replied, accepting the statement as a satisfactory compliment. He laughed. Then he looked toward the professor, whose thoughts were plainly a thousand miles away.

'I've caught an inspiration,' he said softly.

'What is it?' smiled Helen.

There'll be a moon in two or three hours. At best the accommodations here are bad; rooms stuffy and close and hot. If you are not too tired——'

He saw that she understood what he meant, and further that she gave her glad acceptance.

'It will be fun!' she told him. He even detected a something of eagerness in her tone; he had already thought that it would be just he and she this time—they two alone riding together out through the glorious night, chaperoned only by the knowledge that somewhere in the distance behind them the wagon jolted along. He wondered if she, too, had thought of this?

When the three at table finished and went out into the cool of the porch they found only empty chairs; a half-silhouette showed where Barbee leaned against a pepper tree by the roadside. Helen settled herself comfortably, wandering if Mrs. Murray had re-entered the hotel by some side door or if she had business elsewhere. Howard made the suggestion of the return to Desert Valley. Longstreet hesitated, then objected, saying that by now the store would be closed and that the wagon was still to be loaded.

'Tod Barstow will be up at the saloon, probably looking for a game of cribbage,' said Howard. 'It will take me about three shakes to locate him. The store will be open; old Mexican Pete lives in the back. I'll have Tod hitch up at the first peep of the moon; he can load your stuff on in twenty minutes.'

Helen added her voice to Alan's. Longstreet's eyes travelled out to the listless figure against the pepper tree. At the moment Barbee's silhouette disengaged itself from the tree's shadowy trunk and started up the road.

'All right,' said Longstreet. 'But you needn't trouble about looking up Barstow; I'd enjoy the walk. If you and Helen will wait here, I'll see that the wagon is ready about moonrise.' And as though he had just remembered an important engagement, he hurried away.

They saw him overtake Barbee; they heard his cheerful voice, and then a surly rejoinder from the boy. Then, far across the sky, a star fell and their eyes went to it together and they fell silent. When the brief silence was gone, and they talked in lowered voices, they had both forgotten Longstreet and Barbee. And, for one, Alan Howard was in no haste for the rising moon.

CHAPTER VIII

POKER AND THE SCIENTIFIC MIND

Barbee, as he himself would have expressed it, was soured on life. At least for the moment, and after all that is about all that life is, the instant that it is passing. When Longstreet called to him he grunted in disgust. He shoved his hands deeper into his pockets and spat out the cold stump of his cigarette. It was Barbee's natural way to swing along with his hat far back, so that he might see the stars. Now his hat brim was dragged low, and for Barbee the stars were only less remote and frigid than a certain fickle woman.

'I say, Barbee,' called the professor a second time.

Barbee slumped on without turning, but growled over his shoulder:

'Can't you leave a man alone?'

Longstreet doubted his ears; the boy had been so friendly. He tried hurriedly and in vain to recall some trifle in which perhaps, being misunderstood, he had offended. During his mental uncertainty the natural physical hesitancy had resulted in Barbee's gaining a lead of a dozen steps. Hence when a white figure flitted out from the shadows to the boy's side, Longstreet was not near enough to hear the whispered words; the soft trill of a laugh he caught, to be sure, and immediately recognized as Mrs. Murray's. Then she had drawn away from

Barbee, called good night and passed on to the hotel, so close to Longstreet that her skirts brushed him. Barbee stood still watching her until she disappeared under the porch vines. Longstreet came on to his side then. They fell into step and again Barbee was swaggering with his old buoyancy; again his hat was far back, and his eyes were on the stars.

'Hello, old sport,' he said affably. 'Some night, ain't it?'

To know why a man of the type of James Edward Longstreet should be flattered at being called 'old sport' by one of the type of Yellow Barbee is to understand human nature; Longstreet was utterly human. The bonds of environment are bands of steel; the little boy that close to threescore years ago was Johnny Longstreet had been restricted by them, his growth had been that of a gourd with a strap about its middle; he had perforce grown in conformity with the commands of the outside pressure. Had he been born in Poco Poco and reared on a ranch, it is at least likely that he would not have been a professor in an Eastern university. Now that the steel girdles of environment were stricken off it appeared that the youthful heart of him stimulated new growth. As for heredity, environment's collaborator, both he and Barbee were lineal descendants of father Adam and mother Eve. But, be the explanation where it may, 'the everlasting miracle' was the same, and the 'old sport' beamed as he would not have done had the University of Edinburgh bestowed upon him a new degree.

'Let's frolic a few,' suggested Barbee, with a sidelong glance.

'I have some business to attend to,' said Longstreet eagerly. 'I'll hurry through with it. Then—then I assure you that I shall be glad to witness with you the—the gaiety of the—of the places of amusement here.'

He explained what his business was.

'You stop at the store, then,' said Barbee. 'Tell Mexico Pete to have your grub and truck ready; I'll mosey on up to the saloon and scare up Tod and tell him about the team. I'll wait for you up there. And, since we ain't got all night, suppose you shake a foot, pardner.'

When a few minutes later Longstreet reached the adobe saloon of 'Tonio Moraga, he found Yellow Barbee smoking a cigarette outside the deep-set door.

'Kind of quiet,' apologized the young fellow. 'But we'll look 'em over.'

He struck the door open with his shoulder and Longstreet followed him into a big room sufficiently well lighted by a couple of hanging kerosene lamps. At one side was an ancient, battered bar; behind the bar a lazy Mexican in shirt sleeves; at one end Tod Barstow pouring the cool contents of a pint bottle of some pinkish beverage directly from the throat of the bottle into his own throat; lounging idly in chairs of various interesting stages of dilapidation half a dozen men, all dark-skinned, black of moustache and hair. Barstow's position necessitated the fixing of his eyes upon the ceiling; all other glances, ignoring Barbee, centred upon Longstreet. He was smiling and eager.

'Come alive, gents!' called Barbee genially. 'Stack up alongside the bar and I'll buy! Moraga,' to the bartender, 'you know me. I got a real bad case of alkali throat. Roll up, boys!—Say, wait a minute. Moraga, meet my friend Longstreet.' Moraga showed many large white teeth in a friendly smile and gave into Longstreet's keeping a small, moist and very flabby hand. The other men, silently accepting the invitation, came forward; Barbee introduced them all. Longstreet's was the emotion of one being initiated into a new fraternity.

They named their poison, in the parlance of the neighbour-hood, and stood to their glasses like so many valiant gunners. Longstreet, big enough in his views of humanity, to look upon them as so many boyish souls, beamed. Then he noted that they seemed to be waiting for something, wondered what it might be, glanced over his shoulder, looked back at them and understood. They were waiting for him. So he said hastily, and in their own phrase:

'Same thing.'

Which, of course, brought down to his place on the bar a small glass and a large bottle. He had never done a thing like this in all the calm days of his existence, but now the deed came naturally enough. He poured his glass and even echoed the other remarks of 'Here's how.' When the fiery liquor arrived in his stomachical regions he realized with perfect clarity that it was without doubt some newly invented substitute for whisky; perhaps that jackass-brandy which he had heard of. His emotion was twofold: he was glad that Helen was at the hotel and he was determined not to repeat the dose.

'That's the goods,' said Longstreet jocularly, trying to smack his lips.

Barbee led the way to the nearest table and out of the nowhere brought into the here a deck of cards. Longstreet was on the verge of applauding when he noted that every one else accepted the act as a matter of fact, and subsided into himself and into a chair at the same moment.

'Who'll make it four-cornered?' demanded Barbee. 'Short, but lively while she lasts. Little old game, name of stud horse?'

Two of the Mexicans, having hesitated and then looked to Barbee, came forward and deposited themselves carelessly in the two chairs. Barbee shuffled, cut, shuffled again and put the cards down.

'Cut for deal,' he ordered.

When each of the other men had leaned forward and lifted a sheaf of cards, Longstreet divided the remainder. The deal went to Barbee. And what is more, Longstreet understood why; Barbee showed the highest card, a king. Longstreet straightened in his chair and his interest grew; he went over in mind what he had learned at the ranch. A pair beats a stiff, two pair beat a pair, threes beat two pair and so on. It was simplicity itself and here was he, Professor Edward Longstreet, measuring his judgment against that of Mexican Mendoza, Mexican Chavez and Yellow Barbee, cowpuncher. Ready from the flip of the first card to concede that these gentlemen had had a rather wider experience with card-playing, none the less he realized the superiority of his mentality, his greater intellectual training, and fully expected something more than just an 'even break.' He concealed the faces of his cards cannily and gave his scholarly brain entirely to a pleasant task in mathematics.

Through many years of training he was familiar with abstruse problems; hence it may be forgiven him, if, at first blush, this form of poker appeared simplicity itself. He reasoned thus: There were fifty-two cards in the full deck; there were exactly four, neither more nor less, of each ace, deuce, trey and so forth until one got to the king; there were, also, just four men drawing cards; each man, if he played his hand out, could draw five cards. All of this was data; it seemed as though he had x and y given and was merely to find z. His eye, as the game began, registered zest.

He remembered former instructions: Each man's first card, dealt face down, was to remain face down until the hand was played out; the owner of that first card, and no other man, had the right to turn up the corner and discover what it was. So when Barbee tossed his card to him, Longstreet wasted no time in peeking at it. It was the ace of clubs; not a better card in the deck! He lifted his face and beamed; it was a good start. And this time the emotion registered in his frank eye was that of a guileless old gentleman who has an ace in the hole. There was no misreading that triumphant gleam.

Again the cards fell gently from Barbee's practised hand, each of the four faces up this time. Longstreet's was a king; he nodded his acceptance and approval. All of the time his brain was busied with his developing theory of chances: there were four aces, four kings in the deck, and he already had one of each. There were four players in all; there were fifty-two cards; it was unlikely that in this hand another king should turn up. And no other king did; he had the high card. He smiled warmly.

'The high card bets,' drawled Barbee.

'Oh!' exclaimed Longstreet. 'Yes, to be sure. Let me see.'

His sparkling eye roved about the table. Barbee's exposed card was a jack, one of the Mexicans had a ten and the other a four. Longstreet felt both warmed with triumph and yet a little sorry for them. So he did the kind thing by them and bet only a dollar. The two Mexicans lifted their brows at him, looked to Barbee, and then with a splendid show of nonchalance both came in. Barbee chinked his silver dollar down upon the others and dealt the third card. Longstreet waited breathlessly.

This time there came to him another king, the king of spades, and his little exclamation of genuine delight was a pretty thing to hear. But the next second a look of frowning incredulity overspread his features; the king of hearts fell to Chavez and the king of diamonds to Mendoza. Barbee gave himself an ace. But it was not the ace that interested Longstreet; his newly-born theory of chances was a trifle upset. That three kings, when there were only three left in the deck, should come one on the heels of another was a matter for reflection. But evidently there was no time granted for readjustment of preconceived ideas.

'Longstreet's the only man with a pair in sight,' said Barbee. 'It's your bet again, Longstreet.'

Longstreet hurriedly bet a dollar. Chavez, with a king and ten in view, raised the bet four dollars. Mendoza withdrew his hand and his attention and began rolling a cigarette, never once taking his eyes from Longstreet's eager face. Barbee tossed in his five dollars, and Longstreet was brought to realize that if he wished to remain in the game it was in order for him to add another four dollars to his bet. He did so without a moment's hesitation. And again he began his search of the deathless underlying mathematical law of the game of stud poker.

Meanwhile Barbee dealt the fourth card. When the fates had it that a second ace fell to Longstreet's lot they should have been amply repaid by the glowing smile that widened his good-humoured mouth. He now had, and he realized to the full his strategic position in that no one else could have his secret knowledge, a pair of kings *and* a pair of aces. The two biggest pairs in the deck! He looked with renewed interest at the other cards. Chavez now had two tens exposed; before Barbee lay no pair at all, just a jack, an ace and a five. There was but one more card to be dealt. He could therefore count Barbee out of the running. It remained to him and Chavez, and Chavez had only a pair of tens in sight.

'Your bet again, Longstreet,' Barbee reminded him. He started and bet his dollar. Chavez repeated his earlier performance and raised the bet four dollars. Barbee tossed away his cards; Longstreet noted the act triumphantly, and nodded in the manner of a father approving the wise act of a young untried son.

'What you do, *senor*?' asked the Mexican. Longstreet withdrew his eyes from Barbee and gave his attention to his antagonist, a half-bred Mexican of low-grade mentality who was offering a duel of wits! He bet the requisite four dollars.

And now from Barbee's fingers came the last cards, one for Longstreet and one for Chavez. Longstreet drew a queen and went into the silence of deep meditation; to Chavez came a lowly seven. Longstreet needed no prompting that it was time to bet; further he understood that this was the last round, the final opportunity. He did not wait for the customary raise of Chavez, but slipped five dollars into the pot and sat back, beaming.

Nor did the Mexican hesitate. He pushed out to the centre of the table with slow brown fingers two twenty-dollar gold pieces.

'You—you raise me?' asked Longstreet.

'*Si, senor.* Tirty-fife *pesos mas.*'

Longstreet curbed a desire to warn the man, to insist that he reconsider. But in the end he kept his own counsel and made his complementary bet of thirty-five dollars.

'Call you,' he said quite in his best form.

The Mexican extracted from the bottom of his cards the first one dealt him face down and flipped it over carelessly. It was a ten; he had three tens, and the professor's extremely handsome pairs of aces and kings were as nothing. The Mexican's brown fingers drew the winnings in toward him, Longstreet's fifty-one dollars among them. Longstreet stared at him and at Barbee and at the treacherous cards themselves in sheer bewilderment.

It was not that he was shocked at the loss of a rather large sum of money in his present circumstances; his brain did not focus on the point. He was trying to see in what his advance theories had miscarried. For certainly it had seemed extremely unlikely that Chavez would have had three tens. Why, there were only four tens in the deck of fifty-two, there were four men playing, there remained in the deck, untouched, thirty-two cards—

'Deal 'em up,' said Barbee. 'Your deal, old boy.'

'It lies entirely within the scope of conservative probability,' said Longstreet blandly, his eyes carrying the look of a man who in spirit is far away from his physical environment, 'that, after all, my data were not sufficient.'

'Talking to me?' said Barbee. He made a playful show of looking over his shoulder to the invisible recipient of Longstreet's confidences; at the moment a door behind him opened and a new face did actually appear. Barbee's glance grew into a stare of surprise. Then he turned square about in his chair again and snapped out: 'Deal, can't you?' Longstreet saw that the boy's face was red; that his eyes burned malignantly.

'Hello, Barbee,' said the man in the newly opened door. He came fully into the room and closed the door after him.

'Hello, Courtot,' answered Barbee colourlessly.

With an effort Longstreet had withdrawn his analytic faculties from the consideration of the recent problem that had been solved for him by the cards themselves; now he was busied with collecting them, arranging them and getting ready to shuffle. Among the amused eyes watching him he was conscious of a pair of eyes that were not simply amused, the eyes of Jim Courtot. He looked up and took stock of the new-comer, impelled to something more exhaustive than a superficial interest by that intangible but potent thing termed personality. This man who had entered the room in familiar fashion through a back door and a rear room, was of the magnetic order; were he silent in a gathering of talking men he must have been none the less a conspicuous figure. And not because of any unusual saliency of physical attributes; rather for that emanation of personality which is like electricity— which, perhaps, is electricity.

He was tall, thin, very dark; his eyes were of beady blackness; he affected the sombre in garb from black hat and dark shirt to darker trousers and black boots. His face was clean-shaven; maybe he had just now been shaving in the rear room. His age might have lain anywhere between thirty-five and fifty. There are men like Jim Courtot, of dark visages and impenetrable eyes, thin and sallow men, upon whom the passing years appear to work all of their havoc early and then be like vicious stinging things deprived of their stings.

'For God's sake!' spoke up Barbee, querulously and nervously. 'Are you going to shuffle all the spots off? Come alive, Longstreet.'

Longstreet allowed Barbee to cut and began dealing. Jim Courtot, his step quick but strangely noiseless, came to the table. His eyes were for Barbee as he said quietly:

'Just a little game for fun? Any objection if I kick in?'

Barbee frowned. Further, he hesitated—and hesitation played but a small part in El Joven's make-up. Finally he evaded.

'Where've you been all this long time, Courtot?' he asked sullenly. 'The biggest game of six years was pulled off down in Poco Poco last week and you wasn't there. I heard a man say you must be dead.'

Courtot considered him gravely. Longstreet regarded the man, fascinated. He did not believe that the man knew how to smile. To imagine Jim Courtot laughing was to fancy a statue laughing.

'When there's a big game pulled off and I'm not there, kid,' he answered when he was good and ready to answer, 'it's because there's a bigger game somewhere else. And I'm heeled to play in your little game if you think you're man enough to take me on.'

Barbee snarled at him.

'Damn you,' he said savagely.

Jim Courtot drew up his chair and sat down. There was a strange sort of swiftness and precision in the man's smallest acts. Now he brought from his hip pocket a handful of loose coins and set the heap on the table before him. For the most part the coins were gold; he stood ready to put into play several hundred dollars.

'Heeled, kid,' he repeated. The voice was as nearly dead and expressionless as a human voice can be; only the words themselves carried his insolence. 'Please, can I play in your game?'

To Barbee's youth it was plain challenge and, though he hated the man with his whole soul, Barbee's youth answered hotly:

'I'll take you on, Jim Courtot, any day.'

Thereafter Courtot ignored Barbee. He turned to Longstreet and watched him deal five cards face down. Then he appeared to lose interest in everything saving his own hand. Longstreet dealt the second five cards, faces up. They fell in the order of nine, four, jack, ace and, to himself, a seven. He did not believe that the new player had seen any but his own card. Barbee, to whose lot the ace had fallen, placed his bet. There was bright bitter challenge in his eyes as he stared across the table at Courtot.

'Ten bucks to start her off,' he said shortly.

Longstreet had supposed it customary to begin with a dollar; in his mind, however, there was little difference between one and ten. Therefore he made no remark and placed his own money in the pot. The two Mexicans tossed their cards away. Courtot, looking at no one, and without speaking, came in. Longstreet dealt a second round. Now Courtot had two fours in sight; Barbee had two aces; Longstreet a king and a seven exposed, but also a king hidden. When Barbee said, 'Twenty bucks to play,' and said it viciously with a jeering stare at Courtot, Longstreet began counting out his money. But before he had completed the slow process the street door opened.

It was Alan Howard. He stood a moment on the threshold, his look one of sheer amazement. He had come looking for Professor James Edward Longstreet, eminent authority upon certain geological subjects. Had anyone told him that he would find his man playing stud poker with Barbee and two Mexicans and Jim Courtot—

'Barbee!' he cried out angrily, coming on swiftly until he stood over the table. 'What in hell's name do you mean by steering Longstreet into a mess like this?'

'What do *you* mean?' retorted Barbee hotly. 'What business is it of yours?'

'I mean Jim Courtot,' cut in Howard shortly. 'You know better than to drag any friend of mine into a game with him.'

Courtot appeared calm and unconcerned.

'The bet's made, gents,' he said briefly. 'Coming in, Longstreet?'

Longstreet looked confused. Before he could frame his answer, Howard made it for him. And he directed it straight to Courtot.

'I haven't had time to tell Mr. Longstreet about all of the undesirable citizens hereabouts,' he announced steadily. 'No, he's not coming in.'

'I imagine you'll spill an earful when you get going, Alan,' said Courtot. 'I'd like to listen in on it.'

Straightway the two Mexicans rose and left the table. Barbee, though he scorned to do so, pushed his chair back a little and kept his eyes upon the faces of the two men. Longstreet went from confusion to bewilderment. Howard considered the matter briefly; then, watching Jim Courtot while he spoke, he said crisply:

'Mr. Longstreet, you should get acquainted a bit before you play cards out here. Jim Courtot there, who plans to rob you the shortest way, is a crook, a thief, a dirty liar and a treacherous man-killer. He's rotten all the way through.'

A man does not fire a fuse without expecting the explosion. On the instant that Jim Courtot's hand left his pile of coins, Alan Howard's boots left the floor. The cattleman threw himself forward and across the table almost with his last word. Courtot came up from his chair, a short-barrelled revolver in his hand. But, before he was well on his feet, before the short barrel had made its required brief arc, Howard's blow landed. With all of his force, with all of the weight of his body, he struck Jim Courtot square upon the chin. Courtot went over backwards, spilling out of the chair that crumpled and snapped and broke to pieces; his gun flew wide across the room. Howard's impetus carried him on across the table so that he too fell, and across the body of the man he had struck. But when Alan got to his feet, Jim Courtot lay still and unconscious. And, for one, Longstreet thought that he had seen manslaughter done; the man's look was of death.

Howard picked up his hat and then what few of the scattered coins he judged were Longstreet's. Then he took the gaping little man by the arm and led him to the door.

'Miss Helen wanted you,' he said as they passed outside.

'Did you kill him?' Longstreet was shuddering.

'No,' was the cool answer. 'But it looks as if I'd have to some day. Better not say anything about this to Miss Helen.'

'Good heavens, no!' ejaculated Longstreet. 'Not a word!'

CHAPTER IX

HELEN KNEW

Second only to her father's was Helen's eager interest in the world about her. The ride back to Desert Valley through the rich moonlight was an experience never to be forgotten. She and Howard alone in what appeared an enchanted and limitless garden of silence and of slumber, their horses' feet falling without noise as though upon deep carpets, the bright moon and its few attendant stars working the harsh land of the day over into a soft sweet country of subtle allurement—the picture of all this was to spring up vivid and vital in many an idle hour of the days to follow. Little speech passed between them that night: they rode close together, they forgot the wagon which rocked and jolted along somewhere far behind them; they were content to be content without analysing. And at the end of the ride, when she felt Alan's strong hands aiding her from her saddle, Helen sighed.

The next morning early she and her father left Desert Valley, going straight to the professor's destination in the Last Ridge country. They did not see Howard, who had breakfasted and ridden away before dawn, leaving with the kitchen boy a brief note of apology. The note said that his business was urgent and that he would call to see them in a day or so; further that Tod Barstow and Chuck Evans had orders to haul their goods in the wagon for them and to help them pitch camp.

Their departure was like a small procession. The wagon,

carrying all their household goods, went ahead. Longstreet's two pack-horses were tied to the tail end of the wagon and trotted along with slack tie-ropes. Behind them rode the Longstreets upon saddle-horses, which Chuck Evans had brought to the house for them with his employer's compliments.

'Al said you was to ride this one, miss,' said Chuck Evans.

It was the black mare on which Howard had ridden into their camp the first morning—Sanchia or Helen.

'What is her name?' asked Helen quite innocently when she had mounted.

Chuck Evans grinned his characteristic happy grin.

'Funny thing about that mare's name,' he conceded brightly.

'What do you mean?' queried Helen.

'Yesterday,' he explained, 'I heard Al talking to her down to the stable. He does talk to a horse more'n any man I know, and what's more they talk back to him. 'S a fact, miss. And what he said was, "Helen, you little black devil, I wouldn't sell you for a couple million dollars; no, not now." Calling her Helen, understand?'

'Well?' asked the other Helen.

'And,' went on Chuck Evans, 'that mare's been on the ranch six months and never did I hear him call her another thing than Sanchia.'

'Sanchia?' she repeated after him. 'What a pretty name!' And then, more innocently than ever, 'I don't think I ever heard the name before. She was named after somebody, I suppose?'

'Sure,' laughed Chuck. 'After a certain lady known in these

parts as Mrs. Murray. Her name is Sanchia.'

'Oh!' said Helen.

'And,' continued Chuck, 'that ain't all. This morning, just like he knew folks was going to ask her name, he tells me: "Say, Chuck; this here mare's name, if anyone asks you, is Sweet-heart. Don't it just suit her?" he says. And when you come right down to it—'

'Hey, Chuck,' called Tod Barstow from his high seat. 'Get a move on. We better get started before it's hot.'

So Chuck Evans departed and Helen sat straight in the saddle, her eyes a little puzzled. When her father rode to her side she was adjusting a bluebird's feather in her hatband. The feather, pointing straight up, gave a stiff, almost haughty look to the young woman's headgear.

They crossed the big meadow, wound for an hour among the little hills, and then began a slow, gradual climb along a devious dusty road. Less and ever less fertile grew the dry earth under them, more still and hot and hostile the land into which they journeyed. In three hours, jogging along, they came to Last Ridge.

'There's only one spot up this way that's fit to live in for more'n an hour at the stretch,' Barstow told them. 'There's a spring and some shade there. We'll drive right under it, and from there up we'll have to finish the job monkey-style.'

He stopped his horses in a little flat, just under a steep wall of reddish cliff. Here he and Chuck Evans unhitched and here the horses were tethered. Helen looked about her curiously, and at first her heart sank. There was nothing to greet her but rock and sweltering patches of sand and gravelly soil, and sparse, harsh brush. She turned and looked back toward the sweep of Desert Valley; there she saw green fields, trees, grazing stock. It was like the Promised Land compared with this bleak desolate spot her father had chosen. She turned to him, words of expostulation forming. But his eyes were bright, his look triumphant. He had already dismounted and was poking about here and there, examining everything at hand from a sand-storm stratum at the cliff's foot to loose dirt in the drifts and the hardy, wiry grass growing where it could. Helen turned away with a sigh.

From here the two Desert Valley men went forward on foot to show them the spot which Alan Howard had chosen as the most likely site for a camp. They walked to the end of the flat where the reddish, walls shut in; here was an angle of cliff and in the angle was a cleft some three or four feet wide. They passed into this and found that it offered a steep, winding way upward. But the distance was not great, and in ten minutes they had come to the top. Here again was a level space, a wide tableland, offering less of the desert menace and hostility and something more of charm and the promise of comfort. For a gentle breeze stirred here, and off yonder were scattered pines and cedars and in a clump of trees was a ring of verdure. They went to it and saw the spring. It was but a sort of mud-hole of yellowish, thickish water. But water it was, with green grass growing about it and with the shade of dusty trees over it. Beyond were the strange-shaped uplands, distant cliffs and peaks broken into a thousand grotesque forms, with bands of colour in horizontal strata across them as though they had been painted with a mighty brush.

'What though I have never been here until this second?' cried Longstreet triumphantly. 'I know it, all of it, every inch and millimetre of it! I could have made a map of it and laid the colours in. I have read of it, studied it—I have written of this country! Having been right in everything else, am I to be mistaken in the matter of its minerals? I said give me three months to find gold! Why, it's a matter to wonder at if I don't locate my mine in three days!'

The two men grinned readily. Before now they had heard men talk with the gold fever upon them.

'There's gold pretty near everywhere,' admitted Barstow, 'if a man can make it pay. But right now I guess me and Chuck had better start getting your stuff up the rocks. Suit you all right here for a camp?'

Helen turned and looked toward the south. There, broad and fertile below her, running away across the miles, were the Howard acres. She even made out the clutter of head-quarters buildings. Somehow she fancied that the sweep of homely view snatched from these bleak uplands something of their loneliness. When her father announced that this was just the spot he had longed for, Helen nodded her approval. Here for a time was to be home.

Throughout the day and until dusk the four of them laboured, making camp. Barstow and Evans lugged the various articles, boxes, rolls of bedding, up through the cleft in the rocks. They had brought in the wagon-bed some loose boards of various sizes; these they made into a rough floor. At the four corners of the floor they erected studding of two-by-four lumber. These they braced and steadied; they nailed other lengths of two-by-four material along the tops, outlining walls; they hacked and sawed and hammered and nailed to such advantage that in the end they had the misshapen frame of a cabin, rafters and all. Then over the rafters and along the sides they secured the canvas destined for the purpose. Doors and windows were canvas flaps; the sheet-iron stove was set up on four flat stones for legs; the stovepipe was run through a hole in the roof. And when Chuck Evans and Tod Barstow, amateurs in the carpenter's line, stood back and wiped the sweat off their brown faces and looked with fond and prideful eyes at their handiwork, Helen and her father were no whit less delighted.

'If you want more room after a while,' said Barstow, 'it'd be easy to tack more sheds on and run canvas over them, just the same as what we done. Me and Chuck would come up most any time and lend a hand.'

The breeze stiffened and the crazy edifice shivered.

'I don't know as I'd make it much bigger,' said Evans. 'If a real blow come on and the wind got inside—Say, Tod, how about a few guy ropes? Huh?'

Barstow agreed, and they brought what ropes they had in the wagon and 'staked her out, same as if she was a runaway horse,' as Chuck put it. In other words, they ran one rope from the rear end of the ridge of the house to the base of a conveniently-located pine tree; then they secured the second rope to the other end of the ridge-pole and anchored it to a big boulder. Meanwhile Helen opened some cans and made coffee on the newly-adjusted stove and they sat on the grass by the spring and made their evening meal. After which Barstow and Evans went down to their wagon and returned to Desert Valley. And James Edward Longstreet and his daughter sat alone upon their camp-stools in front of their new abode and looked off across the valley and into the distances.

The day departed slowly, lingeringly. The soft night came little by little, a misty veil floating into a hollow yonder, a star shining, the breeze strengthening and cooling. Before the twilight was gone and while one might look for miles across the billowing landscapes, they saw a horseman riding down in the valley; he appeared hardly more than a vague moving dot. And yet—

'It's Mr. Howard!' cried Helen.

Longstreet withdrew his straining eyes and turned them wonderingly upon his daughter.

'How in the world do you know?' he asked.

Helen smiled, a quiet smile of transcendent wisdom.

'Oh, I just knew he'd come over.' she said.

CHAPTER X

A WARNING AND A SIGN

John Carr made a special trip back to Desert Valley ranch for a word with Howard. He rode hard and there was a look of anxiety in his eyes when he came upon his friend smoking thoughtfully in the big living-room of the ranch-house. It was late evening and a week after the departure of Howard's guests.

Howard dragged his boot heels down from the table top when he saw who it was and jumped to his feet his hand outstretched.

'Hello, John old boy,' he cried warmly. What's the good wind blowing you over this way already?'

Carr tossed his hat to the table, drew up a chair for himself and took a cigar before he answered. Then it was quietly and earnestly.

'Met up with Jim Courtot the other night, I hear?' he began.

Howard nodded and waited, his look curious.

'Well,' went on Carr, 'I wish you hadn't. He's a treacherous beast if this man's land ever cradled one. He's looking for you, Al.'

'He knows where to find me,' said Alan shortly. And then,

Jackson Gregory

'Just what's worrying you, Johnnie?'

'I've known Jim for seventeen or eighteen years,' rejoined Carr. 'He's a cold, hard, calculating and absolutely crooked proposition. During that time I've never known him to go on a drunk more than two or three times. And every time there was trouble.'

'He's drinking now, then?'

'He started in right after you got through with him the other night. And he has been talking. There's no use being a fool!' he cut in sternly as Alan shrugged his shoulders. 'Courtot doesn't talk to me, but I've got straight what he has said. He talks to Moraga, and Moraga talks to Barbee, and Barbee passes it on to me. He told Moraga that if it was the last thing he did, he'd get you. And he is carrying a gun every step he takes.'

'The more a man talks, the less killing he does, I've noticed,' said Howard. But his tone did not carry conviction. Carr frowned impatiently.

'He hasn't talked much. He was mad clean through when he made that crack to Moraga. I tell you there's no use being a fool, Al.'

'No. Guess you're right, John. Anyway, it was pretty decent of you to ride over.'

He got up and went into his bedroom. A moment later he came out carrying a heavy Colt revolver in one hand, a box of cartridges in the other. The gun was well oiled; the cylinder spun silently and easily; the six chambers were loaded. He put the gun down on the table.

'I'll ride heeled for a few days, anyhow,' he decided. 'I guess I can shoot with Jim Courtot yet.'

'Did you ever find out for sure that it was Jim the other time?'

'Sure enough to suit me,' returned Howard. 'He was in town that night. And it was his style of work to take a pot shot at a man out of the dark.'

'He's not exactly a coward,' warned Carr.

'No, not a coward. But that's his kind of work, just the same. He would go after a man just as he plays poker—simply to win the surest, quickest, easiest way. Saw Sanchia Murray in town the same day he was there. Are they working together again?'

'I haven't seen either one of them. But I guess so. Barbee, poor kid, is trailing after her all the time, and he comes back hating Courtot worse and worse every day. Seen the Longstreets lately?'

Howard admitted that he had. It was only a little way over, he reminded Carr, an hour and a half ride or such a matter, and the old boy was such a helplessly innocent old stranger, that it didn't seem quite right to turn them adrift altogether.

'The girl is a pretty thing.' said Carr.

'Yes,' agreed Howard. 'Kind of pretty.'

Carr looked at him steadily. And for absolutely no slightest, vaguest reason in the wide world that he could think of, Alan Howard felt his face going red. Carr's look probed deeper. Then, with common consent, they turned to other subjects until bedtime. Nothing of business matters passed between them, although both remembered that a considerable payment was to fall due within ten days.

In particular Howard had cause to remember. He had recently balanced his books and had found that he had cut into his last five thousand dollars. Therefore, meaning to pay on the nail, he had arranged a sale of beef cattle. The range was heavily stocked, he had a herd in prime condition, the market was fair, and his system called for a sale soon and the purchase of some calves. Therefore the next morning, before Carr was astir, Howard and several of his men were riding toward the more remote fields where his beef herds were. Behind them came the camp wagon and the cook.

All day long he worked among his herds, gathering them, sorting them, cutting out and heading back towards the home corrals those under weight or in any way not in the pink of condition for the sale. His men rode away into the distances, going east and south, disappearing over the ridges seeking cattle that had strayed far. Howard changed the horse under him four times that day, and the beast he freed long after the stars were out was jaded and wet. In the end he threw himself down upon the hot earth in the shade of the wagon and turned his eyes toward the uplands of the Last Ridge. He had had no moment of his own to-day, no opportunity to ride for a call on his new friends, and now, after he rested a little and ate, he would go back to work with his men, night-herding. For the rounded-up cattle were now a great milling herd that grew greater as the night went on and other lesser bands were brought in, a stamping, churning mass whose deep-lunged bellowing surged out continuously across the valley stretches and through the passes of the hills.

To-morrow, thought Howard, he would ride toward the Last Ridge, taking it upon himself to gather up the straggling stock there, and, purely incidentally, he would look in upon the Longstreets. He had not seen them for three days. But the night was destined to bring events to alter his plans. In the first place, some of his cowboys whom he had dispatched to outlying districts of the range to round up the cattle there had not yet returned, and he and his men here were short-handed in their task of night-herding the swelling numbers of restless shorthorns. Howard, having had his supper, his cigarette and his brief rest, was saddling his fifth horse to take his turn at a four-hour shift, when he was aware that some one had ridden into camp. And then came a voice, shouting through the din and the dark:

'Hey, there. Where's Al?'

'Here,' called Howard. 'Who is it?'

'It's me,' and Barbee with jingling spurs came on. 'Special delivery letter for you, old-timer.'

Letters came rarely to Desert Valley, and Howard expected none. But he put out his hand eagerly; he had no reason to think such a thing, but none the less the conviction was upon him that Helen had written him. His arm through his horse's bridle, he struck a match and took into his hand a scrap of paper. As his peering eyes made out a sweeping, familiar scrawl, he felt a disappointment quite as unreasonable as had been his hope. It was unmistakably from the hand of John Carr, hastily written in lead pencil upon the inner side of an old envelope and said briefly:

'Better look out for Courtot, Al. He has left Big Run and is headed out your way.—JOHN.'

Howard tore the paper to bits.

'Where's Carr?' he asked quietly. 'Gone on back?'

Barbee chuckled softly.

'He was at your place last night, wasn't he? Well, he headed back and got as far as Big Run. That's where I saw him late this afternoon when he give me this for you. About that time I guess he changed his mind about going home and shifted his trail. He's gone up that way.'

The vague sweep of Barbee's arm indicated a wide expanse of country lying to the north. When Howard was silent, the boy went on lightly and perhaps a hint maliciously:

'Get me? Gone to see how the professor and his girl are making out. Keep your eye peeled, Al, or he'll beat you to it.

Old John's a sure heller with the women.'

Howard snapped out a curt admonition to Barbee to mind his own business and flung himself into the saddle. As he spurred away to the outer fringe of his herd he was not thinking over-much of Carr's warning; somehow Barbee's stuck closer in his mind. A spurt of irritation with himself succeeded that first desire to slap the message-bearer's face. For he knew within his heart that he resented Carr's making himself at home at the Longstreet camp, and he knew that to-night he was an unreasonable beast. Had not Carr once already ridden far out of his way to warn him? Was there any reason in the wide world why Carr should not this time send Barbee and himself ride on wherever it suited him to go? At that moment Howard would have been glad than otherwise to have Jim Courtot present himself.

'Let him start something, damn him,' he growled savagely to himself, 'any time.' And he began wondering if now John Carr were sitting with Helen and her father in front of their little home? Or if perhaps Longstreet had gone in to his books, and Carr and Helen alone, sitting quiet under the spell of the night, were looking out into the shining world of stars? He cursed himself for a fool and an ingrate. Didn't Carr have a man's right to ride where he chose? And had he not already twice in twenty-four hours shown how clearly his thought and his heart were with his friend? A revolver knocked at Howard's side. It was there because John Carr had shown him its need.

Howard's impulse was to stay away from Last Ridge for a little longer. He reasoned that Carr would be invited to stay over-night and would naturally accept the invitation. Why should he not? There is always room in camp for one more, and no doubt both Helen and her father would be glad of company to break their monotony and loneliness. But before Howard had had time for more than an impulse there came the second episode of the night to set him thinking upon other matters.

As he rode he heard several voices and recognized them as

those of his own men. One guffawed loudly and there came the sound of his big hand slapping his leg in his high delight; another swore roundly and impatiently; a third was talking excitedly, earnestly. This third was Sandy Weaver, an old hand, a little man characterized by his gentle eyes and soft voice and known across many miles as an individual in whom the truth did not abide. All up and down these fringes of the desert he was known simply as Lying Sandy.

'What's the excitement, boys?' demanded Howard.

Sandy wheeled his horse, pressing close to his employer's side, and burst into quick explanation. He had been working with Dave Terril over on the east side; they had found only a handful of stock there, and Sandy had left them to Dave, and in order to save time for the morrow had circled the valley and combed over the north end, under the Last Ridge cliffs. Just before dark he had made his discovery. His horse had found it first, shying and sniffing and then trying to bolt; Sandy was nothing if not circumstantial.

'We've got some work to do to-night, Sandy.' cut in Howard shortly. 'If you've got anything to say, go to it.'

'Haw!' gurgled Bandy O'Neil, recently from a California outfit, a man with a large sense of mirth. 'He's got his prize ring-tailed dandy to spring, Al. Don't choke him off or it'll kill him.'

Sandy hearkened to neither of them, but hastened on. He described the hidden sink in a boulder-ringed draw, the difficulty he had had in bringing his horse to the scene and his own stupefaction. And when he had done all of this with his customary detail he declared that he had come upon a yearling bull, dead as a door nail and slaughtered after a fashion that made Sandy's eyes widen in the starlight.

'It's throat was just sure enough tore all to hell, Al,' he said ponderously. 'Like something the size of an elephant had gone

Jackson Gregory

after it. And I says to myself it must have been a wolf, and I go looking for tracks. And, by the Lord, I found 'em! Tracks like a wolf and the size of a dinner plate! And alongside them tracks, some other tracks. And they was made by a man and he was barefooted!'

Bandy O'Neil's roar of mirth was a sound to hearken to joyously from afar.

'And,' he cried, dabbing at his tears, 'Sandy would sure take a man by the mit and lead him to the spot, only just then a big bird, size of half a dozen ostriches, flops down and sinks its claws into that there bull calf and flies right straight over the moon with it! Ain't that what you said, Sandy?'

'You're a fool, Bandy O'Neil, and always will be a fool,' muttered Sandy Weaver stiffly. 'That same calf is laying right there now, and if you don't believe it or Al don't believe it, I'll bet you a hundred bucks and show you the place as fast as a horse can lay down to it.'

He ran on with his tale, having the end yet to recount. He had headed his cattle down to meet Dave Terril; he and Dave had swung in together and moved still further south to herd in with the boys coming up from that direction; and being within striking distance of the ranch-house, Sandy had ridden there alone.

'I wasn't sure but you might be there, Al,' he explained. 'And I wanted to tell you what I saw. I rampsed right in and found somebody waiting for you. Know who?'

'Carr?' suggested Howard.

'No, it wasn't. It was Jim Courtot. There wasn't anybody at the house but old Angela and the Mex kid, and they let him in. He was setting there waiting, and when I went in the door he come up standing and he had his gun in his hand and it was cocked. And, Al, he looked mean.'

There was a pause and a silence. Sandy Weaver might be lying, and then again he might not.

'I got nothing against Jim, and it didn't drop on me right then that he was out to start a row. And, being full of what I saw up there, I spilled him the yarn. And I wish you could have had a look into that man's face! He's no albino to speak on, and yet when I got half-way through he looked it. His face was as white as a rag and his eyes bulged out like he was scared, and the sweat come out on his head and all over, I guess, and he kept looking over his shoulder all the time like the devil was after him. And when I showed him what I found on the rock by the dead calf, he just asks me one question. He says, "Sandy, what way was them tracks pointed?" And when I tells him it looked like they was pointed this way—well, Jim was gone!'

'You lying devil!' shouted Bandy hilariously.

But Howard, wondering, demanded:

'What was it you found on the rock, Sandy?'

Sandy yanked it from his pocket. They crowded closer and some one struck a match. It was a bit of buckskin, and in the buckskin was a little heap of raw gold.

CHAPTER XI

SEEKING

Alan Howard got a lantern from the wagon and said briefly to Sandy Weaver: 'Show me the place.' For he knew that for once Weaver was not lying. When together they came to the hollow where the dead calf lay he dismounted, made a light and verified all that had been told him. He saw dimly the track of the bare human foot where Sandy had left it undisturbed; he passed from that to the other tracks. As his cowboy had said, they resembled a wolf's but were unusually large. As Howard noted for himself, the front feet had made the larger, deeper imprint; the hind tracks were narrower, longer, less clearly defined.

'It carries the bulk of its weight up forward,' he said thoughtfully. 'It would be heavy-chested, big-shouldered, slim in the barrel and small in the hips. And it is the same It that made those other tracks by Superstition Pool—where some gent was scared half out of his hide and clean out of any desire to linger or eat supper.'

'What's all that?' demanded Sandy. 'Seen tracks like that before?'

Howard nodded and went back to his horse in silence. And silent he remained during the ride back to camp, despite Sandy's chatter. For already he had a vague theory and he was seeking stubbornly to render that theory less vague. When they had ridden back to the herd he singled out Chuck Evans and moved with him out of hearing of the others.

'Chuck,' he said soberly, 'I've got a job for you. I've got to go on with the herd to San Juan and I don't know just when I'll be back. To-morrow you move the extra horses up into the hills; it's time, anyway, to feed off the grass in the canons. And I want you to keep in touch with the Longstreets. At night-time make your camp within calling distance of theirs. And keep your eyes and ears open.'

'I get you,' said Chuck, 'only I don't. What's going to hurt them?'

'Nothing that I know of. But I want you on the job. I don't quite like the idea of the old professor and his daughter being out there alone.' And that was all the explanation he gave.

The next afternoon the drive began. Sitting a little aside as his men started the slow procession toward the San Juan trail, Howard watched his carefully bred cattle go by and drew from the moment a full sense of success achieved. As they crowded by in bellowing scores he estimated that they were going to net him above ten thousand dollars, and that every cent of that ten thousand was going to John Carr as a worth-while payment upon Desert Valley. From his own funds in the bank Howard would draw for the purchase of his calves and for running expenses. He would be close-hauled again, but he would have earned a long breathing spell. As the tail-enders pushed by him he dropped in behind them to be engulfed in the rising clouds of dust and to do his own part of his own work.

The wagon had gone ahead to the place appointed for to-night's camp. Since the herd was large, while days were hot and water-holes scarce, Howard had planned the devious way by Middle Springs, Parker's Gulch, the end of Antelope Valley, across the little hills lying to the north of Poco Poco and on into San Juan by the chain of mud-holes where the old Mexican corrals were. Hence, he counted upon being at least four days on the road to San Juan. There his responsibilities would cease, as there the buyers had promised to meet him, taking the herd on into the railroad.

During the days which followed he was as busy as a man should care to be, for the task of moving a large herd across a dry and baking country and through it all keeping the cattle in first-class condition, is no small one. And busy in mind was he when the stars were out and camp was pitched. He lay with his head on his saddle, his pipe in his teeth, his thoughts withdrawn from his business of stock-selling and centred elsewhere. The second night out the boys noted a change in Al Howard; the third night they asked one another 'what had come over the old man.' For whereas formerly his had always been the gayest voice around the camp fire, his the tongue to spin a yarn or start a cowboy ballad, now he withdrew after a silent supper and threw himself down on the ground and stared at the stars, his thoughts his own behind the locked guard of his shut teeth.

'He's figgering on something—hard,' said Dave Terril. 'Might be about Jim Courtot.'

'Or them tracks,' suggested Sandy Weaver. 'The barefoot's and the gigantic wolf.'

'Or,' put in a chuckling voice from the shadows, 'a girl, huh? Having took a good look at old man Longstreet's girl, I wouldn't blame Al overmuch.'

By the time the adobe walls of picturesque San Juan swam into view across the dry lands Alan Howard had at least reshaped and clarified his theory of the tracks, had made up his mind concerning Jim Courtot and had dreamed through many an hour of Helen. As to Helen, he meant to see a very great deal of her when he returned to Desert Valley. As to Jim Courtot, he meant to end matters one way or another without any great delay. For to a man of the type of Alan Howard the present condition was unbearable. He knew that Courtot was 'looking for him'; that Courtot had gone straight to the ranch-house and had sat down with his gun in front of him, waiting for Howard's step on the porch; that when the first opportunity arose Jim Courtot would start shooting. It was not to his liking that Courtot should have things all his way. The gambler would shoot from the dark, as he had done before, if he had the chance. That chance might come to-night or a year from now, and constant expectancy of this sort would, soon or late, get on a man's nerves. In short, if Courtot wanted to start something, Howard fully meant to have it an even break; if Courtot were looking for him he could expedite matters by looking for Courtot.

As to his theory of the tracks; he connected them, too, with Jim Courtot. He knew that for the past three months Courtot had disappeared from his familiar haunts; these were La Casa Blanca, Jim Galloway's gambling-house in San Juan, and similar places in Tecolote, Big Run, Dos Hermanos and San Ramon. He knew that only recently, within the week, Courtot had returned from his pilgrimage; that he had come up to Big Run from King Canon way. He knew that the man who had fled Superstition Pool had turned out in the direction of King Canon, and that that man might or might not have been Jim Courtot. Finally, he had Sandy Weaver's word for it that Courtot went deathly-white when he heard of the slain calf and the tracks, and that forthwith Courtot had again disappeared. The imprint of a man's bare foot spelled an Indian from the northern wastes, and Courtot, during the three months of his disappearance, had had ample time to go far into the north. To Howard it seemed a simple thing to imagine that Courtot had committed some deed which had brought after him the unsleeping vengeance of a desert Indian.

In San Juan Howard found a representative of Doan, Rockwell and Haight, the cattle buyers, awaiting him; and the same day the deal was completed, a cheque placed in his hands and the cattle turned over to the buyers' drivers. His men he dismissed to their own devices, knowing that they would amuse themselves in San Juan, perhaps stir up a fight with a crowd of

Jackson Gregory

miners, and thereafter journey homeward, fully content. They were not to wait for him, as he had business to delay him a day or so. From the corrals he went to the bank, placing his cheque for collection with his old friend, John Engle. Thereafter, while his horse rested and enjoyed its barley at the stables, he turned to the Casa Blanca. For it was always possible that Jim Courtot was there.

As he stepped in at the deep, wide doorway Howard's hat was low-drawn, its brim shading his eyes, and he was ready to step swiftly to right or left, to spring forward or back, to shoot quickly if shooting were in the cards. But he knew upon the moment that Courtot was not here. At the bar were his own men ranged up thirstily; they saw him and called to him and had no warning to give. So he passed on down the long room until he stopped at a little table where three men sat. One of them, a thick, squat fellow with a florid face and small mean eyes, looked up at him and glowered.

'Where's Courtot, Yates?' asked Howard coolly.

Yates stared and finally shrugged.

'Left town day before yesterday,' he replied shortly.

'So he was here? I heard he wanted to see me. Know which way he has gone?'

Yates studied him keenly. Then again he lifted his ponderous shoulders.

'He was looking for you,' he said, his meaning clear in the hardness of his eyes. 'And, if you want to know, he's up Las Palmas way.'

'That happens to be lucky,' Alan told him, turning away. 'I'm going up there now to look at some calves in French Valley. If I happen to miss him and you see him you can tell him for me that I'm ready to talk with him any time.'

He went out in dead silence. Many eyes followed him, many eyes which when his tall form had passed through the door came back to other eyes narrowed and thoughtful. For Alan Howard was well known here in San Juan, and never before had a man of them seen him wearing a gun at his hip. There were bets offered and taken before he was half-way to the stable. His own men, hearing, were thoughtful and said nothing. All except Bandy O'Neil, who smashed his big fist on the bar and stared angrily into the florid face of Yates and cried out loudly that Jim Courtot was a card sharp and a crook and that Jim Courtot's friends were as Jim Courtot. Yates for the third time shrugged his thick shoulders. But his look was like a knife clashing with the cowboy's.

Though it was dusk when he resaddled and Las Palmas was twenty-five miles away, Howard's impatience hastened him on. It appeared that Courtot had made up his mind and, further, was publishing the fact across a wide sweep of country. Then there was no going back for him and Courtot, and like a man borne along in a swift current which offered rapids ahead, he was afire to get them behind him. If Courtot were still in Las Palmas he would find him to-night.

But again, at the end of a tedious ride, he learned that the man he sought had come and gone. No one knew just where, but at the one lodging-house which the little settlement possessed, it was hinted that Courtot had headed still further north, perhaps to Los Robles. Howard went to bed that night wondering what it was that impelled the gambler to this hurried travelling across the land. Was it something that lured and beckoned? Was it something that drove and harassed? His last thoughts were of the tracks he had seen by a dead calf and of the tale Sandy Weaver had told.

Early the next morning he rode out to French Valley for a look at Tony Vaca's calves. They proved to be about what he had expected of them, close to a hundred, of mixed breeding, but for the most part good beef-making stock in fair condition and all under a year old. Vaca was short of pasture this year, hence, he declared, forced to sell at a bargain. Howard nodded gravely, considered briefly, and in ten minutes bought the herd, agreeing to take them at ten per cent. less than Tony's bargain price provided they were delivered in Desert Valley within a week.

Now all of his business of buying and selling was done and there remained but to go home or to look further for Courtot. He rode back into Las Palmas and breakfasted at the lunch counter. There he learned that Courtot had probably gone on up to Quigley, another twenty-five miles to the north-east. And, very largely because of the geographical location of Quigley, Howard decided on the instant to continue at least that far his quest. For, coming the way he had from his ranch, he had described a wide arc, almost a semicircle, and by the same trail, should he retrace it, was a hundred and fifty miles from Desert Valley. But, if he went on to Quigley, a mining-town in the bare mountains, he would be at the mouth of Quigley Pass, which led to a little-used trail through the mountains and almost in a straight line across the arm of the desert known locally as the Bad Lands. Though he had never crossed these weary, empty miles, and though there were no towns and few water-holes within their blistered scope, Howard judged that he could save close to fifty miles of the return trip. So he slipped his foot into the stirrup and swung out toward Quigley, hopeful of finding Courtot and confident of a short cut home.

CHAPTER XII

THE DESERT SUPREME

Considerably to his surprise Howard found absolutely no trace of Courtot in Quigley. He inquired at the pool room, at the restaurant, at the stable. No one had seen the gambler for several months. It struck the cattleman as strange that a man should have ridden out of Las Palmas, taking the Quigley trail, and not have come to Quigley. Where else could a man go? On the west lay the desert, on the east the Lava Mountains and beyond the desert again, and it was a far call to any settlement or habitation. Even the sheepmen did not come up this way; only the Quigley mines brought men here, and yet Courtot had not come to Quigley.

'He turned out somewhere,' mused Howard, 'the Lord knows what for or where. But it's his business, and I'm going home.'

He gave his horse an hour in the stable while he himself made ready for his short cut across the Bad Lands. The preparations were simple; at the store he bought a small pack of provisions, enough to last him three or four days at a pinch and in case of accidents; he filled his canteen; he spent half an hour with the grizzled old storekeeper, who in his time had been a prospector and who knew the country hereabouts as only an old prospector could know it. On a bit of wrapping-paper the old fellow sketched a trail map that indicated the start through the Pass, the general direction and the chief landmarks, the approximate mileage and—here he was very exact and accompanied his sketch with full verbal instructions—the few water-holes.

'You can make it all right, Al,' he said when Howard slipped the paper into his vest pocket. 'It's no trick for a man like you. But I wouldn't send a tenderfoot in there, not unless I wanted to make him over into a dead tenderfoot. And, mind you, every year some of them water-holes dries up; the only ones you can count on for sure are the ones I've marked with a double ring that way. So long.'

'So long,' said Alan, and went for his horse.

The forenoon was well advanced when he rode into the mouth of the narrow pass which gives access, above the mines, into the Lava Mountains and through them into the Bad Lands. In twenty minutes he had entered a country entirely new to him. He looked about him with interested eyes. Never, he thought as he pushed forward, had he known until now the look of utter desolation. The mountain flanks were strewn with black blocks and boulders of broken lava and were already incredibly hot; underfoot was parched earth upon which it seemed that not even the hardiest of desert grasses cared to grow; yonder the Bad Lands stretched endlessly before him, blistering mounds of rock, wind-drifted stretches of burning sand, dry gulches and gorges which one's wildest imagining could not fill with rushing waters. Here and there were growing things, but they were grey with desert dust and looked dead, greasewood dwarfed and wind-twisted, iron-fanged cacti snarling at the clear hot sky and casting no more shade than lean poles.

'A man won't find his trail all cluttered up with folks in here,' thought Howard. 'Wonder who was the last man to poke his fool nose into this bake-oven. Whew, it's hot.'

Hotter it grew and drier and, though such a thing had not seemed possible, altogether more repellent and hostile to life. He climbed a ridge to get his bearings and to locate in the grey distance the black peak which the storekeeper had indicated on his map as the first landmark and steering-point. He found it readily enough, a dozen miles off to the south-west, and jogged down the gentle slope toward it, his hat drawn low to shield his burning eyes. Within an hour the impression obtruded itself upon his fancies that about him the world was dead. He did not see a jack-rabbit or a slinking coyote or a bird; not even a buzzard, that all but ubiquitous, heat-defying bundle of dry feathers and bones, hung in the sky. Why should a rabbit come hither where there was no herbage? Why a coyote when his prey shunned these wastes? Why even the winged scavenger when all animal life fled the Bad Lands? The man's spirit was oppressed and drooped under the weariness of the weary land.

It was a tedious day, and more than once he regretted that he had taken this trail; for it seemed likely, as is so often the case, that the long way round was the short way home. But he was in for it, and plugged ahead, longing for the cool of evening. About noon he found the first water-hole and, what was more, found water in it. It was ugly, hot stuff, but his horse trotted to it with ears pricked forward and nostrils a-twitch and drank long and thirstily. Thereafter, though they came to other spots where there should be water, they found none until after sunset. Howard drew off the saddle, gave his horse a handful of barley and staked it out close to the spring. Then he made his own dinner, had his smoke and threw himself down for a couple of hours' rest and dozing. It was his intention to travel on in the night to the next spring, which was some ten miles farther on and which, because of its location in the centre of a cluster of hills already clear against the skyline, he was sure he could not miss. It was one of the map's double-ringed water-holes.

His horse finished its drink and its barley. He heard it shake itself as a horse does after its sweaty work is done. Without turning his head he knew where it was going to lie down for a roll. Now he did turn a little, seeing through the coming dimness of night the four legs waving in air as the beast struggled to turn over on its back. It was a new horse, one he had purchased some weeks ago with a number of others and had not ridden until now; he recalled how, when a boy, he had

Jackson Gregory

shared other youngsters' superstition in connexion with a horse rolling. If it went clean over, it was worth a hundred dollars, if it rolled back, another hundred, and so on.

But this animal did not complete the one effort. Howard heard its sudden terrified snort, saw it scramble wildly to its feet and go plunging off to the end of its tether, knew that even the strong rope had broken and the horse was running wild. And as the man jumped to his feet he knew why. For before the snort of fear he had heard another sound, one indescribable to him who has not heard it and unforgettable and on the instant recognizable to him who has; that quiet noise resembling as much as anything else the harsh rustling of dead, bone-dry leaves. As he ran forward, Howard prayed in his heart that the snake's fangs had not met in horseflesh.

Because the light was not all gone and he knew just where to look, he saw the rattler slipping away across the sand. He thrust his gun down as close as he dared and with the first shot blew the sinister, flat head off the ugly thick body. Then he went forward, calling soothingly to his horse.

Had it been any one of the horses he rode customarily, his voice might have carried something of quiet to startled nerves. But as it was the horse was frightened, it was free, it was running and the broken end of the tie-rope, whipping at its heels, put fresh terror into it. Howard saw it dimly as it crested a ridge a few hundred yards off; then its vague shape was gone, swallowed up in the night. He hurried after it over the ridge. The stars showed him empty spaces of billowy sand; there were black spots marking hollows and nowhere his horse. But yet he went forward hopefully or at least striving to retain his hope. He had little liking for the plight that would be his were he set afoot here in the heart of the Bad Lands. But at the end of upwards of an hour of fruitless search he went back to the water-hole and his traps, seeing the folly of further seeking now. He would have to camp here until daybreak. Tomorrow he might find his horse and might or might not recapture it; to-morrow he might see the poor beast lying dead and horribly swollen; to-morrow he might find in the empty desert nothing but emptiness. For to-night there was nothing better to do than make his bed and go to sleep under the stars and thank God for food and water.

At the first pale glint of the new day he was astir. With sleep still heavy in his eyes he hurried back to the ridge over which his horse had gone. As he was pretty well prepared to expect, there was no horse in sight. He waited for the light to brighten, probing with eager eyes into the distances. Swiftly the sky filled to the coming day; the shadows withdrew from the hollows, the earth stood forth, naked and clearly revealed. Save for himself, feeling dwarfed in this immensity, there was no living thing within the scope of his vision. He shook his head and turned back to camp and breakfast, frowning grimly. He would have to walk out of this mess, and like any twelve cattlemen out of a dozen he had little love of walking.

While he ate his morning meal he turned matters over in his mind. He saw that he could look forward confidently to a couple of unpleasant days. He did not anticipate any difficulty beyond that of the irksomeness of being obliged to trudge something like fifty miles in the sun. He knew that he would waste no end of time trying to track the vanished horse across such a land as this; he saw only foolhardiness in leaving the trail he had had picked out for him and, with little food and no knowledge of water, turning out across an utterly unknown land of forbidding desolation. He judged roughly that Desert Valley was as near as Quigley. Hence, having filled his canteen and tied his provisions into a bundle, he slung the two over his shoulders, left his saddle where it was and turned his face toward the home range.

Despite his determination to get an ugly task over and done with, he was a full four hours making the first ten miles. He walked as swiftly as he might to take the full advantage of the lesser heat of the earlier hours, but his way led him through loose sand, down into cuts and gorges, up their steep sides, across fields of loose stones, which, shifting underfoot, made

Jackson Gregory

his striving for haste a pure work of Tantalus. At the end of the first hour the heat was already intense; at the end of the second he felt that his skin was as dry as the desert sands and that the moisture of his body was being sucked out of it by the thirsty air and that at every stride the day grew drier and hotter. Thirst clutched his throat, ached throughout his body, that thirst which is like no other, desert thirst. Again and again he drank from his canteen. When he ploughed up the slope of the little hills and then down into their hollow to the double-ringed spring, his canteen was half empty. And when at last he came to the spring itself he found it as dry as a last year's seedpod.

Until this instant the day's adventure had been merely the acme of unpleasantness. Now something more sinister entered into it. He made certain that he had found the place where the water-hole should be. Then he sat down. His eyes were very grave.

'If I don't play this hand right,' he told himself solemnly, 'I'll never get out of this.'

He found a few breast-high bushes and crawled into their thin shade and lay down; before him he spread out the Quigley storekeeper's map. This he studied with thoughtful eyes. The storekeeper had said it would be no trick at all for a man like Howard to make the trip, but he had meant Howard on horseback. On foot it became quite another matter. The next spot where he should find water was some twenty miles ahead of him; at the rate he had travelled this morning it would take him some eight hours to come to it. Further, at the rate he had drank from his canteen this morning, that canteen would be empty when he had gone half the distance. Clearly, he must drink less water, just half what he had drank during the last four hours. Clearly also, it would grow hotter and he would want more instead of less water. Clearly again—and here was the point of points—when he came to the twenty-mile-distant water-hole, it too might be dry. And, after that, there was not another spring for another twelve or fifteen miles. Yes, many things were clear.

He sat up and rolled a cigarette; he sat still while he smoked it. Here was plainly a time for cool thinking; he would take all of the time that he needed to be sure that he had decided correctly. For later there might be no minute to squander. At present he had both food and water. At present he could go on or turn back. There was water where he had left his saddle; he could count on that positively and could get to it before he had emptied his canteen. But, if instead he went forward, there could be no turning back. He studied his map again. So far as he could make out from it, it was as well to go on as to retreat. So, putting his paper into his pocket he took up his food and water, made certain of his bearings and went on. It was a gamble, but a gamble his life had always been, and a fair gamble, an even break, is all that men like Alan Howard ask. He realized with a full measure of grimness that never until now had he placed a wager like this one; he was betting heavily and he knew not against what odds that at the end of twenty miles he would find water.

Hour after hour he trudged on. His feet burned; they ached; his boots made blisters and the blisters broke. Always he was thirsty with a thirst which his whole supply of water could not have slacked and which grew steadily more acute. Now and then he paused briefly and drank sparingly. His bundle of food, small as it was, grew heavy; his feet were heavy; only his canteen seemed to him lighter and lighter. A hot wind rose, blowing direct into his face, flinging at him fine particles of burning sand that sifted through his clothing and got into his boots, torturing further his tortured feet; the wind seared his eyeballs and threatened to blind him. He lifted his head, selected a distant landmark, sought to shelter his eyes with the broad brim of his hat and went on.

Noon found him plunging down the steep bank of a dry gulch, a hideous gash in the breast of the hideous land. He found a spot where there was a little shade under a clump of bushes growing upon the bank's edge. He ate a little of his dried beef; he treated himself to half a dozen big, slow swallows of water; then he lay and rested for half an hour. Again he rose; he moistened his mouth and lips, shut his teeth hard together as he took the first step upon swollen feet; again he wandered monotonously through a monotonous land. There was no wind now save, infrequently, frolicsome little whirlwinds which danced about him and were gone. When he found that their play angered him, that they seemed to mock at his weariness and dying energies, he frowned. This was no time and here was no place for nerves.

In the late afternoon, after having laboured all day through a hell of tedium and distress, he came to the water-hole. He marked it from afar by its dusty willows; he wondered if this time he would find water. It struck him that he must. He began to walk faster; he curbed a heady desire to break into a run. As it was, he came slowly, steadily to the spot. And there was no water. He would not believe it. He walked along the line of willows, looking carefully everywhere. And not until he had looked everywhere did he give up. Oddly, his compelling want at the moment was less for a drink than for a smoke. He began rolling a cigarette. Half-way through the brief task he desisted, returning the thimbleful of tobacco to its sack. For the hot smoke would merely dry out further his already dry mouth.

He lay down in what shade he could find and estimated very carefully the amount of water in his canteen. He weighed the vessel in his hand; he unscrewed the top and held it so as to look into it.

'I've got about three cupfuls,' he told himself.

Again he studied his map. Again he ate sparingly and thereafter took a sip of water. He screwed the top on quickly and tightly, jealous even of a drop which might evaporate in this sponge-air. He stood up, knowing that he must not loiter. For each second his thirst would increase as the arid air took the moisture forth through the pores of his body. Before he had moved a step forward he saw a man coming toward him. He laughed outright, a laugh of suddenly relieved nerves which had been very tense. That man would have water and would know where other water was to be found.

The man came neither from the direction of Quigley nor yet of Desert Valley. Rather he was coming in from the north, would cut Howard's trail almost at right angles. He was on foot. Howard wondered at that. Further, the man had a strange way of walking. He was half naked and about his head a dark cloth was tied. He trotted a few steps, seemed to hesitate and balance, he came on head down. Something seemed to get in the way of his feet; he stumbled, caught himself, stumbled a second time and fell on his face. He got to his hands and knees, slowly rose to his feet and came on, walking crazily. Then Howard understood. The man was an Indian or a half-breed and he was dying of thirst.

CHAPTER XIII

A SON OF THE SOLITUDES

Wonderingly Howard watched the man come on. For a moment he believed that the new-comer had gone both mad and blind. For the roving eyes were terrible to look into, black pools of misery, and the mouth was distended and the stumbling feet did not turn aside for scrub-brush or rock. From the waist up the gaunt coppery body was naked; of a ragged pair of overalls held up by a rawhide thong one leg was gone; the feet were bare.

'Hey there, *companero*,' called Howard. 'Where are you going?'

It was no longer a question of breed or Indian now. Despite the grime that made a mask over the face the features were unmistakably those of a pure-bred Hopi; the shape of the body that of the desert Indian. He had the small shoulders, the thin arms and the powerful iron legs of his people. He was passing only a dozen steps from Howard. He stopped at the sound of the voice, stared wildly and then sagged on by. Howard called again and then followed, bewildered. The Indian fell twice before he came to the spot where there should be water. Here he went down on his stomach, putting his face down as though to drink. Howard heard him groan when the bleared eyes saw that instead of water there was but blazing hot sand. The Indian made no other sound but merely rolled over on his back and lay very still, eyes shut, jaw dropping, hands lax at his sides.

'You poor devil!' muttered Howard.

He came to the prostrate figure. Now he noted that from the string-belt there hung at one hip a little buckskin bag; it might have held a handful of dried meat. Tied at the other hip was a bundle of feathers that made gay colour against the grey monotony, feathers of the bluebird, the redbird, blackbird and dove. Scabbardless, tied with a bit of thong close to the feathers, was a knife with a long blade.

The Indian's chest heaved spasmodically; his breath came in dry gasps. Howard stooped over him and called to him softly. The eyes flew open and, after a heavy gathering of the brows bespeaking the effort made, focussed upon Howard's.

'*Agua*,' pleaded the swollen lips.

Howard took up a sardine tin, the contents of which he had eaten while he rested, and, very careful not to spill a drop of the priceless fluid, poured it half full from his canteen. Then he knelt and put an arm about the gaunt body, lifting it a little, offering the water to the broken lips. Now he noted that the cloth about the black head of hair was stained with blood.

He had expected the man to drink thirstily. Instead, manifesting a display of will power such as the white man had never seen, the Indian took the water slowly, held it a moment in his mouth, swallowed it drop by drop.

'More,' he said when the tin was emptied.

Again Howard filled it. Now the Indian sat upright alone and drank. Afterwards he looked at Howard with a long, piercing regard. A second time he said 'More.'

Howard with his finger indicated how low his water was.

'Not much water, *companero*,' he said quietly. 'Pretty soon all gone.'

'No more?' queried the Indian sharply.

Howard poured out the third small tin; altogether he was giving the poor devil only about a cupful when a quart would have been all inadequate. Again the keen black eyes that seemed clearer now and like a bird's probed at him. Again and as before, the Indian drank.

'Me Kish Taka,' he announced slowly and with a certain dignity. 'Come far, head hurt, much sick, much blood. Pretty soon, no water, die. Now, pretty good.'

Howard grunted. That a man in this fellow's shape should declare himself as being 'pretty good' was worth any man's snort. He looked as though he would be dead in ten minutes as he lay back and shut his eyes. With his eyes still shut, the Indian spoke again:

'You *sabe* other water-hole?'

'No. I found it dry.'

'Kish Taka *sabe* water-hole. Sleep now, damn tired, damn hot, head sick. Sun go down, get cold, Kish Taka go there, you come, get water.'

'Where?' demanded Howard quickly. 'How far?' For he was half inclined to believe that if Kish Taka went to sleep now he would never wake.

The long, thin arm pointed out to the south-west.

'Not too far,' he said. 'Two big high mountain, some tree, water there. Maybe twenty-five mile.'

'Good God!' exclaimed Howard. 'Twenty-five miles! Might as well be a thousand!'

The Indian did not answer. He was breathing regularly, his lips were closed. For five minutes Howard stood looking down upon him and then he tiptoed a few yards away; Kish Taka was evidently asleep. Howard set his canteen down in the shade of a bush, found another bush for himself, and lay as the Indian was lying, on his back, relaxing his body. He did not regret having shared his water with an Indian, but he wondered why his destiny at this time of need had sent to him another thirsty mouth. Further, he allowed himself to wonder soberly if he would ever see his green fields again. He measured his chances with a steady mind, and in the end his mouth grew sterner.

'If I've got to cash in this way,' he muttered as his own sort of prayer, 'I hope I can be as game about it as Kish Taka.'

It struck him that in one thing the Indian was wise. It was as well to rest now until after sunset and then to start on again in what coolness the evening might afford. Further, it was not in him now to get up and sling his canteen on his back and go on, leaving the fellow wayfarer whom his fate had given him. He would try to sleep a little, though he had little enough hope of coaxing the blissful condition of rest and unconsciousness to him. But, physically tired, lulled by the great stillness, it was but a few minutes when he, too, slept heavily.

He woke and sat up. The day had gone, the stars were out, the air was cool against his cheek. He got to his feet and went to the spot where he had left the Indian, half expecting to find the man dead. Instead he found no man at all. He looked about him; there was light enough to see objects at a considerable distance. The desert seemed, as it had seemed all day, empty. He called and got no answer. It was obvious enough that Kish Taka had rested, waked, gone on.

'Got thirsty,' grunted Howard, 'and just trotted over to a spring only twenty-five miles off for a drink! That's the Indian for you.'

His own thirst sprang out upon him, clutching him by the

Jackson Gregory

throat. He stepped to the bush where he had left his canteen and groped for it. When he did not find it, he looked elsewhere, supposing that he had made a mistake in the bush. When the truth dawned upon him his whole body grew rigid, he stood motionless, even for a little his lungs suspended their function. His hands clenched; for some reason and apparently without any act of his will, they were lifted slowly until they were above his head. Then they came down slowly until they were at his sides, still clenched hard. It was his only gesture. He did not speak aloud. Again he stood still. But through his heart and soul and brain, sweeping upward and upward, came such a flood of rage as he had never known. And with it, born of it, came rushing the frenzied craving to kill. At last came his dry whisper:

'I am going to last long enough to kill you, Kish Taka, and may God damn your soul!'

One hand took up his little bundle of food; the, other dropped to the butt of his revolver. He went swiftly to the spot where he had left the Indian whom he had thought half dead. He estimated again and with great care the direction which the lean leathery hand had indicated as the direction of water. Then, walking swiftly, he struck out into the desert. Here was not the way to Desert Valley, not the way to Quigley. But here was the path for one man to follow when he sought another man who had wronged him. The fact that his chances of coming up with the Indian were few did not deter the cattleman; the obscurity of night on the desert did not give him halt or hesitation. The name of his wrath burned high and hot in his brain and in its lurid light he saw his desire fulfilled. Had one tried at the moment to reason with him, Howard would have cursed him and gone on. His anger had spurted up in a brain already mad with the torture of thirst.

And yet that brain was clear enough to guide him in the way he would go. He studied the stars, found the north and set his course painstakingly. Presently he began to walk less hurriedly, bent savagely upon reserving his strength. When there was some object ahead set visibly against the skyline, a hillock or a clump of bushes, he laid his course by it, checking again and again by the stars. When he had walked an hour he stopped and rested, lighting a match to look at his watch. He allowed himself exactly five minutes and floundered up and went on again. Doggedly he sought to shut his mind to the pain stabbing through his weary feet, to the constriction of his throat, to the ache of his body so sorely and so long punished. When, had matters been different, he might have cried out: 'God, for a drink!' he now muttered dully, 'God, put him into my two hands !'

The fine, delicate machinery of a human brain, like any man-made mechanism of great nicety, may readily be thrown into confusion, its exquisite balance disturbed, its functioning confounded. Thirst, near-exhaustion, severe bodily distress and, on top of all, blood-lust anger made Alan Howard over into another man. He was possessed, obsessed. As the night wore on endlessly he created for himself visions; he came a thousand times upon the Indian; he sank his fingers and thumbs into a corded throat; he beat with his fists at the pulp of a face. He grew accustomed to his own voice, muttering ceaselessly. He heard himself praying as another man; the burden of his prayers was always the same: 'Deliver him, O Lord, into mine hands.' He was half mad for water and he cursed Kish Taka; he drove his body on when the agonized muscles rebelled and, driving mercilessly, he cursed Kish Taka.

Somehow the night passed and through it he staggered on. He fell as he had seen the Indian fall; he recalled that the Indian had arisen and he rose. Each time that he failed in something that he tried to do it was as though an imp jeered and taunted him, calling to him: 'Ho! The Indian is a better man. He is off there in the darkness, laughing at you!'

There came a time when he stumbled at every step, when he pitched forward frequently and lay inert and had to gather his strength to get up; when he wondered if he was going mad or if already he had gone mad; when his thirst was a killing agony and he knew that it was in truth killing him; when he crawled on his hands and knees up slight slopes; when the stars danced and he frowned at them stupidly, seeking the North Star, seeking to know which way led to Kish Taka. When the first faint glint of dawn sweetened the air he was lying on his back; he felt, rather than saw, that a new day was blossoming. He collected his wandering faculties, fought with the lassitude which stole upon him whenever his senses were not on the alert and sat up. And he would have cried out aloud at what he saw were not his throat and mouth and lips so dry that he was beyond calling out. For yonder, a blurred moving shape came toward him. The shape was a man's, and he knew that it was Kish Taka.

Somehow he got to his feet, somehow he dragged his revolver out of its holster, somehow he took a dozen tottering steps forward. He saw that Kish Taka had seen him and had stopped; that the Indian carried his canteen; that he was moving again. Howard lifted his gun, holding it in both hands. He was afraid that even now his quarry would escape him, that Kish Taka would run and that he could not follow. His fingers found the trigger and pressed it as he sought to hold the wavering muzzle steady. There was a loud report that seemed to tear his brain to broken shreds, his arms dropped lax at his sides, the revolver fell, its muzzle burying itself in the sand. His knees sagged and he went down, settling slowly. As he fell he saw that Kish Taka was running—but not away from him. Running like a deer was Kish Taka, running straight to the fallen man.

For the first time in his life, Howard fainted, The pink dawn went black in his eyes, his brain reeled, the booming as of a distant surf filled his ears and then unconsciousness engulfed him. When he, knew anything at all it was that he was sitting up, that two thin brown arms were about his body, that water was trickling down his throat.

CHAPTER XIV

THE HATE OF THE HIDDEN PEOPLE

When Alan Howard fully understood, he felt his face go red with shame. There was in his soul something akin to timidity as he put his hand forth for the hand of Kish Taka. And when the Indian nodded gravely and gave his own hand, the white man's fingers locked about it hard. Still East was East and West was West, and again had two strong men met from the ends of earth.

'I have horses and cows and houses and corn,' said Howard, speaking slowly and simply that the Indian might understand clearly. 'What I have is my brother's. When Kish Taka wants a friend, let him come down into Desert Valley and call to Alan Howard.'

The beady, bird-like eyes were void of expression as Kish Taka regarded him steadily. The Indian did not so much as nod again. Like the desert that had mothered him and his progenitors, he had the tricks of silence and of inscrutability.

From the few words which the Indian had spoken and from his own suddenly altered estimate of his new companion, Howard came to understand fully the amazing act which Kish Taka had performed during the night. The Indian had been near the limits of his strength and endurance when the white man had given him generously of his water. Kish Taka had drank sparingly and, because he was desert-bred and because

Jackson Gregory

the stock from which he was sprung was desert-bred, his bodily strength had returned to him. He slept; Howard slept. But the Indian woke, somewhat refreshed, in half an hour. He understood that in the canteen there was not water for both. He promptly drank one of the two remaining cupfuls, slung the canteen over his shoulder and struck off swiftly for the twenty-five-mile-distant spring.

Again, had he been other than a Hopi, less than the superb creature that he was, the thing could not have been done. Down in Oraibi to-day an Indian boy will run eighty miles in a day for ten dollars, and on his return will run races for fun. The American desert has made him just as it has made the thirstless cactus and the desert wolf. He is a special creation, and Kish Taka was but doing the thing he knew. On the run he drained the canteen; at the end of it he stopped and drank and rested briefly. Then with full canteen he turned back to succour and save the man who had befriended and saved him. So it came about that he found Howard in time.

All of that long hot day they sought to rest, lying inert in what scant shade they could find, eating a few bits of dried beef, drinking their water now and then. By the time that the first hint of coming coolness crept into the air Howard sat up, somewhat refreshed and again eager to be moving. He turned to the Indian with a question on his lips, for a thought had come to him.

'Do you know Jim Courtot?' he asked sharply.

Kish Taka's eyes were veiled.

'What man, Jeem Cour'?' he demanded expressionlessly. Then, with the naivete of a child: 'Him your frien'?'

Howard tapped the sagging holster at his hip.

'For Jim Courtot I carry this.' he returned quietly. 'He wants to kill me.'

'Then,' said Kish Taka, and through the veils in his eyes fire flashed and was gone, 'him better be quick! Me, Kish Taka, I kill Jeem Cour' damn quick pretty soon.'

Howard looked at him curiously, wondering just how the trails of the gambler and the desert man had crossed and what wrong Courtot had done the other. For he did not doubt that the sin had been Courtot's.

'You have a big dog,' he said, still looking probingly into the beady eyes. 'Big dog, big head, big shoulders, teeth like a wolf. Where is he?'

If Kish Taka wondered at his knowledge, no sign evidenced the fact. His own teeth, white and strong as a wolf's, showed fleetingly, and into his expression came merely a look of pride.

'You my frien'—See!' With a swift gesture he whipped from his side his long knife, pricked his arm so that a drop of blood came, set his forefinger to the ruby drop and, leaning closer, touched the finger point in the palm of Howard's hand. 'Kish Taka tell you true. No other dog like the dog of Kish Taka! He run with Kish Taka, fight with Kish Taka, hunt with Kish Taka—kill for Kish Taka! He smell out the trail of the man not the frien' of Kish Taka. Now, Kish Taka say, "Dog, go home." And he gone. Yonder.' He swept his long arm out toward the north.

'Far?'

'Running,' answered Kish Taka, 'he go three day and night. Running he come back, other three day and night.'

From other added fragments Howard gathered something of a story: Kish Taka and his brother, the dog with them, had come from 'where they lived' far off to the north, seeking Jim Courtot. Yesterday Kish Taka had sent his dog back across the wastes, carrying a message. The message was in the form of a feather from his belt tied with a lock of hair dipped in blood.

The feather was grey, from a dove's wing, and grey is symbolical of the Underworld with the Hopi; the hair was from the head of Kish Taka's brother. The meaning was plain. The explanation came stoically: Kish Taka pointed to the wound upon his own head. Jim Courtot, more cunning than they had thought, had surprised his pursuers, had even come out into the desert to take them unawares. He had killed the other Indian from ambush, had wounded Kish Taka and had fled. Now Kish Taka's tribesmen would understand and another runner would come to take the place of him who had fallen.

That the dog would understand to make the return across the desert to 'where they lived' was also explained. Each man there had his dog, each man had his friend. These two men, kind to their two dogs, caressed them, fed them, sheltered them. All other men in the tribe abused these two beasts on sight, stoned them, drove them away. Hence every dog had two masters whom he loved with all of the loyalty of a dog heart and all other men he distrusted and feared and hated. Now, in the desert, Kish Taka had but to drive his dog from him, shouting at him, casting a stone at him, and the big brute to whom similar experiences had come before out of as clear a sky, knew that he had a friend in the distant camp, one friend only in the world, and as straight as a dart made off to find him. In three days' time he would be leaping and fawning upon his other master, sure of food and kind words. And, when in turn that other master turned upon him and seized a stick with which to beat him, he would know that Kish Taka would take him into his arms and give him meat and water. For such things had he known since he was a roly-poly puppy.

There was but one matter further about which Howard wondered, and he asked his question point-blank. Point-blank Kish Taka answered it.

Jim Courtot, with lies in his mouth, had come to these desert folk several months ago. He had tarried with them long, swearing that he hated all white men, that he had killed a white and that the whites would kill him, that he would spend his life with the Indians, teaching them good things. In time they came to trust him. He learned of them their secrets, he found where they hid the gold they used now and then to barter with the white men in their towns, he saw their hidden turquoises. Further, he wronged a maiden who was one day to come to the *kiva* of the headman, the Hawk Man, Kish Taka. The maiden now was dead by her own hand; Courtot that night, full-handed with his thievings, had fled; and always and always, until the end came, Kish Taka would follow him.

Howard heard and looked away through the growing dusk and saw, not the scope of a dimming landscape, but something of the soul of Kish Taka. He understood that the Indian had given his confidence freely and he knew that it was, no doubt, the first and last time in his life that he would so speak with a *bahana*. And it was because Howard had shared his last water with him and was, therefore, 'brother.' Kish Taka was an implacable hater; he would follow Jim Courtot until one of them was dead. Kish Taka was a loyal friend, for the Hopi who will bare his heart to a man will bare his breast for him.

Further questions Howard did not ask, feeling that he had penetrated already further into the man's own personal matters than he should have done. He had heard tales such as all men hear when they come into the influence of the desert south-west, wild tales like those he had recounted about Superstition Pool to Helen and her father, wilder tales about a people who dwelt on in the more northern and more bleak parts of the desert. Lies, for the most part, he judged them, such lies as men tell of an unknown country and other men repeat and embroider. There were men whom he knew who maintained stoutly that the old Seven Cities of Cibola were no dead myth but a living reality; that there were a Hidden People; that they had strange customs and worshipped strange gods and bowed the knee in particular to a young and white goddess, named Yohoya; that they hunted with monster dogs, that they had hidden cities scooped out centuries ago in mountain cliffs and that they were incredibly rich in gold and turquoises. Lies, perhaps. And yet a lie may be based upon truth. Here was a high-type Indian who called himself Kish Taka, the Hawk Man; he hunted with such a dog; he camped on the trail of a *bahana* who had betrayed and robbed his people. That *bahana* was Jim Courtot. What had taken Jim Courtot into that country? And now that he was back, Jim Courtot was flush. And, when Sandy Weaver had mentioned certain tracks to him, he had stared over his shoulder and turned white! Truly, there were many questions to ask; but Howard refrained from asking them.

'This Indian has played a white man's part to me,' he told himself. 'And his business is his own and not mine.'

'Come,' said Kish Taka abruptly out of the silence into which they had sunk. 'Cool now, we go.'

They had but little water remaining in Howard's canteen, and Kish Taka scorned carrying water for himself; but he had outlined the trail they would take and appeared confident that they would not suffer from lack of water. They struck out toward the south-east, the Indian swinging along ahead, his body stooped a little forward, his thin arms hanging loose at his sides. Several times Howard stopped to drink; the Indian drank once only before their arrival at the spring. Here they rested and ate. The night was already far advanced and glorious with its blazing stars, and they did not tarry long. In half an hour they moved on again. As day was breaking Kish Taka led the way up a steep-sided mesa and, catching Howard's arm, pointed out toward the east.

'Here we turn,' he explained. 'Not so far that way, maybe two hours, we find more water. Then we go that way,' and he indicated that they must bear off a little to the south, 'and more water. Then we sleep in shade. Then at night, not too far, see your place.'

It came about that all that Kish Taka had predicted was so. They found water; they spent the long day in the shade of some stunted trees; they ate all but a few scraps of their food;

they went on again at sundown. In the pink flush of another dawn they stood together on the uplands back of Last Ridge and saw before them and below them the green of Desert Valley. In the foreground, a thin wisp of smoke arose from the spot where the Longstreets were camped.

'Kish Taka go back now.' The Indian stood, arms folded across his gaunt chest, eyes hard on Howard's. 'Back to the Bad Lands to sit down. Soon Kish Taka's dog comes and with him a man. And while he waits, Kish Taka will make many stones piled up on his brother.'

He swung on his heel to go. But Howard caught at his arm.

'Wait,' he said. 'Two things! One, where that fire is are two people. An old man and a girl. They are my friends, Kish Taka.'

Kish Taka nodded.

'My frien's,' he said simply.

'The other thing,' said Howard. 'Kish Taka, hungry, killed my calves. He left gold. When again Kish Taka is hungry, let him kill as many calves as he pleases. But let him keep his gold.'

Again the Indian nodded. And this time Howard let him go.

The Indian went back toward the Bad Lands, swift, silent, and in a little was lost in the distance. He did not once turn. Howard withdrew his eyes and sent them questing down toward the wisp of smoke. His thoughts were wandering. And last they winged to Jim Courtot.

'Jim Courtot,' he muttered under his breath, as though the man were with him, and as he saw fancied visions of things to be, 'I have it in my heart to be almost sorry for you.'

Then he shrugged, filled his lungs with the fresh clean cool air which rose up across the miles from his own pastures and set his feet into the trail that would lead home—by way of the Longstreets. Now he walked eagerly. In half an hour he had made his way down to the flat upon which the canvas shanty stood. He came on, the fatigue gone from a stride that was suddenly buoyant; there was a humorous glint in his eyes as he counted upon surprising them; he would just say, casually, that he had dropped in, neighbour-style, for breakfast.

Then he saw Helen, her upturned, laughing face rosy with the newly-risen sun. Before her, looking down into her eyes, was John Carr. Howard came abruptly to a dead halt. They saw him, and Helen called something to him. Again he came on, but the joyous spring had gone out of his stride and he realized in a dull, strange fashion that for the first time in his life he was not glad to see his old friend.

CHAPTER XV

THE GOLDEN SECRET

'Good morning, Mr. Howard!' cried Helen gaily. Her cheeks were still rosy, flushed, thought Howard quickly, less with the flood of the dawn than with some sudden rush of blood stirred by something that Carr had been saying. Then as she gave him her hand, inspired by the imp of the moment, she ran on: 'You should have been here last night! Shouldn't he, Mr. Carr? Sanchia was here!'

'Mrs. Murray?' demanded Howard, wondering and therefore floundering into Helen's trap. 'What was she doing here?'

Helen appeared to be in the lightest of spirits this morning. Her laughter was one of sheer joyousness. Her eyes were dancing as she retorted:

'Mrs. Murray? Who said Mrs. Murray? I was talking about Sanchia. Mr. Chuck Evans rode her over last night, asking if we had seen you.'

Howard bit his lip. Carr laughed. Then, seeing the look upon his friend's face, he grew grave immediately and put out his own hand, saying merely:

'We wondered what had become of you, Al. And now to have you come in from that direction—and on foot! What's happened?'

'A side-winder scared my horse into breaking its tie-rope and leaving me on foot. And I've had enough walking to last me seven incarnations. Hello, Mr. Longstreet,' as he saw the professor step out of his canvas house. Howard went forward to meet him, leaving John Carr with Helen.

'Just the man I was wishing to see,' beamed Longstreet, shaking hands enthusiastically. 'I was on the verge of taking up the matter with your good friend Carr last night, but something prompted me to wait until this morning, in hopes you would come. I—I seem to know you better, somehow.' He lowered his voice confidentially. 'Those two out there are just a couple of youngsters this morning. You and I will have to be the serious brains of the occasion.'

Howard glanced over his shoulder. Carr's broad back was turned to him, Helen's eyes, glancing toward the shack, were sparkling.

'Fire away,' he said colourlessly. 'What's in the wind?'

'First thing—Had breakfast yet?'

Oddly, Howard had no longer any appetite for coffee and bacon, though he had hungrily swallowed his last bit of dried meat an hour ago.

'Then,' said Longstreet eagerly, 'come in here where we can talk.' And to Helen he called, 'My dear, I want a few words with Mr. Howard.'

'Oh, we won't disturb you,' Helen laughed back at him. It struck Howard that she would laugh at anything this morning. 'Mr. Carr and I were just going up on the cliff for the view.'

Longstreet came in and dropped the flap behind him. Then he stepped to a shelf and took down a roll of paper which he spread upon the table. Howard looking at it with lack-lustre eyes saw that it was a sort of geological chart of the neighbourhood. Longstreet set his finger upon a point where he had made a cross in red pencil.

'It's there,' he announced triumphantly.

Howard was thinking of the view from the cliff and failed to grasp the other's meaning.

'What's there?' he asked.

'Gold, man!' cried Longstreet. 'Gold! Didn't I say it was as simple as A B C to find gold here? Well, I've done it!'

'Oh, gold.' And even yet Howard's interest was not greatly intrigued. 'I see.'

Longstreet stared at him wonderingly. And then, suddenly, Howard came to earth. Why, the thing, if true, was wonderful, glorious! With all his heart he hoped it was true; for Longstreet's dear old sake, for Helen's. He studied the map.

'That would be right over yonder? About half a mile from here? In Dry Gulch?'

'Precisely. And it has been there since the time Dry Gulch was not dry but filled with rushing waters. It has been there for any man to find who was not a fool or blind. It rather looks,' and he chuckled, 'as though it had been waiting since the Pliocene age for me.'

'You are sure? You haven't just stumbled upon a little pocket—'

Longstreet snorted.

'I am going into the nearest fair-sized town right away,' he said emphatically, 'to get men and implements to begin a moderate development. It is a gold mine, my dear young sir—nothing else or less. Here; look at this.'

Jackson Gregory

It was a handful of bits of quartz, brought up into the light from the depths of a sagging pocket. The quartz indicated high-grade ore; it was streaked and pitted with soft yellow gold.

'By the Lord, you've got it!' cried Howard. He wrung Longstreet's hand warmly. 'Good for you. You've got the thing you came for!'

'One of the things,' Longstreet corrected him with twinkling eyes.

'And the other?'

'Another gold mine! As our young friend Barbee puts it, I'm all loaded for bear this trip, partner!'

'And you haven't told Miss Helen? Or Carr?'

'Never a word. And for two very excellent reasons: *Imprimis*, they both were poking fun at me last night; Helen said that I couldn't find gold if it were in a minted twenty-dollar gold piece in my own pocket. Now I am having my revenge on them; I'll show them! *Secundo*: Next week comes Helen's birthday. I am going to give her a little surprise. A gold mine for a birthday present isn't bad, is it?'

Howard sat down to talk matters over, and since there was still coffee and some bits of toast left he changed his mind about breakfast and ate and drank while he listened to Longstreet. The university man had made certain of the value of his discovery only last evening; it had happened that Carr was staying over with them and therefore, while he and Helen chatted about a great deal of nothing at all, Longstreet had ample time to think matters over. To-day he meant to go into Big Run and on into the county seat, which he had learned was but a few miles further on and was a sizable town. There he would take on a small crew of men and what tools and implements and powder would be needed for uncovering his ledge and there he would attend to the necessary papers, the proving up on his claim, matters upon which he was somewhat hazy. The following day he would return and begin work.

'I've got to go down by the ranch,' Howard told him. 'Then, if you like, I can go on with you. It is possible I might be of service to you. At least, I could steer you into the right sort of people.'

Longstreet nodded vigorously. 'That's fine of you. And I won't say it was not expected. Some day, perhaps, I can repay you for some of your kindnesses to us. Now, if you are ready, I'll go and call Helen. And, remember, not a word to them about our business.'

'Miss Helen will go with us?'

'I can hardly leave her out here alone, can I?' smiled Longstreet. 'And Mr. Carr said that he would have to leave this morning. While he and Helen chat together, you and I can ride on ahead and talk. There are any number of matters to discuss.'

Howard hastily expressed his approval of the plan, and if his tone lacked heartiness, Longstreet did not notice.

'We are all going down to Desert Valley ranch,' Longstreet explained when Helen and Carr came at his calling. 'From there we are going to ride to Big Run and then on into San Ramon. I want to get some—some tools and things there, to scratch around with, you know,' he concluded, beaming with that expression that he wore when he had an ace in the hole. Helen looked at him with keen suspicious eyes.

'Papa is up to something underhanded,' she announced serenely. 'He thinks that he can fool me when he pleases and— look at his face! What is it, father?'

'Never mind,' said Longstreet hastily. 'Just get yourself ready, my dear. You'll ride with us, Mr. Carr?'

Helen, always ready for a ride, hurried for her hat and gloves; now from the end of the room, her eyes bright with mischief and hidden from the men, she called:

'Do come, Mr. Carr. I have to have some one to talk with, you know, and papa and Mr. Howard never let me slip a word in sideways.'

'She wasn't like this when we rode home in the moonlight the other night,' thought Howard, considerably puzzled. 'What have I done, anyway?'

Carr did not give a direct answer. While he cut the end off a fresh cigar, he suggested:

'How about the horses? Al is on foot.'

'That's easy,' Howard answered. 'Chuck Evans is herding a string up this way and I can get one of them. Be back while you are getting ready.' And over his shoulder to Carr, feeling vaguely that in his heart he had been unreasonable and not quite loyal, 'Better come along, John.'

From the edge of the tableland he saw Evans down below. The cowboy saw him and came at his signal.

'So you're back, are you?' said Chuck. 'We'd begun to wonder if you'd hit the trail for some other where. Special,' he added significantly, 'since it's been published kind of wide and large that you and Jim Courtot was both packing shooting-irons.'

'I haven't seen Courtot,' Howard told him carelessly, 'and I'm beginning to believe that he has other calves to brand and has pretty well forgotten all about me. I'm shy a horse, Chuck. Scare one up for me to ride back to the ranch, will you?'

By the time Chuck on his own horse had roped a mount for

Howard the little party was ready. They rode down into the valley four abreast and across the fields to the ranch-house. Helen seemed a new creature this morning, utterly tantalizing and not a little perverse. Howard did not know what a proud and independent little person she was, nor did he know that each day during the week she had expected him to ride over, and had finally told herself point-blank that it did not matter the least snap of her fingers whether he ever came or not. Naturally, she did not know what had kept him away or that he had even wanted to come. Now that she had heard his remark about a lost horse and a long walk she was burning with curiosity. But that was another matter hidden from Alan.

She did remark the big revolver at his hip and when opportunity arose mentioned it to Carr. Wasn't it rather strange, she wanted to know, and even somewhat absurd that a man should go about armed like that? Carr evaded and made a vague remark about a man riding across the Bad Lands perhaps with money in his pocket. But John Carr was a blunt, straightforward type of a man, little given to finesse in circumlocution, and Helen fixed her frank, level gaze upon him and knew that he was holding back something. Still higher rose her curiosity about a man whom she did her feminine best to ignore this morning.

Before they came to the ranch-house Helen and her father were riding ahead, while the two friends dropped further and further back. Carr listened with keen interest as Alan sketched the happenings of the last few days. He whistled softly at what he learned of the man on the trail of Jim Courtot. But he shook his head when Alan predicted that, soon or late, Kish Taka would kill the gambler.

'It's white man and Indian, Al,' he said. 'The thing always works out the same way. Jim got one of the two of them, didn't he? Well, he'll get the other. And what I know of the breed of your friend Kish Taka, they're a pretty low-lived bunch and there'd be precious little harm done if they killed each other.'

But Alan shook his head. 'Kish Taka is a pretty deep shade of dark on the outside, but he's white clean through under the hide of him. And I've got it clear in my head that he'll never quit on the trail until he's squared accounts with Courtot.'

'By the way,' said Carr carelessly after a moment, 'the professor seems all excited about something or other this morning. What's it all about?'

'What do you mean?' countered Howard.

'Oh, nothing. Only from the way he grabbed on to you I fancied that he had told you. I thought that if there were anything I could do for him—'

'No. There's nothing. He did tell me, but he asked me not to say anything about it. I'll tell you as soon as I can, John. To-night, maybe, or to-morrow.'

'Oh,' said Carr. 'I didn't mean to stampede in on a secret.' He turned to other matters and presently they fell silent, jogging along together, their eyes for the most part upon the girl riding ahead of them.

'Papa,' Helen was saying at her first opportunity, 'where has Mr. Howard been?'

'I have no idea, my dear,' said her father placidly.

'What! You mean to tell me that you two have done all the talking you have, and that he hasn't said a word about where he has been hiding himself all this week?'

'Not a word.'

'H'm,' said Miss Helen, 'that's funny.' And then, 'Papa, do you know if he has had trouble with anyone lately?'

'What makes you ask that?' he queried uneasily, and Helen sat straighter in the saddle and looked him full in the face. For now she was positive that Alan had had trouble and that her father knew about it.

Longstreet hesitated. He had no desire to recount his experience at Moraga's saloon in Big Run. He had judged himself fortunate since the affair that Helen had been so absorbed in her new environment that she had not thought to call upon him for an accounting of the family funds. But even so, all along he had had a sort of fatalistic fear that in the end she would know everything; she always did.

'Well,' said Helen commandingly, 'tell me all about it.'

'Eh?' He started guiltily. 'About what?'

'About Mr. Howard's trouble with another man.'

Then Longstreet told her what he must. How, while he was with Barbee, a man named Jim Courtot had joined them. How Howard had happened along, looking for him, and had said that Jim Courtot was no gentleman. Ahem!—he had said it very emphatically, very. Longstreet did not recall the exact terms employed, but their purport was that Courtot was a crook and a—a man-killer. Courtot had whipped out a revolver, Howard had hurled himself upon him and had knocked him down. Table and chairs were overturned, and at first Longstreet thought that Courtot was dead. He was still unconscious when they left.

'Table?' said Helen. 'And chairs? Where were you? In whose house? For this didn't happen at the hotel and there was no table in the store.'

'In the—the house of a man named Moraga, I believe,' Longstreet answered hurriedly.

Helen looked at him severely.

'A saloon, wasn't it?' she asked, quite as a school teacher may put a leading question to a squirming little boy. When he did not answer immediately, Helen did not wait.

'I think,' she informed him judicially, 'that it will be better for you if I don't lose sight of you in these cattle and mining towns after this. And it would be a better thing for Mr. Howard if he did not frequent such places.'

'But you sent him for me!'

Helen merely sniffed at him. She was wondering if Jim Courtot really were a man-killer? She shuddered. Then she set her brain to work upon the name—Jim Courtot. It had a familiar ring; certainly she had heard it before. She and her father rode on in silence. She could hear Alan and Carr talking together again. Suddenly she remembered. It had been that afternoon when they went to Big Run. The two men had spoken of Mrs. Murray, remarking that she was in town. It had been Alan who had said on the heels of this remark:

'I'll bet you Jim Courtot has turned up again!'

That was it! Sanchia Murray—Jim Courtot. What had the one to do with the other? Had the enmity of the two men, Howard and Courtot, begun over Sanchia Murray?

When they came to the ranch-house and Alan was at her side to help her to the ground, Helen said, 'No, thank you,' quite stiffly and slipped down unaided.

CHAPTER XVI

SANCHIA SCHEMES

Chance had it that the very first individual they saw in Big Run was Sanchia Murray. She was in white and looked fresh and cool and girlish and inviting as she sat idling upon the porch at the hotel. When she saw them, she smiled engagingly.

Only a minute ago as they turned into the hot, deserted street Alan Howard had suggested:

'We'd better have lunch at the hotel and ride on to San Ramon afterwards.' Helen now told herself wisely that he had known Mrs. Murray would be at the hotel. She turned to wave to John Carr, who had said good-bye at the outskirts of Big Run; he claimed that he had been away from home long enough and had some business waiting on his return.

'He's perfectly splendid, don't you think, Mr. Howard?' Helen asked brightly, quite as if she had not yet seen Sanchia.

'Yes,' he rejoined warmly. 'He's the best friend a man ever had.'

They dismounted, and Sanchia Murray was not to be ignored longer. She hurried forward and gave both hands at the same time, one to Helen, one to Longstreet. Howard, who held back a pace, fully occupying his own hands with the reins of the three horses, she treated to a quick, friendly nod. He turned away to the stable as the Longstreets and Sanchia took chairs on the porch. Helen was cool but civil; she did not like the woman and yet she had no sufficient cause to be downright rude as she was inclined to be. Longstreet, on the other hand, as he made himself comfortable, considered Sanchia Murray as nice and friendly and pleasant.

They chatted about this, that and the other thing, all inconsequential, and Helen had to admit that Sanchia had her charm, that she was vivacious and clever and pretty. Helen contented herself for the most part with a quiet 'Yes' or 'No,' and sat back and made her judgments. In the first place, Sanchia was no woman's woman, but the type to lead a heedless man to make a fool of himself. In the second place, and even when she was laughing, her dark eyes were quick and filled with a look of remarkable keenness. And, finally, it appeared that she felt a very strong interest in Longstreet.

'She's nothing but a flirt,' thought Helen with something of disgust and utterly without realization that she herself had come perilously close to flirting with John Carr not so long ago—though of course with ample reason! 'She'd look like that at any man, were he in knee-breeches or as old as Dad.'

Howard came, and presently they went into the darkened dining-room. Sanchia was entertaining Longstreet with an account of her first coming into this perfectly dreadful country, and so it came about that Helen and Alan entered together and found chairs side by side. Since for the greater part of the meal Sanchia monopolized the university man, Alan and Helen were left largely to themselves. And, largely, they were silent. He sought to engage her in talk some two or three times, found her quiet and listless, and in the end gave up all attempt at conversation. After lunch, while Mrs. Murray's tongue was still racing merrily for the benefit of the professor, Howard succeeded in getting Helen alone at the far end of the porch.

'Look here, Helen,' he said after his outright style, 'what's the

The Desert Valley   145

matter? What have I done?'

'*Helen?*' she repeated after him.

'Oh, I beg your pardon, Miss Helen, or Miss Longstreet, or Your Ladyship. That Helen just slipped out.'

'So I noticed. Is it a little habit of yours calling girls by their first names when—'

'I don't know any girls,' he cut in vigorously.

She lifted her brows at him.

'How about Sanchia Murray? Isn't she—'

'Damn Sanchia Murray,' he said savagely.

'I'm talking about you! You and me.'

Helen gasped. Either his oath shocked her or she gave a very excellent imitation of a maiden thunder-stricken by such language as she had never dreamed a man could employ. Certainly not a man who had the slightest claim to the title of a gentleman.

'I beg your pardon again,' muttered Howard. 'That's twice. And now tell me, will you, what I've done?'

Just what had he done? Helen had to think fast. He was tall and straight and manly, he stood looking honestly into her eyes, he was good to look upon and he struck her as very much of a man all the way through. Further, he had said 'Damn Sanchia Murray,' quite as though he meant it with all his heart. Just what had he done?

'Are you going to tell me?' he was asking again. 'That's only fair, you know.'

'Don't you know?' countered Helen. She looked the part of a girl who knows very well herself, but is in doubt whether or not she should speak about it.

'No,' he told her vigorously, 'honest to grandma, I don't. But I'm sorry, just the same.'

Then, all suddenly and with no premeditation, Helen smiled and Alan Howard's heart grew warm.

'Maybe sometime I'll tell you,' she informed him. 'If you didn't mean it, we'll forget it now. And I'll try to believe that you didn't mean anything.'

He was considerably puzzled. He scratched his head and wondered. So there was something, then, that he had done to offend her? Then he was a low-lived dog and should have been choked to death. He couldn't know that there was really nothing in the world wrong, and never had been anything wrong; that merely Helen had been musing upon a mare's name, and that she had missed him, and did not intend that he should know it, and had resorted to the ancient womanly trick of smiling upon another man. At least Howard was relieved. The day grew bright again and he could find it in his heart to thank God for Sanchia Murray, who still monopolized Helen's father.

This monopoly was one which continued into the afternoon. For when time came to ride on to San Ramon, Longstreet stated that Mrs. Murray was going with them. It appeared that she had seen a most adorable hat there in the milliner's window and had planned since early morning upon riding over for it. So when Alan brought the other horses he led hers with them, a beautiful white mare, glossy and well-groomed, trim as a greyhound and richly accoutred in Mexican saddle and Spanish bit. Mrs. Murray kept them waiting a moment, hardly more. Then she appeared dressed in a distracting riding habit. They saw her leave an envelope with the hotelkeeper; they did not hear her instructions. Then all mounted, and again

Howard had it in his heart to be grateful for Sanchia. For now he and Helen rode together and far enough in advance to be in a world by themselves.

Until this moment Mrs. Murray had talked about nothing in the world that mattered. But now, her eyes watchful, her manner that of one who has waited long enough and is impatient, she said quickly:

'You are still looking for your gold mine?'

'Yes,' said Longstreet. 'Oh, yes.'

But on the instant in his eye was that look of a man with the ace buried. Perhaps Mrs. Murray had played poker; clearly she knew something of poker faces.

'You have found it!' she cried softly. 'Oh, I am so glad!'

He looked at her wonderingly.

'What makes you say that?' he stammered.

'That I am glad? Why shouldn't I be? Why shouldn't every one be glad? When one's friend—oh, but we are friends, dear Mr. Longstreet! There is the one glorious thing to be said about this country, about all of the West back from the railroads, that two persons don't have to know each other a year to become real, true friends. For your sake and for the sake of your wonderful daughter, am I not to be genuinely glad?'

He had to wait to the end of the rushing words to correct her:

'I meant, what made you say that I had found it?'

She opened her big eyes at him like a baby.

'But you have, haven't you? You came to find gold; you

brought to bear upon the situation your scientific knowledge instead of a prospector's poor brain; and you have found gold, I am sure!' She smiled upon him brightly as she concluded with a semblance of trustfulness and artlessness: 'Tell me the truth; haven't you found it?'

Suddenly he found himself hard beset. She had gauged him pretty accurately and therefore had asked him the question pointedly. He must either say yes or no; true, he might be rude to her and refuse an answer, but that would be equivalent to an admission. If he said 'No,' he would be lying. There was no other word for it.

'Well?' persisted Sanchia. She still smiled, she was still extremely kind and friendly, but it was plain that she would have her answer.

Still he hesitated. What were his reasons for secrecy, after all? Just to spring a surprise for Helen on her birthday. He had already told Alan. A secret is a rather dull and stupid affair unless it is shared. Mrs. Murray was all that was sympathetic; she would rejoice with him.

'I had not planned to say anything about it yet,' he began hesitatingly.

'Oh!' she cried joyously. 'It's wonderful, wonderful, wonderful! I am so glad! Tell me about it. All about it, every word.'

Longstreet's smile answered her own. And, of course, he told.

'Only,' he warned her, 'I am keeping it a secret for a little. Helen doesn't know. Next week is her birthday. I am going to give it to her then.'

Mrs. Murray dropped her reins long enough to clap her gauntleted hands. Then she elicited the whole story. She asked to be informed how he knew he had really found gold; she expressed her child-like wonder at his great wisdom; she was breathless with admiration after a fashion which made him glow; and meantime she learned exactly where the place was and saw his specimens. As she took them into her own hands her eyes were lowered so that they were hidden; but when she looked up they were shining.

'Give me one of them, just one,' she pleaded. 'Won't you? I should so dearly love to keep it for a souvenir of this happiness which is coming to you.' She sighed. Then, in a faint, quiet little voice: 'Maybe I am asking too much?'

'No, no,' returned Longstreet stoutly. He selected the finest specimen and presented it to her quite as a kind father might have given a stick of candy to his little girl. 'It is very kind of you to rejoice with us in the good fortune which is beginning to come our way. Just beginning,' he added with grave assurance.

'I'll have a locket made of it,' said Sanchia. Now for a little it was Longstreet who did the talking. She grew thoughtful, nodding now and then or answering absent-mindedly.

'You'll begin work soon?' she asked abruptly.

'Immediately. That's what I'm going into San Ramon to-day for. There are certain necessary papers to be drawn, you know, in order to file properly. Then I'm going to get some men and teams and explosives and tools and begin development to-morrow.'

More thoughtful still grew Sanchia, biting her lips, frowning, hiding her eyes under her wide hat. Once she looked up quickly and studied his eager face, her eyes keen and searching. Then, still watching him for the slightest change of expression, she said:

'Maybe I can be of assistance to you. You will be busy enough getting your crew and implements. I know everybody in San Ramon; George Harkness, at the court-house, is the man to arrange your papers and he is an old friend of mine. I am going to see him anyway to-day, and if you like I can have him do everything for you and send you your papers next week. It requires several days, you know,' and by now her intent regard had assured her that he knew absolutely nothing in the world about it.

Longstreet demurred. He wasn't certain that it could be done this way, nor did he like the idea of imposing upon her. But, she told him quickly, it *could* be done; she had acted for another gentleman in this capacity, Mr. Nate Kemble of the Quigley mines. She knew all about it. As for imposition, she broke into a timid little laugh.

'I am a rather helpless and, I am afraid, stupid sort of a little woman,' she confessed. 'I have to make my own way in the world, and this is one of the ways I do it. If, when everything is properly concluded, you feel that I have really been of assistance and care to send me a small cheque, just for services rendered, you understand, why—'

He saw the matter immediately in the desired light.

'Then,' he told her heartily, 'I shall be delighted to have you see Mr. Harkness for me. You are very kind, Mrs. Murray. And, as you say, I can give my attention exclusively to the other end of the business. As to the location of the spot so that the papers—'

'Oh, that part is all right! I know just where the Dry Gulch is and so will George when he looks it up on his maps. You won't have to worry about that in the least.'

Again Sanchia grew silent and thoughtful. Before them, side by side, went Helen and Howard. She watched them and held her horse back so that she and Longstreet would not come any closer to them. Finally she made her second suggestion, watching as before the play of Longstreet's expression.

'You have told Mr. Howard?'

'Yes. No one else.'

'He understands that you wish to keep your secret from Helen?'

'Yes.'

'Then, suppose we do this: As we come into town I must leave you a moment to ride by the milliner's and be sure that she holds that hat for me; she lives on a side street. You can ride with the others to the hotel, for you will have to stay all night there; it will be impossible for you to get everything done before dark. And, after all, maybe it would be better if you come with me to the court-house. I want you at least to meet Mr. Harkness. I will attend to everything for you; you can rejoin Helen and Mr. Howard. And I think he will understand if you suggest that he stay with Helen at the hotel while you ride down to the post office to mail a letter, let's say. I wouldn't mention court-house,' she added, 'as Helen might guess.'

During the remaining hour of jogging slowly through the sunshine, Sanchia Murray elaborated her plans, all directed toward the double end of hastening Longstreet's venture and keeping his secret from Helen. She went into detail, secured his consent upon each point or swiftly withdrew it to make another suggestion, and in the end awoke in him a keen sense of her generosity. When they came to the first buildings of the straggling town she waved her hand gaily, swung off into a side street, and he rode on to overtake Alan and Helen. Once around a corner Sanchia put spurs to her mare, struck the sweating shoulders with her quirt and raced on her way through puffing clouds of dust and barking dogs as though all leisureliness were gone before a sudden vital need for haste. Before the party of three had come within sight of the hotel she had swung down from her saddle at the back door of the Montezuma House. And every one who knows San Ramon knows the Montezuma, and every one who knows the place knows a house of sinister reputation.

At the hotel Howard dismounted first to give his hand to Helen. This time she accepted it and even repaid him with a quick smile. Longstreet, while Helen was dismounting, tipped the cattleman a sly wink. It was meant to be full of meaning, but only succeeded in making Howard wonder.

'If you two will wait for me a moment,' said Longstreet, making a perfectly transparent pretence of having nothing of importance on his mind, 'I am going to ride over to the post office. It's just over yonder. You'll be on the porch when I come back?' and without waiting for a reply he clucked to his horse and trotted away. Helen looked after him in surprise.

'Papa's up to something he ought to leave alone,' she decided wisely. She turned to remount.

'We'd better follow him and—'

Suddenly her expression altered. Her eyes softened and she added.

'I know,' she added. 'No, we mustn't follow him. And he'll be gone an hour.'

'What is it?' wondered Alan.

'I am not quite old enough to stop having birthdays,' she explained. 'He's just slipping off mysteriously as usual to buy something expensive and foolish for me. He's just about the dearest old dad in the world.'

So they tied their horses and went into the cool of the shady porch. Because they had matters of their own to talk about, they did not concern themselves further with the eccentricities of a fond parent. Meantime Longstreet, chuckling as he went, rode by the post office to establish a sort of moral alibi and thence proceeded to the court-house. He found it readily, a square, paintless, dusty building upon a dying lawn. Sanchia looking flushed and hot, was waiting for him under a tree in front.

'Mr. Harkness is out,' she told him immediately. 'And as it happens, there is no one in the office. But I have found where his assistant is. He is Mr. Bates, and he has had a hard day, it seems, and is now having a late lunch at the Montezuma House. We are to ride over there.'

This satisfied him, and together they rode through the back street and to the rear entrance of the gambling-house. Here they dismounted and left their horses, Sanchia going before him.

'We'll go in the back way,' she told him, 'as I do not care to come to such places, and if I must come, I'd rather it wasn't known. Tongues are so eager to wag when one is a woman deprived of a protector. The men from the court-house sometimes come here for their meals.'

She showed him the way under a long grape-vine arbour and to a door which she opened. There was a dark, cool hall and another door opening upon a small room in which they could see a man sitting at a table with a cup of coffee and some sandwiches before him.

'I don't know Mr. Bates personally,' whispered Sanchia. 'But he knows who I am and will do quite as well as Mr. Harkness.'

'You are Mr. Bates, aren't you?' she asked from the doorway. 'Mr. Harkness's assistant?'

The man at the table nodded.

'Yes. Come in. You are Mrs. Murray? I have heard Harkness mention you. If there is anything I can do for you?' His eye travelled slowly to Longstreet.

The man was not a pleasant type, thought Longstreet. He was swarthy and squat and had an eye that slunk away from his visitors'. But it appeared that he was kindly and eager to accommodate. He got up and closed the door, and once, after they had begun talking, went on tiptoe to open it again and peered out into the hall as though he suspected that some one was listening. He seemed a broad-minded chap, waving technicalities aside, assuring Longstreet that what he wanted done was quite the simplest thing in the world. No, it was not necessary for him to come in person to the office; Bates himself was authorized to make the necessary entries and draw up the papers. Oh, yes; he knew all about Dry Gulch. But he did not seem in the least excited about the discovery; in fact, at the end of the conversation, he said dryly that he feared that the mine would not pan out. Other men had thought before now that they had found gold in the Last Ridge country, and their findings had never amounted to anything.

'I'll mail the papers to you at Big Run,' he said, rising at the end of the interview. 'There will be a small fee which you may pay at your convenience.'

The three went out together. Bates waved a genial good-bye and strode off toward the court-house. Suddenly Sanchia appeared restless, almost feverish to be gone.

'I must hurry back to the milliner's,' she said. 'Good-bye.'

Longstreet, abruptly deserted by his two companions, mounted to return to the hotel. But Sanchia suddenly came back to him.

'I'd rather you didn't say anything about my helping you,' she said hurriedly. 'I don't like the idea of coming to a place like the Montezuma, even upon a business matter of urgency like yours. Mr. Howard has such old-fashioned ideas, too, and he might misunderstand. And even Helen— You won't mention me at all, will you?'

Again her smile was pleading, child-like. Longstreet assured her that he would respect her wishes.

'You can just say to Mr. Howard that you saw Bates and got everything in shape,' she suggested. 'Good-bye.'

She was gone, racing again, riding toward the milliner's—and, when once out of Longstreet's sight, turning into the road beyond which led to Big Run.

CHAPTER XVII

HOWARD HOLDS THE GULCH

'Look at the mysterious gentleman!' said Helen, laughing, as her father returned to them upon the hotel porch. Longstreet observed that she appeared to be in the best of spirits. 'Look at the light in his eye! Can't you just tell that he thinks he has a secret? Papa,' and she squeezed his arm, 'won't you ever learn that with that face of yours you couldn't hide what you are thinking to save your life?'

For the second time that day Longstreet winked slyly at Howard. His laughter, as gay as Helen's, bubbled up straight from his soul.

'Helen,' he said as soberly as he might, 'I am afraid that we shall have to leave you to your own devices for an hour or so. Mr. Howard and I have a little business together.'

'Oh,' said Helen. She studied her father's face gravely, then turned toward Alan. She knew all along that her father was planning some sort of birthday surprise for her, and now she could not but wonder what it was that had called the cattleman in to Longstreet's aid. For the thought of the two men really having business together struck her as quite absurd.

'I have been dying to be alone,' she said quickly. 'There is an ice-cream shop across the street, and it's so much more comfortable on a day like this not to have a man along counting the dishes you order. Good-bye, business men,' and rather than be the one deserted she left them and ran across the street, vanishing within the inviting door.

'I have already arranged the matter of filing on my claim,' said Longstreet, turning triumphantly to Howard. 'I saw Bates, George Harkness's assistant, and he has undertaken to do everything immediately.'

'I know Bates. He's a good man, better for your work than Harkness even.' He spoke without a great amount of interest in the subject, and there was something of downright wistfulness in his look which had followed Helen across the street.

They walked a short block in silence. Longstreet, glancing at his companion and noting his abstraction, was glad that there were no questions to answer. After all, it was going to be very simple to keep Mrs. Murray's name out of the whole matter. When they came to the corner and he asked 'Which way?' Howard actually started.

'Guess I was wool-gathering,' he grunted sheepishly. 'We go back this way.'

They retraced their steps half the way, crossed the quiet street and turned in at a hardware store. Howard led the way to the tiny office at the front, whose open windows looked out on the street. A ruddy-faced man in shirt sleeves sat with his hands clasped behind his head, his eyes thoughtful. Seeing his callers, he jumped to his feet.

'Put her there, Al, old boy,' he called in a big, booming, good-natured voice like a young bull's. 'Watched you go by and wondered if you weren't coming in. Haven't seen you since old Buck was a calf. Where you been keeping yourself?' His big smile widened. 'Courtot hasn't got you hiding out, has he?'

'So you've heard that Courtot stuff, too? Pony, this is a friend of mine; Mr. Longstreet, Pony Lee.' While they shook hands Howard added: 'Lee here knows more about practical mining than any other foot-loose stranger this side the Alleghanies.'

'Draw it mild, Al,' laughed Lee. 'Glad to know you, Longstreet. Think I've heard of you.'

He indicated chairs and the three sat down. Longstreet, looking curiously at the man, noted that whereas he was florid and jolly and gave the impression at first almost of joviality, upon closer scrutiny that which was most pronounced about him was the keen glint of his probing grey eyes. He came to learn later that Pony Lee had the reputation of being both a good fellow and a fighting man.

'Longstreet wants to spin you a little yarn.' said Howard. 'And if you will see him through, I imagine he's going to have a job open for you.'

'Mine, of course?' suggested Lee.

'Yes.'

'Have a cigar,' invited Lee. He produced a box from a desk drawer. 'See if I can guess where it is. Other side of Big Run?'

Howard nodded.

'Who found it?'

'I did,' answered Longstreet. 'Yesterday.'

'Last Ridge country, then. H'm.' He rolled his cigar in his mouth idly. Then he sat bolt upright and leaned forward. 'How many people have you told about it already? A dozen?'

It was little less than accusation, and Longstreet flushed. He was opening his lips to answer stiffly when Howard spoke for him.

'He is keeping it to himself. He has told no one but me.'

Lee sank back in his chair, and when he spoke again it was in a careless, off-hand manner.

'Half an hour ago I saw Monte Devine. He came tearing down the street, hell-bent-for-election. Down at the saloon on the corner he picked up two men you know, Al. One of them was Jake Bettins and the other was Ed True. The three hit the pike at a regular two-forty clip for the Big Run road. Those birds don't go chasing around on a day like this just to get sunburn, do they?'

Howard frowned. 'Monte Devine?' he muttered, staring at Lee. But Lee, instead of taking the trouble to give the necessary assurance again, turned his eyes upon Longstreet.

'Filed on your claim yet?' he demanded.

'Yes,' retorted Longstreet, feeling inexplicably ill at ease and shifting in his chair. 'Immediately.'

'That's good,' grunted Lee. 'But I would be squatting on my diggings with a shot-gun under my arm. Al, here, can tell you a few things about Monte Devine and his crowd.'

'Next to Lee,' said Howard, 'Devine knows the mining game from hackamore to hoof. And he's a treacherous hound and a Jim Courtot man.'

'You said it, boy,' grunted Pony Lee. 'He's all of that. And he's no nickel shooter, either. If the game ain't big, he won't chip in.'

'But,' continued Howard, 'I guess you've doped it up wrong, Pony. Chances are they've got something else up their sleeves. They couldn't possibly have dropped on to Longstreet's find.'

For a full minute Lee's eyes bored into Longstreet's. Then he spoke dryly:

'As long's the desert wind blows, word of a strike will go with it. Maybe I have got the wrong end of it.' He shrugged loosely. 'I've done that sort of thing now and then. But I got one more thing to spill. Sanchia Murray's in town. Or she was a little while ago.'

Again he fixed his shrewd eyes upon Longstreet's tell-tale face, which slowly reddened. Pony Lee grunted and at last lighted his cigar. Howard, with a look of sheer amazement, stared at Helen's father.

'You didn't tell Sanchia?' he gasped.

They got their answer in a perfect silence. Lee laughed somewhere deep down in his throat. Howard simply sat and stared. Then suddenly he sprang to his feet and grasped Longstreet by both shoulders, jerking him up out of his chair.

'Tell me about it,' he commanded sternly. 'What did you tell her?'

'Everything,' returned the bewildered college man. 'Why shouldn't I? She promised not to say anything.'

Howard groaned.

'Oh, hell!' he muttered and turned away. But he came back and explained quietly. 'She's as crooked as a dog's hind leg; she's running neck and neck, fifty-fifty, with Jim Courtot and Monte Devine on all kinds of deals—Come on. We've got to burn the earth getting back to Big Run. We'll beat 'em to it yet.'

'Wait a minute, Al,' called Lee softly. 'Let's get all the dope first. You say, Mr. Longstreet, that you filed on your claim all right?'

Longstreet began to flounder and half-way through his recital bogged down helplessly. He had met Sanchia Murray, had gone with her to the Montezuma House, had seen Mr. Bates there—

'What sort of a looking gent is this Mr. Bates?' quizzed Pony Lee sharply.

'A short man, dark, black moustaches—'

Again Howard groaned. Lee merely smiled.

'Recognize the picture, Al? She steered him right into Monte to fix his papers! Well, by God!'

His expression was one of pure admiration. In his mind Sanchia Murray had risen to undreamed of heights—heights of impudence, but none the less daring. He could see the coup in all of its brilliance. But not so Howard.

'We saw her leave a letter at the hotel in Big Run!' he cried out. He was half-way to the door. 'She had the hunch then. By now Courtot and Devine and the rest are in the saddles, if they are not, some of them, already squatting on the job at Last Ridge! I'm on my way. Pony, come alive. Chase over to the court-house; take Longstreet with you and file on the claim if it isn't too late.'

As his last words came back to them he was out on the street and running. He knew within himself that it was too late. They would find that Sanchia or one of her crowd had already visited Harkness's office. Well, that was one thing; the other was to take possession. His boots clattered loudly upon the echoing board sidewalk and men came out to look after him.

He came to his horse in front of the hotel, snatched the tie-rope loose and went up into the saddle without bothering about the spurs hanging over the horn. His horse plunged under him and in another moment horse and rider were racing, even as Sanchia Murray's white mare had carried her, out toward Big Run.

He came as close to killing a horse that day as he had ever come in his life. His face grew sterner as he flung the barren miles behind him and higher and higher surged the bitterness in his heart. If Longstreet had found gold, and he believed that he had, it would have meant so much to Helen. He had seen how she did without little things; he had felt that she was just exactly the finest girl in all of the world; it had seemed to him only the right and logical thing that she should own a gold mine. And now it was to go to Jim Courtot and Sanchia Murray. Sanchia instead of Helen! At the moment he felt that he could have choked the lying heart out of the woman's soft white throat. As for Jim Courtot, already he and Howard hated each other as perforce two men of their two types must come to do. Here again was ample cause for fresh hatred; he drove his horse on furiously, anxious to come upon Courtot, thanking God in his heart that he could look to his enemy for scant words and a quick gun. There come to men at times situations when the only solution is to be found in shooting a way out. Now, more than ever before in his life, was Alan Howard ready for this direct method.

Arrived in Big Run he rode straight on until he came to Tony Moraga's. Here, if anywhere in the settlement, he could hope to find his man. A glance showed him one horse only at the rack, a lean sorrel that he recognized. It was Yellow Barbee's favourite mount, and it struck him that if there were further hard riding to be done, here was the horse to satisfy any man. He threw himself from the saddle, left his own horse balancing upon its trembling legs, and stepped into the saloon.

Moraga was dozing behind his bar. Yellow Barbee sat slumped over a table, his lean, grimy fingers twisting an empty glass. No one else was in the room.

'Courtot been here?' demanded Howard of Moraga.

Moraga shook his head. Howard glanced toward Barbee. The boy's face was sullen, his eyes clouded. He glowered at Moraga and, turning his morose eyes upon Howard, snapped out:

'Moraga lies. Jim was here a little while ago. He's just beat it with a lot of his rotten crowd, Monte Devine and Bettins and True. They're up to something crooked.'

'I forgot.' Moraga laughed greasily. 'Jim was in the back room there talking to Sanchia! Nice girl, no?' he taunted Barbee.

'I'll kill you some day, Moraga,' cursed Barbee thickly.

Howard turned back to the door.

'I want your horse, Barbee,' he said quickly. 'All right?'

'Go to it,' Barbee flashed out. 'And if you ain't man enough to get Jim Courtot pretty damn soon, I am!'

'Keep your shirt on, kid,' Howard told him coolly. 'And keep your hands off. And for God's sake, stop letting that woman make a fool of you.'

Barbee cursed in his throat and with burning eyes watched the swing doors snap after the departing cattleman. Howard, his anger standing higher and hotter, threw himself to the back of Barbee's roan and left Big Run riding furiously from the jump. He knew the horse; it could stand the pace across the few miles and there was no time to lose. There was scant enough likelihood as matters were of his coming to Last Ridge before Courtot's crowd. But the men might have failed to change to fresh horses; in that case his chance was worth something. And, always, until a game be played out, it is anybody's game.

As he rode out toward the Last Ridge trail his one thought was of Jim Courtot. Little by little he lost sight of other matters. He had fought with Jim Courtot before now; he had seen the spit of the gambler's gun twice, he had knocked him down.

Jackson Gregory

Courtot had hunted him, he had gone more than half-way to meet the man. And yet that which had occurred just now had happened again and again before; he came seeking Courtot, and Courtot had just gone. It began almost to seem that Courtot was fleeing him, that he had no stomach for a face-to-face meeting; that what he wanted was to step out unexpectedly from a corner, to shoot from the dark. This long-drawn-out, fruitless seeking baffled and angered. It was time, he thought, high time that he and Jim Courtot shot their way out of an unendurable mess. At every swinging stride of Barbee's roan he grew but the more impatient for the end of the ride and the face of Jim Courtot.

The broad sun flattened against the low hills and sank out of sight. Dusk came and thickened and the stars began to flare out. Against the darkening skyline before him the Last Ridge country reared itself sombrely. A little breeze went dancing and shivering through the dry mesquite and greasewood. His horse stumbled and slowed down. They had come to the first of the rocky ground. He should be at the mouth of Dry Gulch in half an hour. And there he would find the men he had followed; they had beat him to it, for not a glimpse of them had he had. They were, then, first on the ground. That was something, he conceded. But it was not everything.

At last he dismounted and tied his horse to a bush. About him were thick shadows, before him the tall bulwark of the uplands. His feet were in a trail that he knew. He went on up, as silently, as swiftly as he could. Presently he stood on the edge of the same flat on which the Longstreets had made their camp, though a good half-mile to the east of the canvas shack. A wide black void across the plateau was Dry Gulch. Upon its nearer bank, not a hundred yards from him, a dry wood fire blazed brightly; he must have seen it long ago except that a shoulder of the mountain had hidden it. It burned fiercely, thrusting its flames high, sending its sparks skyward. In its flickering circle of light he saw dark objects which he knew must be the forms of men. He did not count them, merely prayed within his heart that Courtot was among them, and came on. He heard the men talking. He did not listen for words, since words did not matter now. He hearkened for a certain voice.

The voices broke off and a man stood up. When he was within a score of paces of the fire Howard stopped. The man's thick squat form was clearly outlined. Unmistakably this was Monte Devine. There were two or three other forms squatting; it was impossible to distinguish a crouching man from a boulder.

'That you, Monte?' called Howard.

'Good guess,' came Monte's heavy, insolent voice. 'You've got one on me, though, pardner.'

'Courtot here?' demanded Howard.

Monte Devine laughed then.

'Hello, Al,' he returned lightly. 'You and Jim sure play a great little game of tag, don't you?'

'He isn't here, then?'

'Left an hour ago. There's just me and Bettins and True on the job. Come on in and make yourself at home.'

Howard came on slowly. Monte might be telling the truth, and then again lying came easy to him. Every dark blot was searched out suspiciously by Howard's frowning eyes. Again, having read what was in Howard's mind, Monte laughed.

'He ain't here, Al,' he insisted. 'You and him will have to make a date if you ever get together.'

The two other men rose from the ground and stood a little aside. No doubt they were True and Bettins; still neither had spoken and in this uncertain light either might be Courtot.

　　　　　　　　Jackson Gregory

'Hello, True,' said Howard shortly. True's voice answered him. 'Hello, Bettins,' he said, and it was Bettin's voice replying.

'Where did Jim go?' he asked.

'Search me,' retorted Monte Devine. Then, a hint of a jeer in his voice, 'Going to stay out there in the dark all night? 'Fraid Jim'll be hiding out waiting to pot you?'

The other men laughed.

'That's his sort of play,' muttered Alan coolly.

He took his time to look about. Little by little the mystery shrouding this and that object dissolved and showed him a rock or a bush. He heard a snapping bit of brush off to the right and wheeled toward it. It was a horse moving. He circled the fire and went to it. Beyond were two other horses, only three in all. Then he shrugged his shoulders and jammed his revolver angrily into its holster and came back to the figures by the fire.

'Longstreet is a friend of mine,' he said shortly. 'I am going to see him through, Monte.'

'Who's Longstreet?' demanded Monte.

'I guess you know. He's the man who found gold up here yesterday. He's the man Sanchia Murray brought to you at the Montezuma House. He owns these diggings that you and Jim Courtot and your crowd are trying to jump to-night. Better think it over and jump somewhere else, Monte.'

Monte Devine appeared to be meditating. Howard's angry thoughts were racing. Rage baffled was but baffled again. There seemed nothing concrete that he could lay his hands on; again Jim Courtot had come and gone. To drive the men off the land, even could he succeed in doing it would so far as he could see be barren of any desired result. There was a law in the country, and that law would see the man through who had properly filed on his claim. And yet, for all that, his blood grew hot at the thought of all of this riff-raff of Jim Courtot squatting here upon that which by right was Helen's.

'I reckon we'll stay and see it through,' said Monte at last.

Howard turned and strode away. True laughed. But Howard had seen something showing whitely just yonder in the black void of Dry Gulch. There was the spot where Longstreet's claim lay. He went down into the gulch and to the thing that he had seen dimly. It was a stake and a bit of white paper thrust into the split, and showed him that the three men had not mistaken the spot. Here, at last, was something concrete upon which a man, hot with his anger, could lay his hands. He wrenched it away and hurled it far from him. He saw another stake and another and these like the first he snatched up and pitched wrathfully as far as he could throw them.

'That's something, if it isn't much,' he muttered to himself.

The others had held back, watching him. He could hear them speaking quickly among themselves, Bettins and True angrily. Monte's voice was low and steady. But it was Monte who came on first.

'Hold on there a minute,' called Howard sharply. 'I'm not asking any company down here. Here I am going to stick until morning. By that time, or I miss my guess, this neck of the woods will be full of people who have heard that something's doing here. There'll be a handful of your crowd, but there'll be twice as many square-shooters. You'll stand back with the crowd and take your chance with what is left after Longstreet gets his, or you'll play crooked and take another chance, that of a long rope and a quick drop. Think it over, boys.'

'Better clean out while you can, Al,' said Monte. His own voice had sharpened. 'We're coming down to put them stakes back.'

Howard withdrew half a dozen steps into the deeper shadows of the gulch.

'Come ahead when you're ready,' he retorted. 'I can see you fine up there against the skyline. Start it going any time, Monte.'

His was the position of a man in desperate need for action and with little enough scope for his desire. But he had the hope that Longstreet and Pony Lee might possibly have been the first at the court-house; were that to prove to be the case and were he on the ground when they came in the morning, he would in the end have prevented a tangle and the long delay and intricate trouble of dispossessing Courtot's agents. Further, his mood was one in which he would have been glad to have Monte 'start it going.'

Monte and his companions spoke quietly among themselves a second time. Then, with never another word to him, they withdrew and disappeared. An immense silence shut down about him. He knew that they had not gone far and that they would be heard from before long. For they were not the men to let go so easily. But Monte Devine, plainly the brains of the crowd, was a cool hand who played as safe a game as circumstances allowed.

He sat down with his back to a fallen boulder. He was thinking that perhaps they were waiting for the dawn; by daylight they would have all the best of it and might close in on him from three sides. But when the night wind blowing up the gulch brought him the smell of dead leaves burning, when he saw a quick tongue of flame on one bank and then another, like a reflection in a mirror, on the other bank, he understood. It was like a Monte Devine play. Presently the dry grass would be burning all along the draw; the flames would sweep by him and in their light he would stand forth as in the light of day. Then, if there were a single rifle among the three men, he would have not so much as a chance to fight. Even if they had nothing but revolvers, the odds were all on their side.

And it was like Jim Courtot's play, too, to clear out and leave his agents to deal with the man he hated. All in the world that Courtot ever wanted was to win; the means were nothing. If his enemy went down by another man's bullet than his own, so much the better for Jim Courtot, who had always enough to answer for as it was.

'This belongs to Helen Longstreet,' Howard told himself steadily. 'I am going to hold it for her if it's in the cards.'

He withdrew a little further. Then, with a sudden inspiration, he clambered silently up the sloping bank. The men who had lighted the fires would have circled about to come upon him from the other side. He was right. As he thrust his head above the top of the bank he saw two figures running in the direction that he had judged they would take. He pulled himself up. A loosened rock rolled noisily into the gulch. They heard it and stopped. He knew when they saw him and knew who they were as he heard them call to each other. They were Ed True and Monte Devine. And Ed True, as he called, whipped out his revolver and fired.

'He's on this side, Bettins,' called Monte loudly. 'Take your time.'

He had not fired nor had Howard. Ed True, however, lacked the cool nerve and emptied his revolver. Monte cursed him for a fool.

'You couldn't hit a barn that far off in this light,' he shouted. 'Take your time, can't you?'

Howard's lips tightened. That was Monte Devine for you. Steady and cool as a rock.

'We've got the best of you, Al,' called Monte warningly.

'Better crawl out while you got the chance.'

'Go to hell!' Howard told him succinctly. And knowing that the man had been right when he had said you couldn't hit a barn at that distance and in that light, he came forward suddenly. For in a little the burning grass would be behind him and outlined against it the target of his body would be a mark for anybody to hit.

Suddenly, having reloaded, True fired again. But he was not so hurried now. He fired once and waited. This time the bullet had not flown so far afield as the first shots; Howard heard its shrill cleaving of the air. He saw that Monte was moving to one side. Again he understood the man's intention. Monte planned to put him between two fires. Howard jerked up his own gun.

The two explosions came simultaneously, his and Monte's. There was a brief silence. Plainly no bullet had yet found its mark. True fired again. His bullet whined by and Howard realized that the man was coming closer every time. He turned a little and, 'taking his time,' as Monte was doing, answered True's fire. There was a little squeal of pain from True, a grunt of satisfaction from Howard, a second shot from Monte. Howard saw that True had spun about and fallen. He saw, further, that Monte had come a step nearer and had stopped. In a little Bettins would be to reckon with. It was still close enough for a chance hit, too far for absolute accuracy. Walking slowly, realizing that he had but four shots left and that those gone he would never be given time to reload, Howard came half a dozen paces toward Monte before he stopped. He heard True's groaning curse; a spat of flame from where the man lay showed him that he was still to be counted on. But his shooting would be apt to be wild and he must be forgotten until Devine was dealt with.

He was near enough to make out the gesture as Monte raised his arm. And he was ready. Howard fired first; he saw the flare and heard the report of Monte's gun and knew that he had missed. But Monte had not missed. There was a searing pain across Howard's outer left arm, near the shoulder. The pain came and was gone, like the flash of the gun; remained only a mounting rage in Howard's brain. Three shots left and three men still to fight. A shot for each man and none to waste, or the tale would be told for Alan Howard. And there would be occasion for Jim Courtot's jeering laugh tomorrow.

Before the smoke had cleared from Monte's gun Howard leaped closer, and at this close range fired. He saw Monte reel back. He knew that Ed True was still shooting, but he did not care. Monte was stumbling, saving himself from falling, straightening again, lifting his gun. But before the swaying figure could answer the call of the cool brain directing it, Howard sprang in upon him and struck with his clubbed revolver. And Monte Devine, his finger crooking to the trigger as the blow fell, went down heavily from the impact of the gun-barrel against his head. Ed True emptied his cylinder and cursed and began filling it again.

Howard stood a moment over Monte Devine. Then he took up the fallen revolver in his left hand and turned to True.

'Chuck your gun to me, Ed,' he commanded sternly, 'or I'll get you right next time.'

True damned him violently. Then he groaned, and a moment later there was the sound of his revolver hurled from him, clattering among the stones. Howard took it up, shoved it into his pocket and turned toward the gulch. While he sought for a sight of Bettins he hastily filled the empty chambers of his own weapon.

Now only he realized how brief a time had elapsed since Ed True's first shot. The grass fire was blazing, but had crept up the draw only a few feet. And Bettins had not yet had the time to come from the other side, down into the gulch and up on this side. He saw Bettins; the man was standing still staring toward his fallen companions. The fire leaped higher, its light danced out in widening circles, touching at last the spot where Howard stood, where Ed True and Monte Devine lay.

'Well, Bettins?' called Howard abruptly.

'What about you? Are you coming over?'

Bettins was silent a moment. The light flickered on the gun in his hand. Presently he raised his voice to inquire anxiously:

'Hurt much, Monte? And you, True?'

No answer from Monte. True shrieked at him: 'Come, over and plug him, Bettins. For God's sake, plug the damn cowman.'

Still Bettins hesitated.

'Monte dead?' he demanded.

'How the hell do I know?' complained True.

'Come, plug him, Bettins.'

This time Bettins' reply was lost in a sudden shout of voices rising from the lower end of the flat. The vague forms of several horsemen appeared; there came the thunderous beat of flying hoofs. Howard's lips grew tight-pressed. True lifted himself on his elbow.

'It's Jim coming back!' he called triumphantly.

'This way, Jim!'

But the answering shout, closer now, was unmistakably the voice of Yellow Barbee. And with him rode half a dozen men and, among them a girl.

CHAPTER XVIII

A TOWN IS BORN

The fire, spreading and burning brightly now, shone on the faces making a ring about Alan Howard and the two men lying on the ground. With Yellow Barbee had come John Carr, Longstreet and Helen, and two of the Desert Valley men, Chuck Evans and Dave Terril. They looked swiftly from Howard to the two men whom he had shot, then curiously at Howard again.

'Jim Courtot, Al?' asked Carr, for Monte Devine's face was in shadow.

Howard shook his head.

'No such luck, John,' he said briefly. 'Just Monte Devine and Ed True. Bettins is over yonder; he didn't mix in.'

'I hope,' said Longstreet nervously, 'that you haven't started any trouble on my account.'

'No trouble at all,' said Howard dryly. Yellow Barbee laughed and went to look at Devine. Ed True was still cursing where he had propped himself up with his back to a rock.

'This is apt to be bad business, Al.' It was John Carr speaking heavily, his voice unusually blunt and harsh. 'I saw Pony Lee, and he told me that Longstreet here hasn't a leg to stand on.

Devine filed on the claim; he and his men got here ahead of us; neither Miss Helen nor I nor any one but you can go into court and swear that Longstreet ever so much as said that he had made a find. I was hoping we would get here before you started anything.'

Howard looked at his friend in amazement. He knew that the discovery was Longstreet's by right; to his way of thinking the simplest thing in the world was to hold and to fight for the property of his friends. He would have said that John Carr would have done the same thing were Carr in his boots. He had taken another man's quarrel upon his own shoulders to-night, and asked no questions; he had plunged into a fight against odds and had gotten away with it and no help asked; the fighting heat was still in his blood, and it seemed to him that his old friend John Carr was finding fault with him.

They had all dismounted by now. Longstreet had slid to the ground, let go his horse's reins and was fidgeting up and down, back and forth, in an access of nervous excitement. Now he began talking quickly, failing to understand in the least what effect his rushing words would have on the man who had taken up his fight.

'The thing is of no consequence, not the least in the world. Come, let them have it. It is only a gold mine, and haven't I told you all the time that for me there is no difficulty in locating gold? I am sorry all of this has happened. They're here first; they have filed on it; let them have it.'

Howard's face no longer showed amazement. In the flickering light his mouth was hard and bitter, set in the implacable lines of stern resentment. Between Carr and Longstreet they made it seem that he had merely made a fool of himself. Well, maybe he had. He shrugged his shoulders and turned away.

'I know you did it for me,' Longstreet began, having a glimpse of the bitterness in Alan's heart.

'And you mustn't think—'

Howard wheeled on him.

'I didn't do it for you.' he snapped irritably. 'I tried the only way I knew to help save the mine for Helen. We'd do it yet if you weren't a pack of damned rabbits.'

He pushed by and laid his hand on the mane of the horse Dave Terril rode.

'Give me your horse, Dave,' he said quietly. 'I'm on my way home. You'll find Barbee's down under the cliff.'

Dave Terril was quick to obey. But before his spurred boot-heel had struck the turf Helen had came running through the men about Howard, her two hands out, her voice thrilling and vibrant as she cried:

'There is only one man among you, one real man, and that is Alan Howard! He was not wrong; he was right! And no matter what happens to the gold, I had rather have a man like Alan Howard do a thing like that for me than have all of the gold in the mountains!'

Her excitement, too, ran high, her words came tripping over one another, heedless and extravagant. But Howard suddenly glowed, and when she put her hands out to him he took them both and squeezed them hard.

'Why, God bless you, you're a brick!' he cried warmly. 'And, in spite of the rest of 'em, I'm glad I did make a fool of myself!'

From his wounded arm a trickle of blood had run down to his hand. Helen cried out as she saw the smear across the sleeve of his shirt.

'He's hurt!' she exclaimed.

He laughed at her.

'It would be worth it if I were,' he told her gently. 'But I'm not.' He slipped his foot into the stirrup. 'Dave,' he said over his shoulder, 'you and Chuck had better look at Monte. I don't know how bad his hurt is. Do what ever you can for him. If I'm wanted, I'm at the ranch.'

But Helen, carried out of herself by the excitement of the moment and unconscious that she was clinging to him, pleaded with him not to go yet.

'Wait until we decide what we are going to do,' she told him earnestly. 'Won't you, please?'

'You bet I will!' he answered, his voice ringing with his eagerness to do anything she might ask of him. 'If *you* want me to stay, here I stick.'

He dropped the reins and with her at his side turned back to the others. Already two men were kneeling beside Monte Devine. Chuck Evans, who had got there first, looked up and announced:

'He's come to, Al. He looks sick, but he ain't hurt much, I'd say for a guess. Not for a tough gent like him. How about it, Monte?'

Monte growled something indistinct, but when at the end of it he demanded a drink of whisky his voice was both clear and steady. Chuck laughed. Thereafter those who knew most of such matters looked over both Monte's and Ed True's injuries and gave what first-aid they could. It was Chuck's lively opinion that both gents were due for a little quiet spell at a hospital, but that they'd be getting in trouble again inside a month or so.

'You can't kill them kind,' he concluded lightly. 'Not so easy.'

They called to Bettins, but he held back upon the far side of the gulch and finally withdrew and disappeared. Then Longstreet, who had been restless but quiet-tongued for ten minutes, exclaimed quickly:

'We must get these two men over to our camp right away, where we can have better light, and put them into bed until a physician can be summoned. Think of the horrible situation which would arise if they died!' He shuddered. Then he turned to Howard and extended his hand. His voice shook slightly as he said hurriedly: 'Old chap, don't think that I don't appreciate what you have attempted for us; it was quite the most amazingly splendid thing I ever heard of! But now, with matters as they stand, there is nothing for us to do but withdraw. Let them have the mine; it is blood-stained and ill-starred. I wouldn't have a thing to do with it if they returned it to me.'

'But, papa,' cried Helen hotly, 'just think! They have stolen it from us, they have tried to murder—'

'My dear,' cut in Longstreet sternly, 'I trust that you will say nothing further about it. I have made up my mind; I am a man of the world and an older and cooler mind than you. Leave this to me.'

Howard heard her deep breath, slowly drawn, slowly expelled, and saw her face looking white and tense; he knew that her teeth were set, that her heart was filled with rebellion. But she made no answer, knowing the futility of mere words to move her father in his present mood. Instead, she turned away from him and looked out across the gulch along both banks of which the fires were now raging. Nor did she turn again while Monte and True were placed in the saddles which were to carry them to the camp.

'A moment, Mr. Longstreet,' said Howard, as they were starting. 'Am I to understand that you absolutely refuse to make a fight for your own rights?'

'In this particular instance, absolutely!' said Longstreet emphatically.

'Then,' pursued Howard, 'I have a suggestion to make. We are all friends here: suppose that each one of us stakes out a claim just adjoining the ones you have lost. Certainly they might have some value.'

But Longstreet shook his head impatiently.

'I am through with the whole mess,' he declared, waving his hands. 'I won't have a thing to do with it, and I won't allow Helen to touch it. Further, the other claims would have no value in my eyes; the spot that has been stolen from me is the only spot in the gulch that I would give a dollar for. Come on, Helen.'

'We'll follow you,' said Helen quietly.

The others moved away. John Carr, who had not spoken since his first words, stood hesitatingly looking at the two figures silhouetted against the fire. Then he too moved away, going with the others and in silence.

'Tell me about it,' said Helen. She dropped down and sat with her chin in her hands, her eyes moody upon the rushing flames. 'Just what happened.'

He sat by her and told her. His heart was still filled with his bitterness and his voice told the fact. Presently she withdrew her gaze from the gulch and turned it upon him; she had never seen him so relentlessly stern. Almost he frightened her. Then she noticed again the stain upon his shoulder and this time insisted upon helping him make a bandage. With his knife she slit the shirt sleeve; together they got a handkerchief bound about the wound. It was not deep nor was it in any way dangerous, but Helen winced and paled before the job was done. Then their eyes met and clung together and for a little while they were silent, and gradually the colour came back into the girl's cheeks.

'Are you tired?' he asked presently. 'Or hungry? If not, and you care to sit here with me for an hour or two, maybe a little more, I can promise to show you a sight you will never forget.'

'What is it?' she asked curiously, wondering if he meant a moonrise over the far desert mountains.

'It is the birth of a mining camp. For there will be one here before morning.'

'Surely not so soon? Who will know?'

'Who?' he grunted disgustedly. 'Everybody! Down in San Ramon Pony Lee knows; at the court-house it is known. Men give tips to their friends. Courtot's crowd knows. Out here my men know; Carr and Barbee know. Already there are a hundred men, maybe several times a hundred, who know. And you may be sure that already they are coming like a train of ants. Once gold has been uncovered the secret is out. Pony Lee swears the desert winds carry the news.'

Howard was entirely correct in his surmise, saving in the time he judged they must wait. Less than an hour had passed and the grass fire was still spreading with a fierce crackling sound and myriad sparks, when the vanguard of the gold-seekers came. Helen and Howard heard horses' hoofs, rattling stones, impatient voices, and withdrew a hundred yards from the gulch and into the shadows of a ring of boulders.

With the first came Bettins. His voice was the loudest, coming now and then distinctly; he employed the name of Howard and cursed it; he said something about his 'pals' Devine and True. A man to whom he was talking laughed at him. Thereafter half a dozen forms swarmed down into the gulch; the fire on either side of them was dying out along the gulch's edge; they cursed its heat when it offended them, took advantage of its light at all times, and more like ants than ever appeared to be running back and forth foolishly and aimlessly. But, apparently, Bettins got his stakes and his friends' back and the men with whom he had returned hastily staked out their own claims, all feverishly and by crude guesswork. There was perhaps not a man among them who knew the first thing about mining. Helen watched them in sheer fascination. Down there half in light, half in shadow, darting this way and that, they were like little gnomes playing some wild game of their own.

'They act like madmen,' she whispered. 'They run about as if everything had to be done in a minute.'

'Between them the crowd down there don't own, I'd say, fifty dollars. Each one is figuring that he has his chance to be a millionaire to-morrow. And they know that more men are coming. That's the way men think when they're in the gold rush. Look, there come some more!'

This time there were three men. They broke into a run when they heard voices; perhaps they had hoped to be first. Down into the bed of the gulch they plunged; one of them slipped and rolled and cursed; men laughed, and with the laughter dying in their throats broke off to yell a warning to some one to keep his feet off a claim already staked out. Within an hour after the return of Bettins there were a score of men on the spot; again and again rose sharp words as every man, alert to protect his own interests, was ready for a quarrel. They dragged stones to mark their boundaries; they cut and hammered stakes, they left their chosen sites now and then and altered their first judgments and restaked somewhere else. They swarmed up the banks of the gulch on both sides, they hastened back and forth, they staked everywhere. As the time passed more and more came plunging into the orgy of gold until at last the night was never quiet. Harsh words passed and once blows were struck and a man went down and lay still. Another time there was the report of a gun and a boom of many voices commanding order and that quarrels be taken to a safe distance and out of the way of busy men.

'It's dreadful,' whispered Helen. 'They're like wild animals.'

'It's just the gold fever,' he returned. 'Poor devils! they are drunk with their visions.'

But Helen wondered if they were capable of visions. Down in the shadow-filled sink they were to her imagination like so many swine plunging into a monster trough. When Alan suggested, 'We've seen, and now maybe we had better be going,' she rose without a word or backward glance and went with him. But Howard, looking over his shoulder, saw still other men coming. He himself began to wonder whence they had come: by now, it seemed to him, both Big Run and San Ramon must have emptied themselves like bags of wheat slashed with a knife.

They walked swiftly until the din of the gold-seekers was lost to their ears. Then slowly they strolled on, silence enwrapping them, Helen's eyes wandering away to the glory of the stars, Howard's contented with the girl's face. After a while Helen, feeling the intentness of his look, turned toward him with a strange little smile which came and went fleetingly. She stopped a moment, still looking at him.

'Your country has done something to me,' she said thoughtfully, 'even though I have been out here only a few weeks. For one thing, when I first came I thought that I knew all about men and that they were pretty much all alike. I am finding out that they are not at all alike and that I don't understand them.'

'No, they are not all alike, and some men are hard to make out, I suppose,' he said when she paused.

'Men are more violent than I thought men were nowadays,' she added. 'They are stronger; they are fiercer. I used to think that a girl was a wretched little coward to be afraid of any man. Now I would be afraid of many of them I have seen in this land that you like to call your country.'

He understood that in her brain had formed a vision of his fight with Devine and Ed True, and that, blurring that image, she was still seeing the picture of the dark forms rushing down into the gulch. She began to move on again, and he went at her side making no reply and communing with his own thoughts. She did not stop again until they came close to the canvas-walled cabin and saw the light shining wanly through and the shadows of the men inside. Then she lifted her face so that it was clear to him in the starlight and said to him slowly:

'I am going in and see if I can help with the wounded men now. I should have gone at first, I suppose. Maybe there is something I can do. You wouldn't want them to die, would you?'

'No,' he returned, 'I would not want them to die.'

In the silence which followed he could see that she was seeking to read his face and that she was very, very thoughtful.

'Tell me something,' she said abruptly. 'If one of them were Jim Courtot—would you want him to die?'

At the mention of Courtot's name she made out a quick hardening of his mouth; she even saw, or fancied, an angry gathering of his brows. To-night's work was largely the work of Jim Courtot, and because of it Dry Gulch, which might have poured great heaps of gold at Helen's feet, was being wrangled over by a hundred men. He thought of that and he thought of other things, of how Courtot had fired on him from the dark long ago, of how Courtot was hunting him after Courtot's own tenacious fashion.

'Why do you ask that?' he demanded sharply.

She did not reply. Instead she turned from him and looked at the stars. And then she withdrew her eyes and turned them toward the light gleaming palely through the walls of canvas. But at last she lifted her face again to Howard.

'I'll go in now. And maybe I am tired after all. It has been a day, hasn't it? And please know that I felt that you did the right thing to-night, and that I don't know another man who would have been man enough to do it. Good night.'

'Good night,' he said, and watched her as she went into the house.

CHAPTER XIX

SANCHIA PERSISTENT

Thus, upon the barren flanks of Dry Gulch, a town was born. Mothered by the stubborn desert that appears sterile and is not, it was a sprawling, ungainly, ill-begotten thing. In the night it came; in the dawn it grew; during the first day it assumed lustiness and an insolence that was its birthright. And, like any welcome child, there was a name awaiting it. Men laughed as the unceremonious christening was performed. A half-drunken vagabond from no one knew where had staked out his claim and drained his bottle. 'Here's lookin' at Sanchia's Town!' he cried out, and smashed his bottle against a rock.

It appeared that every one had heard the tale of Longstreet's discovery and of Sanchia Murray's manoeuvre. They made high fun of Longstreet and declared that Sanchia was a cool one. The mere fact that she was a woman enlisted their sympathies in an affair wherein they had no interest. They were doomed to second choice and deemed it as well for Sanchia to have had first as any one. When a narrow-headed individual remarked that he had heard that the widow was getting nothing out of it, but that Courtot and his crowd had cheated her, they hooted and jeered at him until he withdrew wondering at their insane attitude. It was generally taken for granted that Sanchia Murray knew what she was about. If she chose to hunt in couple with Jim Courtot, that was her business.

A town is something more than a group of men encamped. It connotes many social facilities; first among which comes the store and, in certain parts of the world, the saloon. Sanchia's Town was, upon the first day, a town in these essentials. Shortly after dawn a string of three six-horse teams crawled across the lowlands and, by a circuitous way, to the camp. One wagon was heaped with bits of second-hand lumber and a jumbled assortment of old tents and strips of canvas. In it, also, were hammers, saws and nails. The two other wagons were filled with boxes and bags—and kegs. There were two men to each team. Arrived they gave immediate evidence that their employer had chosen well. One of them, a crooked-eyed carpenter named Emberlee, directed, hammer in hand. Before noon he had caused to grow up an architectural monstrosity, hideous but sturdy. It was without floor, but it had walls; wide gaps were doors and windows, but there was a canvas roof.

While his five companions brought their parcels into the place, Emberlee climbed aloft and nailed up a big board upon which his own hand, as the wagon had jostled along, had painted a sign. It spelled: JIM COURTOT'S HOUSE. Then he descended and began a hurried grouping of certain articles upon shelves and in corners. By the time the camp was ready for a noon meal the word had flown about that at Jim Courtot's House one could get food, water and a widely-known substitute for whisky. Meantime Tony Moraga had come: he stood behind a bar hastily made of two planks set on packing cases and sold a tin cup of water for twenty-five cents, a glass of liquor for fifty. There were calls for both. Emberlee, plainly a jack-of-all-trades, began displaying his wares. He offered dried meats, tinned goods, crackers, cheese and other comestibles at several times desert prices. And he, too, chinked many a silver dollar and minted gold piece into his cash-box, because when men rush to gold diggings they are not likely to go empty-handed. Shortly after noon the three wagons returned to Big Run for more supplies.

Obviously, though already Jim Courtot had departed from Dry Gulch when Alan Howard came upon his agents, he was no less active than they with rich gains in sight. It is to be doubted if the man slept at all during the first three days and nights. He had made his own list of foods and tobaccos and alcohols; he had selected men for his work. Down in San Juan men said: 'Jim Courtot is playing his luck again.' For though information was garbled long before it reached the mission town, yet always it was understood that Jim Courtot was playing to win heavily—he and Sanchia Murray.

Those hours which, in Sanchia's Town, had been given over to frenzy and the fury of feverish endeavour, had dragged by wearily and anxiously for the inmates of Longstreet's half-mile-distant cabin. For both Monte Devine and Ed True the night was one of bitter rage and pain. Longstreet was gentle with them, bringing them water, asking them often of their wants; Helen ministered to them silently, a strange new look in her eyes. Often she went to the door and stood looking off into the moonlit night, across the rolling hills and down into the wide sweep of Desert Valley. Carr remained with them all night. It was as well to be on hand, he suggested, if anything happened. He seemed scarcely conscious of the presence of the two wounded men; tilted back in his chair, smoking one cigar after another, he scarcely for an instant lost sight of Helen.

In the morning early there was the sound of hoofs and then men's voices. It was Carr who went to the door.

'It is Bettins and a couple of other men,' he said over his shoulder. 'Come for Devine and True, I guess.' And still without turning, he demanded, 'Ready to go, Monte?'

'Damn right,' said Monte.

Between Carr and Longstreet, Monte shambled to the door. Here he was turned over to his friends, who got him into his saddle. Then, assisted as Monte had been, and cursing at every step, Ed True passed through the door. The men outside accepted the two wounded men with only a few low words; in another moment the five horses were carrying their riders slowly toward Sanchia's Town. Carr returning saw the whisk of Helen's skirt as she disappeared within the little room partitioned off at the rear and knew that she had gone to fling herself down upon her bed. He looked after her as though he still half hoped she were coming back if only to say a belated 'good night.' Then he and Longstreet made coffee and drank it perfunctorily. After breakfast Carr left, saying that he would ride over to have a look at the new camp, and would drop in again some time during the afternoon.

'If I am not making a nuisance of myself,' he said as Longstreet followed him to the door, 'I should like to see what I can of you during the next few days. And of Miss Helen,' he added with utter frankness and clear meaning. 'I have business which will call me back East before long.'

'Come as often as you can, my dear fellow,' invited Longstreet. But his eyes had wandered toward the mining site which should have been his, and his mind seemed to be less than half busied with Carr's words. Carr, turning in the saddle, narrowed his eyes upon the university man's face and, thinking that he had caught his thought, said bluntly:

'It's an infernal shame. It's all yours by right, and—'

'Oh,' cried Longstreet grandly, 'I'm not worrying about a little diggings like that! Let them have it! Next time I'll show them a real mine.'

'Well, I wish you luck,' rejoined Carr. But there was no great conviction in his tone, since in his mind there was little expectation that lightning was going to strike twice in the same place. However, the caution came to his lips involuntarily: 'If there is a next time, I'd be mighty careful whom I told about it. It will pay you to look out for that Murray woman.'

Longstreet's face was puzzled and troubled.

'It does begin to look as though she gave me the—the double

cross, doesn't it?' he said as though he were afraid he must believe the worst of Sanchia Murray despite his wish in the matter.

'It certainly does,' grunted Carr. 'She's absolutely no good. Everybody knows it. Fight shy of her. Well, so long.'

'So long,' repeated Longstreet absently.

Carr rode away. Longstreet's eyes, following the galloping horse, were still puzzled. 'I'm learning a thing or two,' he told himself soberly as he went back into the cabin. Many times he nodded his head thoughtfully. 'I've lived too long in another sort of world; now I am coming to grips with real life, real men and women. There's a new set of rules to grasp. Well,' and he straightened his thin body and a flickering smile played over his lips, 'I can learn. As Barbee says of stud poker: "You've got to set tight and keep your trap shut and your eye peeled."'

Helen slept soundly all morning. Longstreet dozed, studied the maps he had made during the last week and pottered. At noon they lunched together, neither having a great deal to say. Helen regarded her father more than ever as a baby who ought to be scolded and lessoned; still, like any doting mother, she found excuses for him and told herself that he had been amply punished for his indiscretion. She, too, opined that he had learned a lesson. Consequently she coddled him to such an extent that Longstreet remarked the fact and began to wonder just what Helen wanted now; no doubt she was going to ask something of him and was preparing the way after the approved and time-honoured custom.

But the day wore on with never a favour asked. In the drowsy afternoon Helen coaxed her father into her room and dropped the shades and ordered him to sleep, telling him that he looked like a ghost of his former rugged beauty. Then she sank down listlessly upon the doorstep, brooding, her eyes wandering through the green fields of Desert Valley. Her musings were disturbed by the clatter of shod hoofs across the rugged plateau; she looked up quickly, her eyes brightening. Then she saw that it was John Carr returning, and into her look there came an expression much resembling that which had been so much to-day in her father's—one of uncertainty.

Carr staked out his horse before he came to her. Then he sat down on a box near the doorstep and studied her gravely before he spoke. Helen smiled.

'You are thinking unpleasant things about some one,' she stated quickly. 'Has the world turned into a terribly serious place all of a sudden?'

There was little levity in Carr's make-up at any time; just now his speech was as sober as his look.

'I am thinking about you and your father, to begin with,' he replied gravely. 'I have been over yonder all day.' He swept out an impatient arm toward Dry Gulch. 'They call it Sanchia's Town. And it is a town already. I saw Nate Kemble there; he's the big man of the Quigley Mines, and you see how long it has taken him to get on the spot. Your father evidently made no mistake in his location. There's gold there, all right!'

Helen waited expectantly for him to go on. For certainly the fact that her father had been able to find gold was no cause for Carr's frowning eyes.

'My blood has been boiling all day,' Carr blurted out angrily. 'Longstreet should be a rich man to-day and he has gained nothing. I saw Nate Kemble pay one man ten thousand dollars for his claim; Kemble wouldn't pay that if the thing were not worth a great deal more. Kemble doesn't make many mistakes. Your father stumbled on to the place and then he couldn't hold it. When do you think he will make another discovery? And, if his lucky star should lead him aright again, is he the man to cash in on his luck? Don't you see, Helen, that James Edward Longstreet in this man's land is a fish out of water?'

'I understand what you mean,' Helen nodded slowly. Again her look wandered through the fields stretching out far below. 'And you are right. I didn't want papa to come in the first place; now, as you say, he is only wasting time.' She smiled a little tenderly. 'He is just a dear old babe in the woods,' she concluded softly.

Carr's approval of her mounted swiftly to admiration. They lowered their voices and spoke at length of the professor and of what should be done for him. They agreed perfectly that, while he was an unusually fine technical man and an able instructor in matters of geological theorizing, he was not the man to wander with a prospector's pick across these rugged lands.

'Even grant the extremely unlikely,' concluded Carr hastily as they heard the subject of their discussion moving about in the cabin, 'and admit that he may chance upon a second strike. What then? Why, Sanchia and Devine and Courtot and a crowd of hangers-on have their eyes on him. They'd oust him again with not the shadow of a doubt or a second's hesitation.'

Helen nodded and they went in together.

Carr stayed on to supper. Longstreet looked rested from his nap, bright and eager and as usual interested in everything in the world. Carr had bought a new hat yesterday; Longstreet tried it on and approved of it extravagantly. He asked what it cost and jingled his few coins, admitting ruefully that he'd have to wait until he uncovered his 'real mine.' Just the same, he proclaimed brightly, clothes did help make the man, and inside a year when he was decked out entirely to his own liking and a tenderfoot saw him, there would be no suspecting that Longstreet was not a Westerner born and bred. He put the hat away and sat down with them at the table. As he mentioned in such a matter-of-fact way his intention of tarrying a year, Carr and Helen glanced at each other significantly. And Carr after his direct fashion opened his campaign.

'There are other things than gold mines, and you were not

made for this country,' he said. 'What would you say to going back East if I showed you the chance there to clean up more money than you'll ever see out here? I have been thinking about you, and I know the place where you'll fit in.'

This was all news to Helen, and her look showed her eager interest. Longstreet smiled and shook his head.

'That's kind of you,' he said warmly. 'But I like it out here.'

'But, papa,' cried Helen, 'surely you should hear Mr. Carr's proposition! It is not merely kind of him; it is wonderful if he can help us that way, and it is wise.'

'No,' said Longstreet. 'Carr won't think me ungrateful. I told them in the East that there was nothing simpler than the fact that a man like me, knowing what I know, can discover gold in vast quantities. First, it is universally conceded that the auriferous deposits remaining untouched are vastly in excess of those already found and worked. Second, all of my life I have made a profound study of geognosy and geotectonic geology. Now, it is not only the money; money I count as a rather questionable gift, anyway. But it is my own reputation. What I have said I could do, I will do.' And though his words came with his engaging smile, he seemed as firmly set in his determination as a rock hardened in cement.

Helen, who knew her father, sighed and turned from him to Carr. Then her eyes wandered through the open door, across the flat lands and down to the distant hills of Desert Valley.

'I should not speak as I am going to speak,' Carr was saying, 'if matters were not exactly as they are. To begin with, I take it that I have been accepted as a friend. Hence you will forgive me if I appear to presume and will know that I have no love of interfering in another man's personal affairs. Then, I must say what I have to say now: in a few days I am leaving you. I've got to go to New York.'

'Oh,' said Helen. 'I am sorry.'

'You are kind to me,' he acknowledged gravely. 'And I am sorry to go. Unless you and your father will consent to come also. Now, I am going to have my say—and, Mr. Longstreet, I hope you will forgive me if I am assuming a privilege which is not mine. I take it that you have no great amount of ready cash. Further, that your income has been that of most college men, who are all underpaid—say, three or four or five thousand a year. I have talked with Nate Kemble about you. His concern is a tremendously big affair with head offices in New York. Kemble is a friend of mine: I own stock in his company: he will acknowledge, quite as I am prepared to acknowledge, that there is a place for an expert of your type in the company. And the place will pay you, from the jump, ten thousand dollars.'

Helen fairly gasped. Despite her father's talk of the extravagant sums he meant to wrest from the bowels of the earth, she had never dreamed of so princely an income for them. Longstreet, however, merely shook a smiling head.

'You're a real friend, John,' he said. 'But here we stick. And, when you come down to dollars and cents, I'll eat your new hat for you if I can't make ten times your ten thousand in the first year.'

Before such amazing confidence Carr stalled. But he did not give up; it wasn't his habit of thought to relinquish anything which he had undertaken. Still for a little he was silent, studying his man. Again Helen was staring out through the open door.

'Some one is coming,' she announced. Then, her tone quickening, 'It is Mr. Howard; I knew he would be riding over before night. I know his horse,' she explained hastily, flushing a trifle under Carr's eyes which told her that he was surprised that she could tell who it was at such a distance. 'It is the horse he rode the first time we ever saw him. There is some one with him. It looks like—'

She did not say whom it looked like. Carr and Longstreet looked out. The second rider was a woman; her horse was not Sanchia Murray's white mare, but none the less they all knew that with Alan Howard came Sanchia. Carr's heavy brows gathered blackly. The flush died out of Helen's face and her lips tightened. Longstreet sprang up and went to the door.

'If it is Mrs. Murray,' he called back, something like triumph in his excited voice, 'and if she is coming here—why, then maybe there was a mistake after all.'

'She is not coming here!' cried Helen hotly. 'Papa, I will not have that woman in the house. After the way she has cheated you, fooled you, lied to you—'

'Come, come, my dear,' chided Longstreet. 'No one must be judged and condemned unheard. And remember that she is coming with Mr. Howard.'

Helen looked hopelessly at Carr. There were times when she utterly despaired of her father. But she could find comfort in the thought that if that Sanchia woman sought to perpetrate any more of her villainy and deceit, she was going to stand at her father's side through all of it. Meantime the two riders came on swiftly. As they drew up at the door Helen saw that Howard looked worried and ill at ease and that Sanchia Murray's eyes were red as though with copious weeping. Whereas Helen sniffed audibly.

'The horrid cat,' she said.

Sanchia began pouring out a torrent of confused words which Howard's curt speech interrupted. As he lifted his hat his eyes were for Helen alone: she flashed him a scornful look and turned away from him. Then he turned to Longstreet.

'Mr. Longstreet,' he said sharply, 'I want you to know my

position in this matter. As I was starting Mrs. Murray came to the ranch. I was naturally astonished when she said that she was on her way to see you. I had thought, from what has happened, that you would be the last man in the world whom she would care to meet. She said, however, that she must speak with you and that she hoped she could do something to right matters. When she asked for a fresh horse I loaned her one. That,' he concluded harshly, 'is all that I have to do with Sanchia Murray and all that I want to do with her. The rest is up to you.'

The spite in Sanchia's quick sidelong look was for Howard alone.

'Alan is rather hard on me, I think,' she said quite simply as she turned her eyes upon the three at the cabin door. 'Especially,' and again she gave him that look for him alone, 'after what has been between us. But I must not think of that now. Oh, Mr. Longstreet, if you only knew how this thing has nearly killed me—'

She broke off, hiding her face in her hands, her body swaying in the saddle as though surely she would fall. Longstreet looked concerned.

'Get down and come in,' he exclaimed. 'You are utterly exhausted. Helen, my dear, a cup of coffee, quick. This poor lady looks as though she hadn't slept or rested or eaten since we saw her last.'

'How could I eat or rest or sleep?' cried Sanchia brokenly. 'After all that has happened? Oh, I wish I were dead!'

Helen did not budge for the coffee. Her eyes were blazing. Sanchia slid down from the saddle and came to the door. Longstreet hastened to her side and the two went in together. Helen, without looking toward Howard, followed, determined that she would hear whatever it was that Sanchia Murray had to say.

'Come in, Howard,' Longstreet remembered to say. 'We're having supper. Both you and Mrs. Murray will eat with us.'

Sanchia bathed her eyes and they all sat down. When Howard looked toward Helen she ignored him. Outside Carr had demanded, 'What in hell's name made you bring that woman here?' and Alan had rejoined, 'I couldn't stop her coming, could I?' And now the two had nothing to say to each other. Longstreet, nervous and impatient for whatever explanations were coming, fidgeted constantly until Sanchia began speaking.

'When I learned what had happened,' she said, 'I thought at first that I could not live to endure it. I could have shrieked; I could have killed myself. To think that I had been the cause of it all. Oh, it was hideous! But then I knew that I must live and that I must seek somehow to make reparation. All of my life, as long as I live, I shall hope and try and work to undo what I have done.'

She was watching them all through her handkerchief, which she was using to dab her eyes; of Longstreet she never for an instant lost sight. She saw the eagerness in his eyes and knew that it was an eagerness to believe in her. She saw Helen's anger and contempt; she saw Carr's black looks; she saw, too, how Howard kept his eyes always on Helen's face, and she read what was so easy to read in them. It was her business, her chief affair in life just now, to keep her two eyes wide open; hence she saw, too, the look which Helen had flashed at the cattleman. And while she observed all of this she was speaking rapidly, almost incoherently, as though her one concern lay in the tragic error she had made. Had she been less than a very clever woman who had long lived, and lived well, by her wits, she must have found the situation too much for her. But no one of her hearers, excepting possibly the one chiefly interested, failed to do Sanchia Murray justice for her cleverness. As it was, she did not fear the outcome from the outset.

She told how she had been so overjoyed at Longstreet's news;

how, for that dear child Helen's sake, she had rejoiced; how she had for a little felt less lonely in sharing a secret meant for a wonderful birthday surprise; how she had yearned to help in this glowing hour of happiness. She had tried to help Mr. Longstreet with Mr. Harkness at the court-house; she had learned that he was out of town; she had been told that his assistant was at the Montezuma House. In spite of her abhorrence of going to such a place she had gone, carried away by the high tide of excitement. And there she had been tricked into introducing Mr. Longstreet to no less a terrible creature than Monte Devine. She hastened to add that she told Mr. Longstreet that she did not know this man; he would bear her out in this; she too had been tricked. But she would never, never forgive herself.

'Nor,' said Helen's voice coldly, 'will I ever forgive you. Nor am I the fool to believe all these tales. Maybe you can make a fool of my father, but—'

'Helen, Helen,' expostulated Longstreet sternly, 'you are being hasty. At times like this one should seek to be kind and just.'

Again Helen's sniff was audible and eloquent.

'Do you mean,' she demanded, 'that you believe all of this nonsense?'

'I mean, my dear, that one should be deliberate. Mrs. Murray has made an explanation, she is plainly sick with grief at what has occurred. She has ridden straight to us. What more could one do? When you are older, my dear, and have seen more of life you will know that the world sometimes makes terrible mistakes.'

'You are so great-hearted!' sobbed Sanchia. 'So wonderful! There is not another man in the world who would be even tolerant at a time like this. And to think that it is you—you whom I have hurt.' Her sobs overcame her.

Helen flung herself angrily to her feet.

'Papa,' she cried, 'can't you see, can't you understand that this woman is determined to make a fool of you again? Hasn't she done it once already? Oh, are you going to be just a little baby in her hands?'

Sanchia lowered her handkerchief for a swift glance at Helen and then at the other faces in the room. The sternness on Howard's and Carr's faces did not greatly concern her, for she saw written across Longstreet's countenance just about what she had counted on. And Helen's words had simply succeeded in drawing his indignation toward his daughter. Hence, wisely, Sanchia was content to be silent for a spell. Matters seemed to be going well enough left alone.

Helen had meant to run out of doors, to close her ears to this maddening discussion. She felt that it was either that or deliberately slap Sanchia Murray's face. Now, however, she sat down again, deciding with a degree of acumen that Sanchia would prefer nothing to a *tete-a-tete* with Longstreet.

'After all,' said Helen more quietly and with a look which was hard as it flashed across Sanchia's face to Howard's and then on, 'threshing all this over is valueless. Forgive her, father,' she went on contemptuously, 'if either of you will feel better for it, and don't detain her. We are going back East in a few days, anyway.'

Howard stared at her wonderingly as Carr nodded his approval of the speech. But Longstreet spoke with considerable emphasis.

'Aren't you rather premature in your announcement, my dear? I am not going back East at all.'

There might have been no discussion of the matter had he ended there. But seeing the various expressions called by his words to the faces about the table, he added the challenge:

'Why should I go? Haven't I already demonstrated that I know what I am doing? Isn't this the place for me?'

Helen answered him first and energetically. He should go, she cried hotly, because he had demonstrated nothing at all save that he was a lamb in a den of wolves. He was a university man and not a mountaineer or desert Indian; he knew books and he did not know men; it was his duty to himself and to his daughter to return home. The girl's colour deepened and grew hot with her rapid speech, and Sanchia, sitting back, watching and listening, lost never a word. Before Longstreet could shape a reply John Carr added his voice to Helen's plea. He said all that he had said once before to-day; he elaborated his argument, which to him appeared unanswerable. When he had done, always speaking quietly, he turned to Howard.

'Don't you think I am right, Al?' he asked.

'No!' replied Howard emphatically. 'I don't. Mr. Longstreet does know his business. He has located one mine in this short time. It was not chance; it was science. There is more gold left in these hills. Give him time and a free swing, and he'll find it.'

Carr appeared amazed.

'I can't imagine what makes you talk like that, Al,' he said shortly. 'It's rather a serious thing with the Longstreets which way they move now. You are deliberately encouraging him to buck a game which he ought to leave to another type of man.'

'Deliberately is the right word,' said Howard. 'And I can't quite understand what makes you seek to discourage him and pack him off to the East again.'

Carr was silent. Sanchia's eyes, very bright, grew brighter with a keen look of understanding. Very innocently she spoke.

'Are you thinking of going East, too, Mr. Carr?' she asked.

'Yes,' snapped Carr. 'I am. What of it?'

'Oh, nothing,' said Sanchia. But she laughed. Then as Longstreet was opening his mouth to make his own statement, she cut in, turning to him, speaking directly to him, in some subtle way giving the impression that she was quite oblivious of anyone but of him and herself.

'You mustn't go,' she said softly. She studied his face and then put a light hand on his arm. Helen stiffened. 'How shall I say all that I feel here?' She gave an effective gesture as she pressed the other hand against her own bosom. 'You have come into a land of nothing but ignorance and into it you have brought the brain of a scholar. You said, "I will find gold," and they laughed at you—and you found it! It was not chance; Alan was right. It was the act of a man who knew. This land has many kinds of men, Mr. Longstreet. It has no other man like you. It needs you. You must stay!'

'Oh,' said Helen. It was scarcely more than a gasp, and yet it bespoke profound disgust. The woman was insufferable. Here, upon the top of her treachery, was most palpable flattery. Surely her father would not fail to see now the woman's true character; surely he must baulk at such talk as this. But he was beaming again as though the clouds of a storm had passed and the sunlight were streaming upon him; he rubbed his hands together and spoke cheerfully.

'Sanchia is right; Alan is right. These two understand me. I shall show to the world that they have not misjudged me. I know my own limitations. I am no superman. I have made blunders in my time. But I do know my own work, and I am the only man here who does! In a way Sanchia is right when she says that this country needs me. It does. And I need it. We are going to stay, my dear.'

Sanchia flashed Helen a look of triumph; her eyes, passing on to Howard, held briefly a sparkle of malice.

Jackson Gregory

'Alan and I are very grateful to have your approval,' she said sweetly. 'Aren't we, Alan?' and again her look was for Helen and was triumphant.

Helen pushed her plate away and for a second time rose abruptly.

'I'll choke if I stay in here,' she said. And, with breast heaving, she went to the door and out into the fading afternoon. Sanchia's glance followed her and then returned placidly to the men.

'The dear child is high-strung, and Heaven knows she has been through enough to upset anyone,' she said condoningly. Then, 'Mr. Carr and you, Alan, don't seem to be hungry any more. I would like a word with Mr. Longstreet, and if you two went out to Helen perhaps you might soothe her. Remember she is only a child after all.'

Glad of the excuse to be gone, both men rose. As they went out they saw how Sanchia was already leaning toward Longstreet, how her hand had again found its way to his arm. Then they lost sight of her and saw Helen standing upon the cliff edge looking off to the lowlands of the south. In silence they joined her.

'I don't know whether I love this country or hate it most,' Helen said without withdrawing her troubled eyes from the expanse of Desert Valley. The sun was down, the distances were veiled in tender shades, pale greens of the meadowlands, dusky greys of the hills. 'If it were only all like that; if there were only the glorious valley and the peace of it instead of this hideous life up here!'

It was in Alan Howard's heart to cry out to her, 'Come down into the peace of it; it is all mine. Come down to live there with me.' It may have been in John Carr's heart to whisper: 'It is mine until the last cent is paid on it; if you love it so, there may still be the way to get it back for you.' But neither man spoke his thought. The three stood close together, the girl with troubled eyes standing between the two friends, and all of their eyes searched into the mystery of the coming dusk.

From the cabin came the sound of a laugh. It was Longstreet's, and it was like a pleased child's.

Jackson Gregory

CHAPTER XX

TWO FRIENDS AND A GIRL

Howard and Carr rode down into the darkening valley side by side. The silence of the coming dusk was no deeper than that silence which had crept about them while the three stood upon the cliff's edge. Longstreet's laugh had whipped up the colour into Helen's cheeks and had lighted a battle fire in her eyes. She had whisked away from them and gone straight back to the cabin, meaning to save her father from his own artlessness and from the snare of a designing widow. She had remembered to call out a breathless 'Good-night' without turning her head. They had taken their dismissal together, understanding Helen's tortured mood. Each man grave and taciturn, like two automatons they buckled on their spurs, mounted and reined toward the trail.

Then Howard had said merely: 'Come down to the ranch-house, John. I want to talk with you.' And Carr had nodded and acquiesced. Thereafter they were silent again for a long time.

The coming of night is a time of vague veilings, of grotesque transformations, of remoulding and steeping in new dyes. Matter-of-fact objects, clear-cut during the day, assume fantastic shapes; a bush may appear a crouching mountain cat; a rock may masquerade as a mastodon. This is an hour of uncertainties. And doubtings and questionings and uncertainties were other shadow shapes thronging the demesnes of two men's souls. Silence and dim dusk without, dim dusk and silence within.

Once Howard, the lighter spirited of the two, sought to laugh the constraint away.

'Something seems to have come over us, John,' he said. But as he spoke he knew that what he should have said was that something had come between them. Further, he knew that Carr would have amended his words thus in his own mind and that that was why he did not reply. He recalled vividly how they three had stood on the cliff, he on Helen's left, John on her right. He and John were friends; in the desert lands friendship is sacred. Further, it is mighty, stalwart, godly, and all but indomitable. They had shared together, fought together. One friend would do to the uttermost for the other, would die for him. He would rush into the other's fight, asking no questions, and if he went down the chill of coming death would be warmed by the glow of conscious sacrifice. The friendship of Howard and Carr had stood the many tests of time. But only now had the supreme test come. Until to-day, either of them in the generousness of his spirit would have stepped gladly aside for the other. But now? A girl is not a cup of water that one man, dying of thirst, may say of her to his friend: 'Take her.' Their friendship was not changed; simply it was no longer the greatest thing in life. The love of a man for a man, though it be strengthened by ten thousand ties, is less than the love of a man for his chosen mate, though to the other eyes and minds that love may be inexplicable. Set any Damon and Pythias upon an isolated desert island, then into their lives bring the soft eyes of a girl, and inevitably the day will dawn when those eyes will look upon the death of a friendship. This knowledge had at last become a part of the understandings of Alan Howard and John Carr.

'You are going East, John?' asked Howard when at length his spirit sought a second time to shake off the oppression of the hour.

Even these words came with something of an effort. He tried to speak naturally. But behind his words were troops of confused thoughts; Carr was going East, and had said nothing to him; if Carr left, what then of Helen? Carr had tried to persuade the Longstreets to go with him.

And to Carr the query sounded more careless, more lightly casual than Howard had intended. His own thoughts were quick to respond though his reply came after a noticeable hesitation. Alan did not appear to care whether he went away or remained; he had not asked if this were to be a brief absence or an indefinite sojourn.

'Yes,' Carr's answer at last was short and blunt; 'I have business there.'

Carr thought that if Alan were interested he would ask naturally, as one friend had always asked the other, to know more. Howard thought that if Carr cared to speak of his own personal affairs he would do so. Hence, while both waited, neither spoke. Perhaps both were hurt. Certainly the constraint between them thickened and deepened in step with the engulfing night; they could not see each other's faces, they could not glimpse each other's souls. Both were baffled and into the temper of each came a growing irritation. One thing alone they appeared to have in common—the desire to come to the end of the ride. Their spurs dipped and they raced along wordlessly.

When Howard dismounted at the home corrals and began unsaddling, Carr rode on to the house.

'You're going to stay all night, John,' Howard called after him. 'Put your horse in the barn.'

But Carr swung down at the yard gate and tied his horse there.

'Can't this time,' he said. 'I'll have to ride on, Al.'

Thus each made his pretence, less to his friend than to himself, that everything was all right. They sought to be natural and failed, and knew that they had failed. Carr waited for Howard, smoking at the gate; Howard hastened up to the house and went in. He struck a match, lighted the table lamp and filled the pipe lying beside it. Carr tossed his hat to the table and sat down. Their eyes roved about the familiar room. Here were countless traces of both men; Carr had lived here, Howard lived here now. Helen had been here, and she too had left something to mark her passing. They both saw it. It was only a bluebird's feather, but Alan had set it in a place of conspicuousness just above the fireplace. Even into a room which had been home to each, which they had held must always be home to both, something of Helen came like a little ghost.

'You'll have use for some money about now,' said Howard abruptly. He drew out the table drawer; inside were scraps of paper, a fountain-pen, a cheque-book and some old stubs. 'Time's up for a payment, too. I sold a pretty fair string the other day.'

'I could use a little cash,' Carr admitted carelessly. 'I've got in pretty deep with the Quigley mining outfit. I made Longstreet a proposition—I am a trifle short, I guess,' he concluded lamely.

'I see,' responded Howard, whereas he saw nothing at all very clearly. He busied himself with his pen, shook it savagely, opened his cheque-book. 'Ten thousand this trip, wasn't it?'

Carr hesitated.

'I had figured on twelve five,' he said. 'Wasn't that the amount due now?'

Howard hunted through the back of the drawer and finally found a little memorandum book. He turned through the pages upon which he had scribbled notes of purchases of cattle and horses and of ranch equipment, passed on to a tabulation

Jackson Gregory

of his men's wages, and finally stopped at a page devoted to his agreement with his friend.

'Here you are,' he said when he had found it. 'Ten thousand, due on the eleventh of the month. I'm pretty near a week late on it, John,' he smiled.

Carr however had his own note-book with him; readily he found his own entry.

'I've set it down here as twelve thousand five hundred,' he said quietly. 'You remember we talked over a couple of methods of payment, Al. But,' and he snapped the rubber band about his book and dropped it into his pocket, 'what's the odds? Let it go at ten.'

'No,' said Howard. 'Not if you've counted on more.' A flush ran up into his face and his eyes were inscrutable. He was conscious of being in the absurd mood to note trifles; John had come with his memoranda, John had meant to ask him for the money. 'I'd just as lief pay twenty-five hundred extra now as at any time.' And with lowered head and sputtering pen he wrote the cheque.

'I don't want to inconvenience you, Al,' Carr accepted the cheque with certain reluctance. 'Sure it's all right?'

'Sure,' said Howard emphatically. He tossed the pen and book into the drawer. Now the awkwardness of the silence upon them was more marked than ever before. Carr tarried only a few minutes, during which both men were ill at ease. Only an expressionless 'So long!' passed between them when he got up to go. They might see each other again before Carr went East; they might not. Howard went back to his chair at the table, staring moodily at the bluebird feather.

Nothing of the instinct of a clerk had ever filtered into the habits of Alan Howard. His system of books was simple. He set down in one place the amounts which came in; in another place those expended. He added and subtracted. He deposited his money in the bank and checked it out. He must bank more when the last was gone. That was about all. It was seldom that he knew just how far his assets were above his liabilities or below. But to-night he knew that he had strained his account. He had counted on paying ten thousand and had paid twelve thousand five hundred. He turned first to his cheque-book, which had not been balanced for a couple of months. No adept at figures he spilled much ink, scratched out many calculations and went through them again, grew hot and exasperated and finally before he got anywhere was in a mood to damn everything that came under his hand. It was midnight when he had assembled upon one sheet of paper an approximately truthful statement of his financial condition. And then he sat back limply and lifted his eyebrows and whistled.

Within something less than thirty days he must take up a note which Pony Lee held for a thousand dollars; Pony would want the money and had said as much when he had advanced it. Then there were the calves, due within the week, from French Valley; Tony Vaca was rushing them, was selling at a very low figure and would want his money on the nail. Well, he must have it. That was another seven hundred dollars. There was another note held by Engle, down in San Juan. The banker might extend it; he might not. It was for fifteen hundred dollars, and would fall due within sixty days. On top of this were the running expenses: the ranch was working full-handed, the men would want their wages a week from Saturday: this was Tuesday. He turned to their accounts; three or four of them had not drawn down last month. They would all want their money when next pay-day came. He estimated the amount. In the neighbourhood of seven hundred dollars. He totalled all of these forthcoming payments. The aggregate was close to four thousand dollars. And his cheque-book, balanced to date, indicated that he had overdrawn to make the payment to Carr. He could have paid the ten thousand and have had something over two thousand in cold cash to run on; now he had not enough in the San Juan bank to make his own cheque good.

'If Carr had only been satisfied with the ten thousand,' he muttered. 'Or if he had given me warning ahead that he wanted the extra twenty-five hundred. Now what?'

None of these issues were clouded, and in due time he decided upon all points. He gave up all thought of bed, made himself a pot of coffee and sat up all night, devoting himself to details. The cheque he had given Carr must be honoured; hence he must ride to-morrow to San Juan to see Engle, the banker. He was only a few hundred dollars short there and Engle would help him to balance the account. The fifteen hundred he owed the bank on his personal note could no doubt be extended if necessary. There remained the money for the calves, the thousand due Pony Lee and another thousand to pay his men and for such necessities as would arise. All of this he would talk over with Engle. It might be that the bank would take a mortgage on his equity in Desert Valley and advance a considerable sum on it.

But he must not forget that the present crisis was not all to be considered. Another year would bring the time of another payment to Carr. In the meantime the ranch must be operated, it must be made to pay. He had already planned on asking extensions from Engle; but it did not enter his thought now to ask John Carr to wait.

'I've got my work cut out for me,' said Howard grimly. 'I've got to work like hell, that's all. I've got to carve down expenses, fire men I can manage without, be on the job all the time to buy in stock cheap wherever it can be got and unload for a quick turnover and some ready cash. I've got to go in for more hay and wheat another season; the price is up and going higher. And real soon, the chances are, I've got to sell some more cows.'

Before dawn he was at the men's bunk-house. He woke Chuck Evans and told him to hurry into his clothes and come up to the house. When Chuck came the two men sat down at the table, pencil and paper in Howard's hand, Chuck's eyes keen upon his employer's set face.

'I'm right down to cases, Chuck,' said Howard bluntly. 'I am in up to my neck, and that's all there is to it. As soon as I get through with you I am off to San Juan to see if there is any real money left in the world. I'll be back as soon as I can. But you get busy while I'm gone. First thing, here are five men you will have to give their time. Tell them why; tell them there's always a job open for them here when I've got the cash for pay-day. Then you and what's left will get your necks into your collars and go to it, long hours and hard work until we pull out. Get the boys out this morning for another round-up. Bring in every hoof and tail that will size up for a decent sale. If you can get time, ride down to San Ramon and see if there's a chance to sell a string of mules to the road gang. That's about all this time; look for me back in two or three days.'

'All right, Al,' said Evans. 'So long.' He went to the door and paused. He wanted to say something and didn't know just what to say or how to say it. So he coughed and said again, 'Well, so long, Al,' and went out.

In the first flush of the dawn Howard rode away toward San Juan. He turned in the saddle and looked back toward the Last Ridge country. He fancied that he could make out the Longstreet cabin even when he knew that his lover's desire was tricking his sense. He thought of Helen; she would be sleeping now. He would not see her for several days. He thought of John Carr; Carr would see her every day until he was forced to go East. Carr had not confided in him when he expected to leave. His eyes left the uplands lingeringly and wandered across the sweeping fields of Desert Valley. He straightened in the saddle and his lungs filled and expanded. The valley was his, his to work for, to struggle and plan for, to make over as he would have it—to hold for Helen. For Helen loved it no less than he loved it. And he loved Helen.

'. . . One should be loyal to one's friends.' He held to that stoutly, insistent and stubborn to play his part. Something had come over him and Carr, or between them; but none the less he obstinately sought to refuse to harbour thoughts which came again and again and which always angered him with himself. There was the suspicion: 'Carr was unfair in seeking to take Helen and her father away with him to the East.' He told himself that that was Carr's right if Carr held it so. There came the accusation: 'Carr had been hard on him last night.' He told himself that it was easily granted that they had misunderstood each other when, long ago, they had arranged for the payments; further, that no doubt Carr, too, was hard up for cash. The thought suggested itself: 'Carr had no right to berate him for allowing Sanchia to ride to the Longstreet cabin.' Carr had spoken quickly, unthinkingly, and they all were under stress. He would play fair and give a man his due—and his thoughts switched to Helen and Carr was forgotten and, with a half-smile on his lips, he rode on through the brightening morning, dreaming of the ranch that should be when Helen came with him to ride and their hands found each other and she whispered: 'I love it and—it is ours!'

John Engle, the banker of San Juan, was something more than a banker. Not only was he a fine, upstanding, broad-minded man; he was a man, no longer in the first flush of youth, who had made himself what he was and who from forty-five vividly recalled twenty-five. He had learned caution, but he had known what it was to plunge head-first into deep waters. That now, a man established, he no longer had to take long chances, was due largely to the successes met in long chances taken when all of life lay before him, inviting. When now Alan Howard came to him in his office at the bank and put his case before him straightforwardly and without evasion or reservation, he came to the one man in the world who because of his position and his character could best help him.

'Take it slow, Alan,' said Engle quietly. 'I can give you the whole day, if necessary. I've got to know just where you stand and just which way you are headed before I can get anywhere.'

He drew out his pad and very methodically began to set down

figures as the cattleman talked. Finally:

'It's the bank's money, not my own, that I'll be advancing you, you know. I am pretty well sewed up personally as usual. Consequently, while I can see you over a few of the immediate bumps in your trail, I can't give you all that you'll want. But I fancy you can get across with it.' His keen eyes took fresh stock of the cattleman, marking the assertive strength, the clean build, the erect carriage, the hard hands, the lean jaw and finally the steady eyes which always met his own. The personal equation always counts, perhaps with the banker more than most men imagine, and John Engle found no sign of any deterioration in the security offered by Alan Howard's personality. 'It's a good thing, anyway,' he went on, with the first hint of a twinkle in his regard, 'for a youngster like you to have to scrap things out after the old fashion. Not married yet, are you?'

'No,' said Alan.

Engle laughed.

'But hoping to be? Well, it's time. That's a good ballast for a man. Now, I've got this pretty straight, let's have your plans. You hope to swing the ranch all right, or you wouldn't be calling on me. You're in deep already and, of course, if it's a human possibility you've got to swing it. What do you figure to do?'

Howard during his long ride had considered his problem from all angles, and now, leaning forward eagerly, told in detail what he had decided. Engle, a rancher himself with broad experience, nodded now and then, asked his few pertinent questions, made an occasional suggestion. Then he rose to his feet and put out his hand.

'Drop in and see us when you're in town and have the time,' he said cordially. 'Mrs. Engle was speaking of you only the other day. You'll want to be on your way now. I'll let you have five thousand on your equity and let the other fifteen hundred ride with it, making one note for sixty-five hundred. I think that if you work things right and hold down expenses and make the sales and purchases and other sales you have in mind, you'll get away with your deal. Just the same, my boy,' and for an instant there came into his eyes the fighting look which had been there frequently in the day when he fought out his own battles, 'you've got a man's-sized job on your hands.'

'I know it,' said Alan. And when, the proper papers signed, he said good-bye, his eyes brightened and he said directly: 'It's a great thing, John Engle, to have a man's-sized man to talk things over with.'

From his window Engle musingly watched the tall form go out to the horse at the hitching-post and swing up into the saddle.

'Now what's happened between him and John Carr?' he asked himself. And without hesitation he answered his own question: 'A girl, I suppose. Well, she ought to be a real girl to do that.'

Howard, riding joyously back toward Desert Valley, thought first of Helen. But not even Helen could hold all of his thoughts when at length his horse's hoofs fell again upon the rim of Desert Valley Land. Upon the bordering hills of the southern edge of the valley he drew rein and sat, lost in thought. He saw herds feeding, and they were his herds and he himself did not know their exact number. He must know; the game was swiftly becoming one where pawns count. He saw a man riding; it was his man, whom he must direct and pay. He saw water running in one of his larger creeks, and thought how it too must be made to work for him. Yonder were colts running wild; there were more than he required at present. They must be broken; they could be sold. He looked across empty acres, rich pasture lands void of grazing stock. A slow, thoughtful frown gathered in his eyes; he must somehow put stock into them, stock to be bought skilfully and sold skilfully. All of this glorious sweep of country stretching to the four corners of the compass was his, his very own, if he were man enough to go on with the work to which he had somewhat lightly set his hand. He had loved it always, since first he had come here as John Carr's guest. He loved it now with a mounting passion. It flashed over him that when, at some far-distant time, he should die, this was the one spot upon God's great earth where he should want his ashes scattered on the little wind which came down from the hills. It was a part of him and he a part of it. And as he loved it and yearned for it utterly, so did Helen love it.

'It is going to be mine and yours, my dear.' He spoke aloud, his voice stern with his determination. 'For us to have and to hold.'

And because of the thought and the knowledge of what lay ahead of him, he knew that for the present he must forego that to which he had looked forward all day. He must for a little postpone a ride to see Helen. For already he foresaw the calls upon his time; short-handed, it was to be work for him from long before day until long after dark. As he started down the hill into the valley he saw a herd of cattle coming from the north. He had a round-up on his hands to begin with, and it was already beginning.

CHAPTER XXI

ALMOST

Long hours and hard work in the cattle country mean that a man slips from his saddle into his bunk and to sleep, and from his bunk into his saddle again, with only time to bolt his food and hot coffee infrequently and at irregular intervals. Chuck Evans had obeyed orders; the ranch was short-handed and the 'old-timers' remaining cursed a little, to be sure, at the new order of things, but understood and went to work. Howard, when he met them all at supper long after dark, noted how their sunburned eyes turned upon him speculatively. And he knew that in their own parlance every mother's son of them was ready to go the limit if the old man set the pace. That night, when the others trooped off to bed, he detained Chuck Evans and Plug Oliver and Dave Terril for a brief conference. To them he gave in what detail he could his latest plans. Also, since they were friends as well as hired hands, he told them frankly of his difficulties and of his success with Engle. When the men left him they had accepted his fight as their own.

The first man in the saddle the next day was Howard. He ordered the tally taken of every head of stock on his ranch. This alone, since his acres were broad and since his stock grazed free over thousands of acres lying adjacent to Desert Valley on three sides, was a big task. Already, during his absence, a number of the best of the beef cattle had been moved to the meadowlands. He set a man to close-herd there; he sent other men to bring in still other straying stock; he himself judged every single head, cutting out those he deemed unfit; finally he saw the growing herd driven down into the choicest of his meadow grazing land to fatten.

All of this required days. Between breakfast and supper every man with the outfit changed his horse several times; Howard, the hardest rider of them all, changed horses five times the first day. He and his men showed signs of the strain they put upon their bodies; they were a gaunt, lean-jawed, wild-eyed lot. There was little frolic left in them when night came; they were short-spoken, prone to grow fierce over trifles. But there was not a sullen or discontented man among them. They took what came; they had known times of stress before; they could look forward to a day to come of boisterous relaxation and money to be spent in town. Though the subject had never been mentioned, they fully understood that there would be a bonus coming and a glorious holiday. They would see the old man through now: later he would square the account.

Eat, sleep and work; there was nothing else in their schedule. The times when Howard had a few moments over a cigarette to think quietly of Helen were times when he could not go to her: in the dimness of the coming day when he was going out to saddle and she would still be asleep; in the dark of the day ended when she would be going to bed. But he held grimly to his task here, saying to himself that in a few days he would ride to her and with something to say; wondering how she would listen; sometimes aglow with his hope, sometimes fearing. And, as he thought of her, so did he think often of John Carr. He did not know if Carr had gone East or if still he were a daily guest at the Longstreet home. Not a man of his riders had been beyond the confines of the grazing lands; no one had come in from the outside. There was no news.

So a full week sped by. Then for the first time came both opportunity and excuse for Howard to leave the ranch. Chuck Evans had ridden into San Ramon to see if there were a market for a string of mules; he brought back word that a teamster named Roberts in the new mining-camp had been making inquiries. It seemed that he wanted high-grade stock and had the money to pay for it. Everything was running smoothly on the ranch, and Howard rode this time on his own errand. But, before starting for Sanchia's Town, he slipped into the ranchhouse and shaved and changed to a new shirt and chaps and recently blackened boots. Thereafter he brushed his best black hat. Then from a bottom drawer of his old bureau, where it was hidden under a pile of clothing, he brought out a parcel which had come with him from a store in San Juan.

As good a way as any to see Roberts in Sanchia's Town led by way of the Longstreet camp on Last Ridge. Howard took the winding trail up which his horse could climb to the plateau, and once on the level land came swooping down on the well-remembered spot joyously. The spot itself was hidden from him by the grove of stunted pines until he came within a couple of hundred yards of it. Then he jerked his horse down to a standstill and sat staring before him incredulously. The cabin was gone quite as though there had never been a cabin there in all time.

At first he wouldn't believe his eyes. Then swiftly his wonder-ment altered to consternation. They had gone! Helen and her father had gone. Carr had prevailed upon them; Howard had not come to see; by now they were flying eastward upon the speeding overland train, or perhaps were already in New York.

The splendour of the day died; the joyousness went out of his heart; he sat staring at the emptiness before him, then at the parcel in brown paper clutched so foolishly in his hand. He looked all about him; through the trees as though he expected to see Helen's laughing face watching him; across the broken ridges beyond the flat; down into his own valley. Down there, too, the glory had passed. When he had stood here with Helen and they two had looked across the valley lands together, it had been to him like the promised land. Now it was so much dirt and rock and grass with cows and horses browsing stupidly across all of it.

For a long time he sat very still. Then his face hardened.

'If she has gone, then I am going, too,' he told himself. 'And I am going to bring her back.'

He turned his horse and rode swiftly to Sanchia's Town. They would have gone that way, on to Big Run, San Ramon and down to the railroad. In such a case he would have word of them in the mining-camp. In his present mood he required only a few minutes to come to the new settlement. Had he been less absorbed in his own thoughts he must have been amazed at what he saw about him. He had known men before now to make towns upon dry bare ground and in a mere handful of days; not even he, with his first-hand knowledge of such venturings, had ever seen the like of Sanchia's Town. The spirit which had initiated it into the world was still its driving spirit. It sprawled, it overflowed its boundaries incessantly, it hooted and yelled and sang. It grew like a formless mass lumped about fermenting yeast. Already there were shacks and tents up and down both sides of Dry Gulch and strung along in the gravelly bed. There were gambling-houses, monstrosities which named themselves hotels and rooming-houses, stores, lunch counters. The streets were crooked alleys; everywhere dust puffed up and thickened and never settled; teams and jolting wagons and pack burros disputed the congested way; there were seasoned miners, old-time prospectors, going their quiet ways; there were tenderfeet of all descriptions. Not less than five thousand human souls had already found their way to Sanchia's Town and more were coming.

In all of this to-day, Howard took scant interest. His major emotion was one of annoyance. Among such a seething crowd where should he ask of the Longstreets? He sat his horse in a narrow space between a lunch counter and a canvas bar-room and stared about him. Then he saw that the solitary figure perched upon a box before the lunch counter was Yellow Barbee. He called to him quickly.

Barbee's young eyes, which he turned promptly, were still

eloquent of an amorous joyousness within Barbee's young soul. He bestowed his glance only fleetingly upon Howard, said a brief 'Hello, Al,' and turned immediately to the cause of the obvious flutter in Barbee's bosom. Howard expected to see Sanchia Murray behind the counter. Instead he saw a young girl of a little less than Barbee's age, roguish-eyed, black-haired, red-mouthed, plump and saucy. Her sleeves were up; her arms were brown and round; there was flour on them.

'Where are the Longstreets, Barbee?' asked Howard.

'Gone,' announced Barbee cheerfully. And as though that closed the matter to his entire satisfaction, he demanded: 'Come on, Pet; be a good kid. Going with me, ain't you?'

Pet laughed and thereafter turned up her pretty nose with obviously mock disdain.

'Dancing old square dances and polkas, I'd bet a stack of wheats,' she scoffed. 'Why, there ain't any more real jazz in your crowd of cow-hands than there is in an old man's home. What do you take me for, anyway?'

'Aw, come on,' grinned Barbee. 'You're joshing. If it's jazz you want—'

'Look here,' said Howard impatiently. 'I'm just asking a question, and I'll get out of your way. Where did they go?'

'Who?' asked Barbee.

'The Longstreets.'

'Dunno,' Barbee shrugged. Then, as an afterthought, 'Sanchia Murray could tell you; she's been sticking tight to them. She's got a tent up yonder, back of the Courtot House on the edge of town.'

Howard hurried on. The lunch counter girl, following him

with critical eyes, demanded for him or anyone else to hear:

'Who's your bean-pole friend, Kid?'

But the answer Howard did not hear. He swung out to the side to be free of the town and galloped on to Sanchia's tent, which he found readily. Sanchia herself was in front of it, just preparing to saddle her white mare.

'Hello, Al,' she greeted him carelessly, though her eyes narrowed at him speculatively.

'Where have the Longstreets gone?' he asked without preliminary.

'Back in the hills, Bear Valley way,' she replied, still scrutinizing him. She marked the look of relief in his eyes and laughed cynically and withal a trifle bitterly. 'On the Red Hill trail. Going to see them?'

'Yes.' He reined away, and then added stiffly, 'Thank you.'

'Wait a minute,' she called to him. 'I'm just going up there myself. You might saddle for me, and I'll ride with you.'

He paused and looked her sternly and steadily in the eyes. His voice was cold and his words were outspoken.

'I had rather ride alone, and you know it. Further, after the way you have tricked that man, I'd think you'd draw off and leave them alone. You can't do a thing like that twice.'

For an instant the look in her eyes was baffling. Then there shot through the inscrutability of it a sudden gleam of malice that was like a spurt of flame. It was the fire which before now Howard's attitude had kindled there.

'What you men see in that little fool, I don't know!' she cried hotly. 'What has she that I haven't? I could have made you the biggest man in the country; I would have given everything and held nothing back. I am even honest enough to say so, and I am not afraid to say so. And you are stupid like every other man. Oh, I am done with the crowd of you!' she broke out violently, half hysterically. 'Laugh at me, will you? Turn your back on me, will you?' She paused and panted out the words. 'Why, if you came crawling to me now I'd spit on you. And, so help me God, I'll ruin the last one of you and your precious flock of lambs before I have done with you. If Jim Courtot can't do the trick, I'll do for you first and Jim next.'

He wheeled his horse and left her, groping wonderingly for an explanation of her fury. He had not spoken with her above a score of times in his life. He had merely been decent to her when, in the beginning, it struck him that after all she was only a defenceless woman and that men were hard on her. That his former simple kindness would have awakened any serious affection had failed to suggest itself to him.

But swiftly he forgot Sanchia and her vindictiveness. She had mentioned Courtot; for a little as he rode into the hills he puzzled over Courtot's recurrent disappearances. He recalled how, always when he came to a place where he might expect to find the gambler, he had passed on. Here of late he was like some sinister will-o'-the-wisp. What was it that urged him? A lure that beckoned? A menace that drove? He thought of Kish Taka. There was a nemesis to dog any man. Jim Courtot had dwelt with the desert Indians; he had come to know in what savage manner they meted out their retributive justice. Was Kish Taka still unsleeping, patient, relentless on Courtot's trail? Kish Taka and his dog?

But his horse's hoofs were beating out a merry music on the winding trail that led toward the Red Hill country, and at the end of the trail was Helen. Helen had not gone East. The frown in his eyes gave place to his smile; the sunlight was again golden and glorious; the emptiness of the world was replaced by a large content.

'They just couldn't stand being so close to what they had lost,' he argued. 'It was a right move to come up here.'

He found the new camp without trouble. As he entered the lower end of the tiny valley he saw the canvas-walled cabin at the farther end, under the cliffs. He saw Helen herself. She was just stepping out through the door. He came racing on to her, waving his hat by way of greeting. He slipped down from the saddle, let his bundle fall and caught both of her hands in his.

After this long, unexplained absence Helen had meant to be very stiff when, on some fine day, Alan Howard remembered to come again. But now, under his ardent eyes, the colour ran up into her cheeks in rebellious defiance of her often strengthened determination and, though she wrenched herself free from him, something of the fire in his eyes was reflected in hers.

'Good afternoon, Mr. Cyclone,' she said quite as carelessly as his sudden appearance permitted her vaguely disturbed senses. 'What are you going to do? Run over me?'

He laughed joyously.

'I could eat you,' he told her enthusiastically. 'You look just that good to me. Lord, but I'm hungry for the sight of you!'

'That's nice of you to say so,' Helen answered. And now she was quite all that she had planned to be; as coolly indifferent as only a girl can be when something has begun to sing in her heart and she has made up her mind that no one must hear the singing. 'But I fail to see why this very excellent imitation of a man who hasn't seen his best friend for a couple of centuries.'

'It has been that long, every bit of it—longer.'

Helen's smile was that stock smile to be employed in answer to an inconsequential compliment paid by a chance acquaintance.

'Three or four days is hardly an eternity,' she retorted.

'Three or four days? Why, it's been over nine! Nearly ten.'

She appeared both amazed and incredulous. Then she waved the matter aside as of no moment.

'I was going out to the spring for a drink,' she said. 'Will you wait here? Father will be in soon.'

'I'll come along, if there's room for two.' He picked up his parcel, which Helen noted without seeming to note anything. 'Look here, Helen,' as she started on before him to the thicket of willows, 'aren't you the least little bit glad to see me?'

'Why, of course I am,' she assured him politely. 'And papa was wondering about you only this morning. Isn't it pretty here?'

He admitted without enthusiasm that it was. He had not seen anything but her. She had on a blue dress; she wore a wide hat; her eyes were nothing less than maddening. He recalled the prettiness of Barbee's new girl at the lunch counter; he remembered Sanchia's regular features; these two were simply not of the same order of beings as Helen. No woman was. He strode behind her as she flitted on up the trail and felt thrilling through him an odd commingling of reverence, of adoration, of infinite yearning.

She came to the spring and stopped, watching him eagerly though she pretended to be looking anywhere but at him. And for a moment Howard, marvelling at the spot, let his eyes wander from her. The spring had been cleaned out and rimmed with big flat rocks. About it, as though recently transplanted here, were red and blue flowers. Just at hand close to the clear pool was a delightful shade cast by a freshly constructed shelter. And the shelter itself made him open his eyes. Willow poles, with the leaves still green on them, had been set in the soft earth. Across them other poles had been placed cunningly woven in and out. Still other branches, criss-crossed above, and piled high with foliage, offered a thick mat of verdure to shield one from the hot rays of the sun. Within the elfin chamber was a rustic seat; everywhere, their roots enwrapped in wet earth, were flowers.

'It's wonderful!' he told her, and now his enthusiasm had been awakened. 'And, of course it's your own idea and your own work.'

'Oh my, no! It was John's idea and John made it!'

'John?'

'John Carr. He has been a perfect dear. Isn't he wonderful?'

Yes, Carr was wonderful. But already Howard's enthusiasm had fled.

'The leaves will wilt pretty soon,' he found fault in spite of himself. He was a little ashamed even while he was speaking. 'The flowers will die, and then—'

Helen was already seated within, smiling, looking placid and unconcerned.

'By then,' she announced lightly, 'I'll be gone; so it won't matter.'

'Gone?' he demanded sharply. 'Where?'

'East. Mr. Carr has gone on ahead. We are to meet him in New York.'

He sat down upon a rock just outside her door and made no attempt to hide what was in his heart. He had thought to have lost her when he came to the spot whence the cabin had vanished; he had found her here; he was going to lose her again. . . . Helen's heart quickened at his look, and she lowered her head, pretending to be occupied exclusively with a thistle that had caught on her skirt, afraid that he would know.

'Why are you going like this?' he asked suddenly.

She appeared to hesitate.

'I ought not to say anything against one of your friends,' she said with a great show of ingenuousness. 'But, Mrs. Murray—'

Explosively he cut her short. 'You know that she is not a friend of mine and that she has never been and never will be a friend of mine. Why do you say that?'

She shrugged her shoulders and went on smiling at him. That smile began to madden him; it appeared to speak of such an unruffled spirit when his own was in tumult.

'I beg your pardon, I'm sure. I was merely going to say that Mrs. Murray shows too great an interest in papa. Of course I understand her, and he doesn't. Dear old pops is a perfect child. She has tricked him once; she seems to think him worth watching; she is unbearable. So I am going to do the very natural thing and take him away from her. Back where he belongs by the way; where we both belong.'

'That is not true; you don't belong anywhere but here.' He began speaking slowly, very earnestly and with little show of emotion. But little by little his speech quickened, his voice was raised, his words became vehement. 'You belong here. There is no land in the world like this, just as there is no girl like you. Listen to me, Helen! For your sake, for my sake—yes, and for your father's sake—you must stay. You were speaking of him; let's think of him first. He is like a child in that he has kept a pure, simple heart. But he is not without his own sort of wisdom. He knows rocks and strata and geological formation; he found gold once, and that was not just accident. He lost, but he lost without a whimper. He is a good sport. He will find gold again because it is here and he knows how to find it and where to find it.'

He paused, and Helen, though with no great show of interest and no slightest indication of being impressed, waited for him to go on.

'The fault in what has occurred is less his than mine. Knowing the sort Sanchia Murray is, I should not have given her the opportunity that day of a long talk alone with him. But,' his meaning was plain as he caught and held her eye, 'I was in the mood to forget Sanchia Murray and Professor Longstreet and every one else but the girl I was with.'

Helen laughed lightly, again passing the remark by as a mere compliment of the negligible order.

'Don't do that, Helen,' he said gravely. She saw that a new sort of sternness had entered into his manner. 'I have been working, working hard not alone for myself but for you. Desert Valley has always been to me the one spot in the world; you saw it and loved it, and since then there is no money that would buy it from me. If it were really mine! And I have been working night and day to make it mine. So that some day—'

She was not ready for this, and, though her colour warmed, she interrupted swiftly:

'You speak as though there were danger of losing it.'

He explained, plunging into those matters which had absorbed his mind during so many hard hours, telling her how he had paid Carr twelve thousand and five hundred dollars when he had expected to pay only ten thousand, how he had been obliged to ride to San Juan for money, of his success with Engle, of his plans for sales, of cutting down his force of men; all that he had done and all that he hoped to do. She caught something of the spirit of the endeavour and leaned forward tense and listening.

'But surely Mr. Carr, being your best friend, would not have driven you like this?'

Howard did not answer directly. This hesitation, being unusual in him, caught Helen's attention.

'I imagine John needed the money,' he said quietly. 'I didn't say anything to him about being short of cash. By the way, while in San Juan I got this for you. I thought you'd like it.'

He unwrapped the bundle. In it were a beautiful Spanish bit, richly silvered and with headstall and reins of cunningly plaited rawhide, and a pair of dainty spurs which winked gaily in the sunshine. Helen's eyes sparkled as she put out her hand for them. Her rush of thanks he turned aside by saying hastily:

'I've got the little horse to go with them. I'd like mighty well to give him to you. I don't know whether you can accept yet, but I'm rounding up a lot of horses and when we get a rope on Danny I'm going to lend him to you. To keep indefinitely, as long as you'll have him.'

Long ago Helen's fancies had been ensnared by the big picturesque ranch; long ago her heart had gone out to a fine saddle horse. No longer did she seek to hold her interest in check; she asked him quick questions about everything that he had overlooked telling her and exclaimed with delighted anticipation when he suggested that she and her father ride down and watch at the round-up. He'd have Danny ready for her and would have ridden him enough to remind him that his long frisky vacation was at an end.

They were very close together and very happy just then, when a laughing voice broke in upon their dreamings.

'Isn't he the most adorable lover in the world? But look out for him, my dear child. He nearly broke my heart once. Hello, Al! Sorry I couldn't come up with you. But, you see, I followed as dose as I could!'

They had not heard Sanchia's horse, and Sanchia had drawn her own deduction from the fact. Helen stiffened perceptibly, drawing slowly back. Howard's face reddened to his anger.

CHAPTER XXII

THE PROFESSOR DICTATES

Sanchia was cool and bright and merry. She sat flicking at her gleaming boot with her whip, and laughing. Helen, who had stood very close to a great happiness, now shivered as though the day had turned cloudy and cold. But she was still Helen Longstreet, her pride an essential portion of the fibre of her being. Because she was hurt, because suddenly she hated Sanchia Murray with a hatred which seemed to sear her heart like a hot iron, she commanded her smile and hid all traces of agitation and spoke with serene indifference.

'Mr. Howard was telling me of the work on the ranch. Isn't it interesting?'

'So interesting,' laughed Sanchia, 'that no doubt the heartless vagabond forgot to mention that he had just left me and that I had sent word by him that I was coming?'

'I don't believe you did say anything about it, did you?' Helen's level regard was for Howard now; the red of anger still flared under his tan and looked as much like guilt as anything else. 'Although,' and again she glanced carelessly toward the trim form on the white mare's back, 'we were speaking of you only a moment ago.'

If Sanchia understood that nothing complimentary had been spoken of her she kept the knowledge her own.

'We just had a little visit together in the mining-camp,' she said, veiling the look she bestowed upon Howard so that one might make anything he pleased of it. 'Alan knows he'd better always run in and see me first when he's been away for ten days at a stretch; don't you, Boy?'

For Howard the moment was nothing less than a section of purgatory. He was no fine hand to deal with women; he stood utterly amazed at Sanchia's words and Sanchia's attitude. He had not learned the trick of saying to a woman, 'You lie.' He had a confused sort of impression that the two girls were merely and lightly teasing him. But having eyes that were keen and a brain which, though a plain-dealing man's, was quick, he understood that somehow there was a stern seriousness under all of this seeming banter. Single-purposed he turned to Helen; bluntly he intended to tell how he had seen Sanchia and how he had left her.

But Helen's quick perception grasped his purpose, and in an anger which included him as well as herself with Sanchia, she wanted no explanations. It was enough for her that he had seen Sanchia Murray first; that he had come direct from her. She left the new bridle and spurs lying on the ground, passed swiftly by him and as she walked on said carelessly:

'If you both will excuse me a moment I must run into the house. I have something to do before papa comes in.'

Sanchia's face glowed triumphantly, and her triumph was clearly one of sheer malevolence. Howard lifted his face to hers, letting her read his blazing wrath. She only shrugged her shoulders.

'I wish to God you were a man!' was all that he said.

'I don't,' she rejoined coolly. 'It's a whole lot more fun being a woman. Men are such fools.'

She saw a tremor shake him from head to foot. He came a

Jackson Gregory

quick step toward her, even laid a tense hand on her horse's mane as involuntarily his other hand was lifted; for the instant a wild fear thrilled through her. She thought that he was going to drag her from the saddle; she had driven him hard, perhaps too hard. But she saw beyond him Helen hurrying down the trail, she saw even that Helen was turning to glance back. Resourceful in a crisis had Sanchia Murray always been; resourceful now. She leaned forward, and, for Helen to see, patted the rigid hand on her horse's neck. She laughed again as she saw that Helen was almost running now; she could fancy that she had heard a gasp catch in the girl's throat.

'You'll keep your hands off my affairs, Mr. Alan Howard,' she said evenly. 'Or I'll spoil every dream of your life.'

He held back his answer, his throat working. He saw the forsaken spurs and bridle near the bower which John Carr had constructed; he saw the sunlight and shadow across the trail down which Helen had vanished. Then, his own spurs clanking to his long strides, he too went down the trail, his back and shoulders to Sanchia, stiff and belligerent.

Helen was in the cabin, the door closed. He called, and she did not answer. He could hear her within, rummaging about, evidently very busy with something or other; had it not been for the little snatch of song which came out to him he could have thought that she was in the grip of a frenzy no less than that riding him. He rapped on the door and called again.

'Is that you, papa?' Helen's song was suspended briefly.

'No,' answered Howard. 'Won't you let me have a word with you?'

'I'd love to,' she rejoined. 'But I'm terribly busy just now. I'll be out in a minute.' And again he heard her humming and stirring about.

He tried to open the door. It was locked. He turned away and sat down on the doorstep.

'I'll wait here,' he told her. 'I'll wait all day and all night if I have to.'

But there is nothing harder than an indefinite waiting. He saw that Sanchia still sat upon her white mare where he had left her, that her head was bent, and she seemed to be in a profound study. Now and then he heard Helen; she appeared to be re-arranging their scant furnishings. Ten minutes passed. He called softly:

'Aren't you coming out, Helen?'

'Presently.' By now Helen had commanded and subdued her agitation entirely to her own satisfaction. 'I know it seems rude, but I simply *must* get a few things done.'

'What sort of things? Can't I help you?'

'Help?' She laughed. 'Men are such funny animals when it is a matter of helping indoors.

Sanchia had just said men were such fools. Well, come right down to it, he was rather inclined to accept the statement as largely true. And women were so utterly beyond comprehension.

'Anyway, can't I just come in and watch you?'

He wondered why she should seem so highly amused.

'In this little house you always seem about seven feet tall,' she laughed at him. 'You'd be terribly in my way. And you haven't waited half a day yet, let alone all night.'

He saw that Sanchia had suddenly lifted her head and had jerked her horse about in the trail. But she was not riding this way. She had turned toward the cliffs and was waving her hand. Then he saw Longstreet, grotesque in the various bits of Western accoutrement which he had incorporated into his wardrobe, humorously militant as to swinging revolver, miner's pick in hand, high-booted and red-shirted.

'Your father is coming,' he offered. 'That Murray woman is going to meet him.'

Helen had paused in her activities. But he could not guess how her expression had changed. 'That Murray woman,' as he spoke the words, did sound convincing. Still she did not come out. She knew that it would be a full ten minutes before Longstreet would make his way down the steep slope and come to the cabin. She resumed her occupation and remembered to accompany it with her tantalizing bit of song. Howard began to hate that air whole-heartedly.

The longest day has its end, the longest ten minutes fall something short of an eternity. At length, walking side by side, leading the white mare and chatting gaily, Longstreet and Sanchia approached the house. Longstreet saw Howard and put out a friendly hand.

'Glad to see you, my boy,' he called warmly. 'Helen and I have talked of you every day; we've missed you like the very mischief. Where is Helen, by the way?'

'Inside,' Howard told him sombrely. 'Changing things around and making them all over.'

Helen opened the door. Howard wondered how she had found the time to lay aside her hat, give a new effect to her hair and pin on those field flowers. Her cheeks were only delicately flushed, her eyes were filled with dancing lights.

'Back again, pops?' She appeared to see only her father, though Howard still had a foot on the step and Sanchia was fluttering close at his elbow. 'And no new gold mine to-day!' It was quite as though a gold mine were virtually an everyday occurrence.

She patted his dusty shoulder.

'No,' said Longstreet lightly. 'No new mine to-day, my dear. But I'm right; I'm getting all the signs I want and expected. To-morrow or maybe the next day, we'll have it. I know right where it is. Take the trail by—'

'Papa,' said Helen hastily and a trifle impatiently, 'can't you ever learn, even after you have been bitten? If you do stumble on anything, I should think you would remember and not talk about it.'

'But, my dear,' he expostulated, 'we are among friends.'

'Are we?' Helen demanded coolly. 'We were among the same friends before.'

Longstreet looked frankly displeased, vaguely distressed. Sanchia was listening eagerly, her eyes stony in their covetousness. Howard, staring only at Helen, had hardly heard.

'Well, well,' said Longstreet. 'I haven't found anything, so that's all there is to to-day's tale, anyway.' He got his first view of the cabin's interior. 'What in the world has happened in there?' he demanded, in amazement.

'Nothing,' answered Helen. 'I'm just packing; that's all.'

'Packing, my dear? Packing what? And, pray, with what intention?'

'Packing everything, of course. And with the intention of travelling.'

Longstreet looked perplexed. He turned to both Howard and Sanchia as though he suspected that they must share the secret.

'If you'll come in, pops,' Helen informed him, 'we'll arrange for everything. I wanted to get the worst of it done before you came, as you're so frightfully upsetting when there's anything like this to be done. Mr. Howard and Mrs. Murray,' she added, explaining sweetly, 'just ran in for a minute's call. They are both in a hurry, and we had better not detain them.'

Howard flushed. But his jaw muscles only bulged, and he did not withdraw his foot from the doorstep. Sanchia bestowed upon the girl a long searching look; it may have suggested itself to Sanchia's open mind at that instant that Helen was likely to prove a more troublesome factor than she had counted on.

'If you don't mind,' Howard said with slow stubbornness, 'I'd like just a few words with you and Miss Helen. Mrs. Murray came alone, and no doubt would prefer to return alone.'

Sanchia's eyes flashed and she bit her lip. Then, though her words came quickly, they were smooth and quiet and had a note of bantering laughter in them.

'Dear me, we must all be tired and hungry like a lot of children who have played too hard! We'll be quarrelling in another moment. But I am not going to be so sensitive as to feel hurt and run off and cry; we are too good friends for that, as you've just said, Mr. Longstreet. And I did so want to ask you some questions; I sent right away for the books you told me of, and I am simply mad over them. And I got one of yours, too; the one on south-western desert formations. It is the most splendid thing I ever read. But it is so erudite, so technical in places. I was going to ask if you would explain certain parts of it to me?'

'Delighted to,' ejaculated Longstreet. His old beaming cheeriness enwrapped him like a rosy mist. 'Come in, come in. And you, too, Alan.'

They entered, Sanchia with a sidelong look at Helen, Howard grave and stubborn. Everything was in a state of confusion which Sanchia was quick to mark, while Howard saw nothing of it. He saw only Helen looking a far-off princess, cold and unapproachable. And only a few minutes ago she had been just a winsome girl who leaned toward him, whom he dared to hope he could gather up into his arms.

Helen's expression was one of set determination. She breathed quickly and deeply. Her anger rose that her two guests had overridden her expressed wish. She watched her father hand Sanchia a chair. She saw them sit down together at the table, Longstreet beginning to talk largely upon his hobby, Sanchia encouraging him with her sympathetic smile and her pertinent questions. It appeared that Sanchia had really read and understood and was interested.

'Papa,' said Helen quietly, though her voice shook a little, 'I suppose that a time for very plain talking has come. We will never get anywhere without it. I have shown Mrs. Murray as plainly as I could that I don't trust her and further that I do not like her. She should not come into my house. You should not ask her, if she has not enough pride to refuse your invitation. Do you want me to go? Or will you ask her to go?'

Longstreet had not expected this, and for a moment was utterly at a loss. He looked at his daughter in bewilderment; he turned from her to Howard and finally to Sanchia herself as though for help. His face was puckered up; he looked ridiculously as though he were on the verge of tears. Sanchia had the effrontery to pat his arm and whisper:

'Dear friend, that you should be distressed because of me.'

But she did not offer to go. She sat still again and watched and waited.

'I have begun packing for both of us,' Helen went on. 'You should come back home. If you refuse to go I shall have to go alone.'

To her amazement her father appeared suddenly relieved. He had never been parted from her for forty-eight hours consecutively since she could remember; he had never seemed competent to get through the day without her countless ministrations; he had leaned on her more than she on him; and yet the stupefying certainty was that now his face cleared and he actually smiled as he accepted her threat as a sensible solution of the problem.

'No doubt you are right, my dear,' he nodded vigorously. 'This is a wild sort of country after all; it is hard for a girl, bred as you have been. Perhaps if you went East it would be better. I could stay here; I'd find my mine very soon; I'd take some one in with me in order to raise a large sum of money immediately. And then, when I had builded a fine home and had everything ready for you, you'd come back to me!' He was carried away with his dream. He rubbed his hands together, and had he been playing poker you would have known he held nothing less than a royal flush. 'You always rise superior to the situation, my dear; always.'

But Helen's face would have indicated that the situation had mastered her. Her own eyes filled with vexation; she dashed the tears aside and her anger rose. Of all men in the world her father, with his gentle innocence, could at times be the most maddening. And, withdrawn a little behind her father, she saw Sanchia laughing into her handkerchief.

On the instant Helen had the clear vision to know that in this skirmish she was defeated. She had thought her father would follow her; she knew that she would not go without him. At least not yet. In a moment her anger would get the best of her; she went quickly to the door and outside. Howard came quickly behind her.

'Helen,' he said harshly, 'you've got to listen to me.'

'Well?' She whirled and confronted him, her body drawn up rigidly. 'What have you to say?'

'You mustn't leave like this. You must stay.'

'I am not going to leave,' she retorted. 'I am going to stay!'

'But,' he began, at sea once more, 'I thought—'

'Think what you please, Mr. Howard,' she told him hotly. 'But here's one thing you don't have to speculate upon. I am not going to leave my father in the hands of that Murray woman to do as she pleases with. She can have whatever I don't want,' and he knew she meant Alan Howard, 'but I am not going to give her the satisfaction of having all of the mines and horses in the world named after her.'

The last came out despite her; she could have bitten her tongue to hold back the words which came rushing forth with such vehemence. She did not know what had put that thought into her mind at this crisis; perhaps it had always been there. But it was this which had chief significance for Howard.

'I have a horse named Sanchia,' he said. 'The one I rode the first day I saw you. You think that I named it after her?'

'What if you did?' she demanded. 'Do you suppose that I care?'

'That horse,' he went on steadily, 'I bought a long time ago from Yellow Barbee. It was before I had so much as heard of Sanchia Murray. He named the beast.'

Helen's old familiar sniff was his answer. The matter, he was to know, was of no moment to her. But she knew otherwise, and looked at him swiftly hoping he had something else to say.

'You've got to stay here,' he continued gravely. 'And we both know it. I believe in your father and in his ultimate success. We must watch over him, we must see that Mrs. Murray does not worm his secret out of him again and steal what he finds. And you've got to know that when a man loves a girl as I love you, he is not going to tolerate any further interference from a lying, deceitful jade like that woman in there.'

Helen laughed her disbelief.

'I rode first of all to the place where your cabin used to stand,' he went on, his big hat crumpled in his hands. 'You had left, and I was afraid you had gone East. I rode into the mining-camp to get word of you. I saw Barbee; he said that Sanchia Murray knew where you had moved. I asked her. When she said she was coming up this way, I did not wait for her. She appears to have it in for me; she hates you for standing between her and your father. She knows that I love you, and—'

Longstreet was calling from the door,

'Helen, I want you and Howard to come back. We must talk everything over. Mrs. Murray has much to explain; she hates Jim Courtot and his crowd, she is working against them instead of with them. Be fair, young people; remember these words,' he paused, lifted his hand oratorically and then made his statement with an unusually deep gravity,—'Every one, though appearing guilty, must be given an opportunity to prove himself innocent. That's it and that's fair: *the opportunity to prove his innocence*.' He emphasized the words in repeating them. 'That's all that I ask now. Please let's talk things over.'

Helen returned slowly to the cabin.

'I must go back,' she said to Howard. 'After all, I must keep my head and watch over papa every minute while she is with him.'

'May I come in, too?' he asked gently.

'Won't you believe me, Helen? And won't you let me help you?'

She hesitated. Then she turned her head so that he could see her eyes.

'I am apt to have my hands full,' she admitted. She even smiled a little. 'Maybe there *will* be work for both of us.'

But when he sought to come to her side, she ran on ahead of him. The face which she presented at the door for Sanchia's vision was radiant. Even Sanchia was at a loss for the amazing alteration. How these two could have come to an understanding in two minutes baffled her. But as Howard presented his own face at the door there was no misdoubting that he and Helen had travelled far along the road which she had thought to close to them.

'What in the world has happened?' Guarded as was the tongue of Sanchia Murray it was human after all.

Helen laughed merrily and gave her eyes for an instant to Howard's. Then, lightly, to Sanchia:

'We were just laughing over a story Alan was telling me. Yellow Barbee has a new girl.'

Sanchia understood, and her face went red. Howard merely knew that for the first time Helen had called him Alan. Of trifles is the world made.

CHAPTER XXIII

THE WILL-O'-THE-WISP

For the hour, if for no longer, the tables plainly were turned upon Sanchia. The high content which so abruptly had enveloped Helen and Howard was comparable to the old magic armour of the fairy tales which the fortunate prince found always at his time of need. Through it venomed glance and bitter tongue might not pass; as Sanchia's anger rose the two lovers looked into each other's eyes and laughed. Again Sanchia bit her lips and sat back.

'Dear old pops,' said Helen, going to her father's side and slipping both arms about his neck, ruffling his scant hair and otherwise making free with his passive person, thereby achieving the dual result of coming between him and Sanchia and giving a joyous outlet to a new emotion. 'I am not going to leave you, after all. And the West is the nicest country in the world, too. And Alan and I were wrong to run off and leave you as we did. We'll stay right with you now, and it will be so much jollier that way; won't it, Mrs. Murray?'

Longstreet patted her hand; Sanchia Murray measured her anew.

'And I too,' ran on Helen, 'must take more interest in your work, your books. Now that we live right on the spot where the things are, the strata and eroded canons and—and relics of monster upheavals and fossils of the Pliocene age and all that—it will be so much fun to study about them, all together. Alan thinks so, I'm sure. Don't you agree, Mrs. Murray?'

Helen's eyes were dancing, Longstreet imagined with newly inspired interest, Alan knew with the light of battle; Sanchia's eyes were angry. The girl had stated her plan of campaign as though in so many words. If time came when Longstreet had a second golden secret to tell, she meant to hear it and to have Alan hear it at least not an instant later than Mrs. Murray; thereafter, with odds two to one against the widow, they should see what they would see.

Sanchia did much thinking and little talking. She remained an hour. During the last half-hour she developed a slight but growingly insistent cough. Before she left she had drawn the desired query from Longstreet. Oh, hadn't he noticed before? It had been coming on her for a month. The doctors were alarmed for her—but she smiled bravely. They had even commanded that she move away from the dust and noise of a town; that she pitch a tent somewhere on the higher lands and live out-doors all of the time. Helen saw what was coming before the actual words were spoken. It was Longstreet who was finally led to extend the invitation! Why didn't she move into a tent near them? And with a look in which gratitude seemed blurred in a mist of tears, Sanchia accepted. She would move to-morrow and pitch her tent right up there near the spring.

'If you don't mind, Helen dear?' she said. 'Your little summer house by the spring may be sacred ground?'

Promptly Helen made her a present of it. All that she wanted were some things she had left there, a pair of spurs and a bridle; Sanchia was perfectly welcome to the rest.

They all went out together for Sanchia's horse. And Sanchia, accepting the altered battle-ground to which Helen's tactics had driven her, seeing that she was to have little opportunity of getting Longstreet off to herself, began a straight drive at her main objective. She laid an affectionate hand on his arm as though thrown upon that necessity by the irregularities of the trail in which she had stumbled, and turned the battery of her really very pretty eyes upon him. With her eyes she said, boldly yet timidly: 'You splendid man, you have touched my heart! You noble creature, you have made Sanchia Murray love you! Generous man, you have come to mean everything to a poor little woman who is lonely!'

It is much to be said in a glance, but Sanchia had never travelled so far on her chosen road of life if she had not learned, long ago, how to put into a look all that she did not feel. And she did not stop with the one look; again she appeared to stumble, again her eyelids fluttered upward, her glance melted into his; again she flashed sufficient message to redden Longstreet's cheeks and make his own eyes burn with embarrassment. And since it was obvious that henceforward the combat must be waged in the open, she did not await the unlikely opportunity of some distant tete-a-tete to emphasize her intention. Before she mounted she managed to allow the glowingly embarrassed man to hold her two hands; and she told him whisperingly:

'I would to God that you had come a few years earlier into the life of Sanchia Murray!' She sighed and squeezed his hands. Then she smiled a wan little smile. 'You have come to mean so much, oh, so much, in my poor little lonely existence.'

She mounted and rode away, waving her farewell, looking only at Longstreet. They all saw how, before she reached the bend in the trail, her handkerchief went to her eyes. Longstreet appeared genuinely worried.

'I am sorry for that little woman,' he said thoughtfully.

'She's making love at you, papa,' laughed Helen, as though the matter were of no moment but delightfully ridiculous. 'Fancy Sanchia Murray falling in love with dear old pops!'

He looked at her severely.

'You should not speak lightly of such matters, my dear,' he chided her. 'Mind you, I am not admitting that there is any ground for such a suspicion as you express.'

'But if there were ground for it?'

'Is there any reason why a pretty woman should not fall in love?' he asked her stiffly. 'Further, is your father such a man that no woman could care for him?' He stalked away.

Helen gasped after him and was speechless.

In due course of time Howard recalled that there was a man named Roberts, a teamster in Sanchia's Town; and that on the Desert Valley ranch there were mules which should be sold; and that, though there was a golden paradise here in Bear Valley, there remained a workaday world outside the charmed confines where time was of the essence. He made Helen understand that if he were to make good in his acquisition of the cattle range he must be down there among his men and his herds during every working hour of the day, but that the nights were his own. He was to come up every night that it was possible. She was to guard her father from Sanchia during the days; he was to seek to be on hand if ever the golden news broke again; they two were to check the adventuress' move. And Helen was to keep the spurs and bridle; she was to take Danny not as a loan but as a gift, of which only they were to know; she was to induce her father to ride down to the lower valley to watch the round-up. Then, lingeringly and with many a backward look, Alan Howard went on his way.

He found his man and, while Howard sat sideways in the saddle and Roberts whittled at a stick, they drove their bargain. The mules were sold for two thousand dollars, if they were as Roberts remembered them and as Howard represented them; Roberts would ride down the next day for them and would pay six hundred dollars as the first payment and thereafter not less than two hundred a month. Howard was satisfied. He would have a little more cash for running expenses or for the purchase of more stock if he could find another chance like that when he had bought the calves from Tony Vaca in French Valley.

The week rolled by, bursting with details requiring quick attention. Danny was found, roped, saddled and bridled. Longstreet rode him, delighting in the pony's high spirits, more delighted to see how he 'came around.' Gentled sufficiently and reminded that he was no longer a free agent to fling up his heels at the wind and race recklessly where he would, but that he was man's friend and servant, Danny was presented to Helen. He ate sugar that she gave him; he returned bit by bit the impulsive love which she granted him outright. In his new trappings, to which Howard had added a saddle from his own stables, Danny accepted his new honours like a thoroughbred.

Helen rode him the day she and her father came down from the hills for the round-up. Longstreet out-Romaned the Romans: his spurs were the biggest, his yell when he circled a herd was the most piercing, his borrowed chaps struck the eye from afar; his hat was a Stetson and amazingly tall. Now and then, when his horse swerved sharply to head off a racing steer, he came near falling. Once he did fall and rolled wildly through the dust of a corral; but he only continued his occupation with the more vim and was heard to shout over and over: 'It's the life, boys! It's the life!'

Helen, often riding at Howard's side, saw how the herds were brought down from the hills; how they were counted and graded; how the select were driven into the fattest pasture lands. She watched the branding of those few head that had escaped other round-ups. At first she cringed back as she saw the hot iron and the smoke rising from the hides and smelled the scorching hair and flesh. But she came to understand the necessity and further she saw that little pain was inflicted, that the victims though they struggled and bellowed were soon grazing quietly with their fellows. And at last the time had come when she had learned to ride. That was the supreme joy of the moment.

To Howard, no less, was it a joy. He watched her race, with whip whirling over her head, to cut off the lunging attempt at escape made over and over by the wilder cattle; he saw that with every hour her seat in the saddle became more secure; he read that she was not afraid. He looked forward to long rides, just the two of them, across the billowing sweep of Desert Valley, in the golden time when the title rested secure with them, in the time when at last all dreams came true.

Of any world outside their own happy valley they knew little. Sanchia had pitched her tent near the Longstreet camp, but these days she was left very much to herself. They did not pass through Sanchia's Town on their way back and forth and knew and cared nothing of its activities. The Longstreets, keenly interested in all that went forward on the ranch, were persuaded to accept Howard's hospitality for three days and nights. They rode early and late; there were the brief before-bedtime talks together; Helen saw the bluebird feather and laughed about it; she claimed it, but was in the end, after a deal of bantering argument, content to leave it where it was. She allowed Howard to talk what she branded as foolishness about certain alterations in the old house which he prophesied would be necessary before long; she grew into the custom of speaking of the room which she had occupied on her first visit to the ranch as 'my room.' She was very happy and forgot that her father was a troublesome childlike parent who fancied that he knew how to discover gold mines. What did mere gold amount to, anyway?

Then came the drive. The pick of the herd were to be moved slowly down to San Juan. Howard had communicated with his former buyers, and they were eager for more of his stock and at the former price. He wanted Helen and her father to come with them. But Longstreet shook his head smilingly.

'I'm two-thirds cowboy now,' he chuckled. 'A few more days

of this and I'll be coming to you and asking for a job! It won't do, my boy. It won't do. Especially at a time like this. You make your drive and I'll make mine. And I'll bet you a new twenty-dollar hat that when you get back I'll have found gold again.'

So the Longstreets went back to Bear Valley and the drive began. Howard started his cattle moving at three o'clock the next morning. And almost from the beginning, although everything started auspiciously, he encountered hardship. At ten o'clock that morning he came upon a dead calf, its throat torn out as though by a ravening monster wolf; a section of the flesh seemed to have been removed by a sharp knife. That was nothing; to him it merely spelled Kish Taka, and Kish Taka was his friend and welcome. But as he rode on, reflecting, he read more in the omen. If Kish Taka were here, in the hills, then somewhere near by Jim Courtot had passed. Then shortly after noon he came upon what he knew must be the work of Jim Courtot. And he surmised with rising anger that recently Courtot had seen Sanchia and that again Courtot was Sanchia's right hand. Here was a little hollow; on two sides were steep banks. Along these banks lay four big steers, dead, a rifle bullet through each one. Already the buzzards were gathering.

Dave Terril came upon him and found him bending over one of the big stiffening bodies. Howard's face was white, the deadly hue of rage.

'Who done that for you, Al?' muttered Dave wonderingly.

'Jim Courtot!'

'Why don't you go get him, Al?'

'Why don't I?' said Howard dully.

Why did he not lay a fierce hand upon the wind that danced over the hills? It was no more elusive than Jim Courtot. Why did not Kish Taka, the eternally vigilant, come up with his prey? Nowhere in the world is there so baffling a quarry as a hunted man. Jim Courtot struck and vanished; he played the waiting game; he would give his right hand for Howard's death, his left hand for the Indian's. But in his heart, his visions his own, he was afraid.

Before they came to Sunderberg's Meadows, where it had been arranged that the herd was to pasture that night, they saw the wide-flung grey films of smoke. Accident or hatred had fired the dry grass; flames danced and sang their thin songs of burning destruction; the wide fields were already black. Howard had bought and paid for the pasture land; the loss was his, not Sunderberg's; Courtot, if Courtot it was, or perhaps Monte Devine or Ed True, had been before him. Sanchia's venom—for, be the hand of the agent whose it may, he recalled always the look in Sanchia's eyes and the threat from Sanchia's lips—seemed to travel with him and in front of him. His cattle browsed that night on a rocky, almost grassless ground, making the best of what poor shrub growths they could lay their dry tongues to. There was no water; the pools lay in the heart of a smouldering tract too hot to drive across.

When the cattle had rested, without waiting for full day Howard was forced to start them on and to make a wide swerve out of his intended direction to come soon to feed and water. Otherwise the drive would become a tremendous misfortune and loss. His cattle would lose weight rapidly under privation; they would when delivered in San Juan only vaguely resemble the choice herd he had promised; scrawny and jaded, under weight and wretched, their price would drop from the top to the bottom of the scale. He would make for the San Doran place; Doran, though no friend, would at least sell him hay; the figure would be high, since Doran, no man better, knew when the other man was down and in a ditch. But water and food must be had.

Howard, toward noon, rode ahead to Doran's house. Doran was out in front of his barn, breaking a team of colts, working one at the time with a steady old mare, and in a hot and unpleasant mood. He saw Howard and behind him the dust-clouds of an advancing herd.

'Got any hay?' demanded Howard.

'Two barns full,' said Doran.

'Sell me enough to take care of my cows? Sunderberg's pastures were burned out; I'm up against it for feed.'

'Can't,' said Doran. 'Guess I'm sold out already for all I can let go.'

Howard wondered who was buying up hay at this time and by the big barnful.

'A fellow came by here yesterday,' explained Doran, and took an option on my whole lot.' His shrewd eyes gleamed. 'And at my own figure, too! Which was four dollars the ton higher'n the market! That's going a few, ain't it?'

'Who was the man?' asked Howard.

'Fellow named Devine. Know him?'

Howard pondered swiftly. Then he demanded: 'Just an option? Mind saying how much cash you got, Doran?'

'Why, no. He said he was short of cash, but he slipped me twenty bucks to tie the option. I'm expecting him back to-morrow or next day to close the deal.'

Howard sought swiftly to explain what Devine's play was; it was his suspicion that the twenty dollars would be forfeited and that Doran's hay would remain in his barns a thousand years if he waited for Devine to come back for it. But Doran, though he seemed to reflect, was stubborn. He hadn't a bale to sell, and that was all there was of it. He even grinned behind

Howard's departing back.

The drive continued. Slowly the panting brutes were urged on; at every water-hole and every trail-side pasture they were rested. In the afternoon Howard found a rancher who could spare half a dozen bales of hay; they were promptly purchased, opened and thrown to the herd; to disappear instantly. That night camp was made on the upper courses of the Morales Creek. It was less than satisfactory; it was better than nothing.

Thus the journey into San Juan required twice the time Howard had counted upon. And when at last he and his men urged his lagging cattle to the fringes of the village, he knew that the herd was in no condition for an immediate delivery. He rode ahead and saw Engle at the bank; from Engle he rented the best pasture to be had at hand and bought hay; then, impatient at the enforced delay, he pitched camp and strove in a week to bring back his stock to something of its former condition.

Alone, he rode that night into San Juan, his eyes showing the rage which day after day had grown in his heart. His revolver loose in its holster he visited first the Casa Blanca, Crook Galloway's old place of sinister reputation. Some day he must meet Jim Courtot; might not that time have arrived? God knew he had waited long enough. But Jim Courtot was not to be found here; nor anywhere in San Juan, though Howard sought him out everywhere. No, men told him; they had not laid eyes upon Courtot since Howard had last sought him here.

Finally the delivery was made at the local stock pens; the cattle crowded through the narrow defile, were counted and weighed and paid for. The purchasing agent looked at Howard curiously.

'You had higher grade stuff last time,' he said. 'This bunch isn't in the same class with the other shipment.'

'Don't I know it?' Howard flared out at him, grown irritable here of late.

He took his cheque, banked it and left town, advancing his men a little money and telling them to cut their holiday short. Then he saddled his best horse and headed back for Desert Valley the shortest way. His expenses had been far heavier than they should have been; his receipts lower. He knew that look he would see in Sanchia's eyes when again they met; he prayed that the time might come when he could come close enough to Jim Courtot to read and answer his look. He thought of Kish Taka, and for the first time with anger; Kish Taka should keep his hands off.

CHAPTER XXIV

THE SHADOW

There was something awaiting Alan Howard at his ranch house that for a little at least made him forget Sanchia and Courtot and hard climbs ahead in the road he must travel. Tired as he was and dispirited when he got home late that night he went to bed glowing with content. At dawn he was in the saddle. The Longstreets, early risers as they had grown to be, had only finished breakfast when he came racing into Bear Valley, waving his hat to them and calling cheerily. A first frown came when he saw that Sanchia Murray was breakfasting with them, but the frown did not linger.

'Good morning, everybody,' he greeted them. Helen, sitting in the sun on the doorstep, got to her feet; her father came smiling out to shake hands; even Sanchia, pushing her plate back, rose. She looked at him searchingly, appearing to note and wonder at his gay mood.

'No, I won't light down and have coffee with you,' he laughed at the invitation. 'And I won't stop to eat, having devoured a day's rations before I hit the saddle. No, there's nothing you can do for me, Mr. Longstreet; there's nothing in the world I want.' Helen had given him her hand; he held it a little before he would let it free and looked straight down into her eyes and kept on laughing gaily as he declared with certain unmistakable boldness: 'Right now I've got every blessed thing in the wide world I want.'

Sanchia said sharply: 'You must have been unusually successful in your latest deal?'

'It's the next deal I'm thinking of,' he told her lightly, letting her have the words to ponder on if she liked. But he had scant time for Sanchia and his eyes came back to Helen. 'I've got to ride into the new camp to see Roberts,' he told her. 'He's seen my mules and is buying. How would an early ride suit you? And I'll show you how easy it is to collect six hundred dollars before most folks have had breakfast!'

'My, what a lot of money,' laughed Helen. 'Of course I'll come. You know where I keep Danny. If you'll saddle for me I'll get ready and be out in two minutes.'

When they rode away down the trail together, Longstreet was smiling, and Sanchia frowning after them.

'She even eats with you?' queried Howard.

'I just thank Heaven she hasn't brought her bed in yet,' answered Helen. 'She is as transparent as a piece of glass, and yet dear old pops lets her pile the wool over his eyes as thick as she pleases. I'm just giving her plenty of rope,' she added philosophically. 'Do that, and people always get tangled up first and then hang themselves next, don't they?'

'Give me plenty of rope!' he said eagerly. 'I'll just tie myself up, hand and foot, and give you the end of the rope to hold.'

She laughed at him, touched Danny with her new spurs and shot ahead.

'You're nearly dying to tell me some good news,' she said when he had come up with her again. 'Aren't you?'

'I want to show you a letter I got when I came in last night. But I'd just as soon think of handing it over to a whirlwind as to you at the rate you are going.'

They drew their horses down to a walk. From his pocket Howard took an envelope; from the envelope brought forth a long blue slip of paper, torn in two, and with a few words penned across the fragments in a big running scrawl. He held the two pieces together for her to read; by now the horses had stopped and, being old friends, were rubbing noses. Helen read:

'Dear old Al: It took me a few days to see straight. Instead of blocking your game, let me help whenever I can. Don't need this now; won't have it. Take your time, Al. Good luck and so long.

JOHN.'

'Turn it over!' cried Howard.

Helen obeyed, only then fully understanding. It was a cheque for twelve thousand five hundred dollars, signed by Alan Howard and payable to the order of John Carr. Again she looked at the brief note; it was dated, and the date was eight days old. Her face flushed suddenly; the colour deepened.

'He wrote that the day after I sent my telegram to him!' she cried breathlessly.

'Telegram?'

'Yes.' She hesitated, then ran on swiftly: 'When Mr. Carr left I let him think that maybe father and I would follow soon. I don't know that I had been exactly what you men call square with Mr. Carr. I wanted to be square with everyone. So I sent him a telegram, saying that we appreciated his generosity but that we would stay here.'

Howard studied the date on the fluttering paper and his mind ran back.

'You sent that wire the day after I came back last time!'

'And if I did?' She met his look serenely.

'You did so because you cared—'

But Helen laughed at him, and again Danny, touched with a sudden spur, shot ahead down the trail.

They clattered like runaway children into the crooked rocky street of Sanchia's Town. Had their thoughts been less busied with themselves and with a hint of a rosy future and with the bigness of the thing which John Carr had done for them, they would have marked long ago that here something was amiss. But it was only when they were fairly in the heart of the settlement that they stopped abruptly to stare at each other. Now there was no misunderstanding what had happened! Sanchia's Town, that had been a busy, humming human hive no longer ago than yesterday was this morning still, deserted, empty and dead. Those who had rushed hitherward seeking gold were gone; be the explanation where it might, shacks stood with doors flung wide; tents had been torn down, outworn articles discarded, dumped helter-skelter into the road. The atmosphere was like that of a circus grounds when the circus was moving on, only a few things left for the last crew to come for.

'It feels like a graveyard,' whispered Helen. 'What has happened?'

'The old story, I suppose.' He turned sideways in the saddle, looking about him for a sign of remaining life. 'It grew in the night; somehow it has pinched out; the bottom has dropped out of it. Nate Kemble of Quigley bought up two or three claims; I've a notion the rest were worthless. Anyway, like many another of its kind, Sanchia's Town was born, has lived and died like old Solomon Gundy.'

Helen's face was that of one in deep study.

'Papa was saying only day before yesterday,' she said

thoughtfully, 'that this was going to happen. He said that was why he hadn't taken the trouble to make a fight for his rights here. He said that Kemble had bought up all of the land that was worth anything; and that he, himself, had given Kemble the right tip. It begins to look as though papa knew, doesn't it?'

Howard nodded vigorously.

'He knows gold mines and he knows gold signs,' he said positively. 'I've felt that all along. But—'

'But,' she took the words out of his mouth, speaking hastily, 'he doesn't know the first thing about people; about a woman like Sanchia Murray. And now that he says he is going to locate his real mine and we are leaving him with her—'

'We mustn't be away too long,' he agreed.

'Look. There's some one down there at the lunch counter; at least there's a little smoke from the stovepipe. Shall we see who it is?'

It was love among the ruins. Or, in other words, Yellow Barbee leaning halfway across the lunch counter, toward the roguish-eyed, plump maid who leaned slowly toward him.

'Hello, Barbee,' called Alan. And when Barbee greeted him without enthusiasm, he asked: 'What's happened to the town?'

'Hit the slide,' said Barbee carelessly. 'Bottom fell through, I guess, and at the same time somebody started a scare about gold being found down toward Big Run. The fools,' he scoffed, 'piled out like crazy sheep. You can find the way they went by a trail of old tin cups and socks and such stuff dropped on the run.'

'Roberts, the teamster, has gone, I suppose?'

'He'll be back. Pet's old man is still packing his stuff and Roberts is going to haul it this afternoon. I'm sticking along, helping pack,' he grinned. Pet eyed him in high mock scorn.

'A lot of help you are,' she told him. Barbee laughed.

Howard and Helen were reining their horses about to leave when Barbee came out into the road and put a detaining hand upon Howard's horse's mane.

'Saw Jim Courtot last night, Al,' he said quietly.

'Here?' asked Howard quickly. So long had Courtot seemed the embodiment of all that was elusive that it came with something of a shock of surprise that any man had seen him.

'Yes,' Barbee nodded. 'He's trailing his luck with that Murray woman again. They're a bad outfit, Al; better keep your eye peeled.'

Howard did not smile at Barbee's reference to Sanchia. He hardly remarked it.

'Tell me about Courtot,' he commanded.

'Something's come over him,' said Barbee vaguely. 'He's different somehow, Al; and I can't just get him. If he ain't half crazy he ain't much more than half right. He's got a funny look in his eyes; he's as nervous as a cat; he jumps sideways if you move quick. Last night I thought he was going to break and run for cover at a little sound no man would pay any attention to,'

'What kind of a sound?'

'Just a fool dog barking! Well, so long, Al. I got to help Pet do her packing.' And winking his merry eye, Barbee turned back toward the lunch counter.

Howard and Helen rode again toward the hills. Across the girl's face a shadow had fallen. Howard wondered if it were there because the odd sadness of a forsaken town had tinged her spirit with its own weird melancholy; or if she had been disturbed by word of Jim Courtot. Barbee had spoken quietly, but Helen might have heard. They rode in silence until Sanchia's Town was lost behind a ridge. Then Helen asked steadily:

'Is there no way out for you and Jim Courtot but the way of violence?'

He sought to evade, saying lightly that it began to look as though he and Courtot could no more meet than could spring and autumn. But when she asked directly, 'What would happen if you did meet?' he answered bluntly. His mood was not quarrelsome this morning; he wanted no needless fight with any man. But if Jim Courtot stepped out into his trail and began shooting . . . Well, he left it to her, what would happen. Then he began to speak of Barbee and his new girl, of anything that offered itself to his mind as a lighter topic. But Helen was in no responsive mood. It seemed to her that a shadow had crept across the sky; that the warmth had gone out of the sunlight. A fear crept into her heart, and like many a baseless emotion grew into certainty, that if Alan Howard and Jim Courtot came face to face it would be Alan who fell. When she saw how straight and virile Howard sat in the saddle; when she marked how full of life and the sheer joy of life he was; when she read in his eyes something of his own dreams for the future; when then she saw the gun always bumping at his hips, she shivered as though cold. Her own senses grew sharpened; her fancies raced feverishly. From every boulder, from every bend in the trail, she feared to see the sinister face of Jim Courtot.

CHAPTER XXV

IN THE OPEN

There came that night a crisis. Half expected it had always been, and yet after the familiar fashion of supreme moments it burst upon them with the suddenness of an explosion. Howard and Helen were sitting silent upon the cabin doorstep, watching the first stars. In Sanchia's near-by tent a candle was burning; they could now and then see her shadow as she moved restlessly about. Longstreet had been out all day, prospecting.

The first intimation the two star-gazers had of any eventful happening was borne to them by Longstreet's voice, calling cheerily out of the darkness below the cliffs. His words were simply 'Hello, everybody!' but the whoop from afar was of a joy scarcely less than delirious. Sanchia ran out of her tent, toppling over her candle; both Helen and Howard sprang up.

'He has found it!' cried Helen. 'Look at that woman. She is like a spider.'

Longstreet came on down the trail jauntily. Sanchia, first to reach him, passed her arm through his and held resolutely to his side. As they came close and into the lamp-light from the cabin door their two faces hid nothing of their two emotions. Longstreet's was one of whole-hearted triumph; Sanchia's of shrewdness and determination.

'Now,' cried Longstreet ringingly, 'who says that I didn't know what I was talking about!' It was a challenge of the victor, not a mere question.

Before any other reply came Sanchia's answer.

'Dear friend,' she told him hurriedly, 'I always had faith in you. When others doubted, I was sure. And now I rejoice in your happiness as—'

'Papa!' warned Helen. She ran forward to him. 'Remember and be careful!'

Longstreet went into the cabin. The others followed him. Sanchia did not release his arm, though she saw and understood what lay in Helen's look and Howard's. The main issue had arrived and Sanchia meant to make the most of it.

Longstreet put down his short-handled pick. Howard noted the act and observed, though the impression at the time was relegated to the outer fringes of his concentrated thought, that the rough head of the instrument and even a portion of the handle looked rusty. Longstreet removed from his shoulders his canvas specimen-bag. Plainly, it was heavy; there were a number of samples in it, some as small as robins' eggs, one the size of a man's two fists. He was lifting the bag to dump its contents out upon the table when suddenly Howard pushed by Sanchia and snatched the thing from Longstreet's hands. Longstreet stared at him in astonishment; Sanchia caught at his coat.

'Just a minute,' said Howard hastily. Even Helen wondered as he turned and bolted out through the door and sped up the trail toward the spring. Longstreet looked from the departing figure to his daughter and then to Sanchia, frankly bewildered. Then all went to the door. In a moment, Howard returned, the bag hanging limp over his arm, his two hands filled with the fragments of rock which glistened in the lamp-light.

'I washed them off,' he said lightly. 'If there really is gold here we can see it better with all the loose dirt off, can't we?' He put them down on the table and stood back, watching Sanchia keenly.

The fine restraint which, in her many encounters with the unexpected, Sanchia had been trained so long and so well to maintain, was gone now in a flash. Her eyes shone; a rich colour flooded her face; she could not stop her involuntary action until she had literally thrown herself upon the bits of quartz, snatching them up. For they were streaked and seamed and pitted with gold, such ore as she had never seen. The avarice gleaming in her eyes for that one instant during which she was thrown off her guard was akin to a light of madness.

But she had herself in hand immediately; she was as one who had slipped slightly upon a polished floor but had caught herself gracefully from falling. She thrust the rock into Longstreet's hands; she smiled upon him; she made use of her old familiar gesture of laying her hand upon his arm, as she hardly more than whispered:

'Dear friend—and wonderful man—I am glad for your sake, so tremendously glad. For now you have vindicated yourself before the world. Now you have shown them all'—and in her flashing glance Sanchia managed to include both Alan and Helen sweepingly with an invisible horde whose bitter tongues had been as so many dogs yelping at the excellent Longstreet's heels—'now you have shown them all that you are the man I have always contended you were.' She crowded her smile fuller of what she sought to convey than even she had ever risked before as she murmured at the end, her tones dropping away like dying music: 'This is a happy hour in the life of Sanchia Murray!'

'There's truth there, if nowhere else,' cried Helen pointedly. 'Papa, if you have stumbled on a real gold mine at last, aren't you wise enough this time to keep still about it?'

'That word "stumbled," my dear,' Longstreet told her with great dignity, 'is extremely offensive to me at a moment like this. It is a word which you have employed in this same connexion before to-day, yet it is one to which I have always objected. In that sure progress which marks the path a scientific brain has followed, there are no chance steps. Surely my own daughter, after the evidence I have already given—'

'That isn't the point,' said Helen hurriedly. 'The only thing that counts now is that you mustn't go shouting of it from the housetops.'

'Am I shouting, my dear? Am I seeking the housetops?' His dignity swelled. Also, it was clearly read in his unusually mild eyes that Helen, in her excitement with her ill-chosen words, had hurt him. Sanchia Murray, for one, who was older and of wider worldly experience than Longstreet's other companions of the moment, and who surely knew as much of human nature, saw something else in his clouded look. It was an incipient but fast-growing stubbornness. Therefore Sanchia closed her lips and watched keenly for developments.

'There's a good old pops,' Helen cajoled. She slipped between him and Sanchia, sending Howard a meaning look. She made use of certain of the widow's own sort of weapon, putting her two round arms about her father's neck. Before he quite understood what was happening to him, she had managed to get him through the door which led to her room at the rear, and to close the door after them and set her back to it. Forthwith her cajolery was done with, and taking him by the two shoulders Helen looked severely into his wondering eyes.

She began speaking to him swiftly, but her voice lowered. She had marked how Sanchia had sought to follow, how Howard had put his hand on her arm and Sanchia had shown her teeth. The woman was in fighting mood, and Helen from the beginning was a little afraid of what she might succeed in doing.

'Papa,' she said, 'anyone can see what that woman is after. She robbed you once, and anyone can see that too. You are a dear old innocent thing and she is artful and deceitful. You are not safe for a minute in her hands; you must stay right in here until Mr. Howard and I can send her away.'

She felt Longstreet's body stiffen under her hands.

'If you mean, my dear, that your father is a mere child; that he cannot be trusted to know what is best; that you, a chit of a youngster, know more of human nature than does he, a man of years and experience; that—'

'Oh, dear!' cried Helen. 'You are wonderful, pops, in your way. You are the best papa in the world. But, after all, you are just a baby in the claws—or hands of a designing creature like that hideous Sanchia. And—'

'And, my dear,' maintained Longstreet belligerently, the stubbornness now rampant in his soul, 'you are mistaken, that is all. You and I disagree upon one point; you condemn Mrs. Murray outright, because of certain purely circumstantial evidence against her. That is the way of hot-headed youth. I, being mature, even-minded and clear-eyed, maintain that one accused must be given every opportunity to prove himself innocent. When you say that Mrs. Murray is untrustworthy—'

'I could *pinch* you!' cried Helen. 'If she robs you again I—I—' She could think of no threat of punishment sufficient unto the crime. Suddenly she pulled the door open. 'Come in here,' she called to Alan. And as he obeyed, leaving the baffled Sanchia without, Helen said swiftly: 'See if you can't talk reason into papa. I'll keep *her* out there.' And she in turn passed out, again closing the door.

'You little vixen!' Sanchia's cheeks were red with anger as, Helen's manoeuvre complete, the girl stood regarding her with defiant eyes. Sanchia's hands clenched and the resultant impression given forth by her whole demeanour was that upon occasion the little widow might be swept into such passionate rage that she was prone to resort to primal, physical violence. Helen, though her own cheeks burned, smiled loftily and made no answer.

From beyond the closed door came Alan's eager voice. Sanchia bent forward, straining her ears to hear; Helen, the light of battle flaring steadily higher in her eyes, began suddenly to sing, the same little broken snatches of song which not so long ago had irritated her impatient lover and which now confused the words spoken beyond the door and which made Sanchia furious.

'Stand aside,' commanded Sanchia. 'I am going in.'

Helen stood firm. Then she saw that Sanchia meant what she said. And, on the table near the discarded pick, she saw Longstreet's big revolver. She made a quick step forward, snatched it up in both hands and pointed it directly at Sanchia's heaving breast. Now the colour went out of Helen's face and it grew very white, while her eyes darkened.

'If you move a step toward that door,' she threatened, 'I am going to shoot!'

Sanchia sneered. Then she paused. And finally she laughed contemptuously.

'You little fool,' she whispered back, cautious that no syllable might enter the adjoining room. 'I don't need to go rushing in there, after all. And you know it. That stuff,' and she glanced briefly at the rock on the table, 'got into my blood for a second. I'll take my time now; and I'll get what I want.'

As they stood in silence, Helen making no answer, they heard what the men were saying.

'—just this if nothing more,' came the end of Howard's entreaty. 'Don't tell Sanchia.'

Promptly came the angry answer:

'Mind your own business, young man! And, until you are asked for advice, hold your tongue!' At the end of the command the door snapped open and Longstreet popped into the room.

Sanchia, her cool poise regained, made no step toward him but contented herself by a slow comprehensive and sympathetic smile. Howard came quickly to Helen, stooped to her and whispered:

'I can't do a thing with him. But come outside with me a second; I think I know what to do.'

She flung down the heavy gun and went with him. Ten paces from the cabin they stopped together.

'Did you glimpse the specimens before I ran out to the spring with them?' he asked sharply. She shook her head, her eyes round.

'Do you have any idea,' he hurried on, 'just where your father has been prospecting lately?'

'Yes, I went with him for a walk two or three times during the last week. He—'

But he interrupted.

'Has he shown any interest in a flat-topped hill about three miles back? Where there is a lot of red dirt? They call it Red Dirt Hill.'

'Yes!' Her tone quickened. 'That is why—'

They had no time for complete sentences.

'I saw the red dirt on his pick first; then on the rock. That is why I washed it off, hoping that she had not seen. It's more than a fair gamble, Helen, that your father's claim is on Red Hill.'

Her hand was on his arm now; she did not know, but through all other considerations to him this fact thrilled pleasurably. He put his own hand over hers.

'If Sanchia saw, too?'

'I don't think that she did. Nor am I half sure that it would mean anything to her. I know every foot of these hills; she doesn't. We'll go in now and see what we can do. If your father does give it away—well, then we'll play our hunch and try to beat her to it.'

But though they had been out so brief a time, already Sanchia met them at the door. Her eyes were on fire; her slight body seemed to dilate with a joy swelling in her heart; she looked the embodiment of all that was triumphant. Behind her, rubbing his two hands together, and looking like a wilful and victorious child, was Longstreet. Sanchia ran by them. In her hands, tight-clutched, was the finest specimen.

'You haven't told her, papa! Oh, you haven't told her!'

'And what if I have?' he snapped. 'Am I not a man grown that I am not to—'

Again no time for more than a broken sentence.

'Will you tell us?' demanded Howard.

'In due time,' came the cool rejoinder. 'When I am ready. I should have told you to-night, had you trusted to me. Now I shall not tell you a word about it until to-morrow.'

They knew that Sanchia was going for her horse. Here was no time for one to allow his way to be cluttered up with trifles.

Howard turned and ran to his own horse. They lost sight of him in the dark; they heard pounding hoofs as he raced after Sanchia and by her; they heard her scream out angrily at him as she was the first to grasp his purpose. And presently at the cabin door was Howard again, calling to Helen. She ran out. He was mounted and led two horses, her own and Sanchia's white mare.

'Hurry!' he called. 'We'll play my hunch and beat her to it yet.'

Helen understood and scrambled wildly into her own saddle. She heard Sanchia calling; she could even hear the woman running back toward them. Then her horse jumped under her, she clutched at the horn of her saddle to save herself from falling, and she and Howard were racing up trail, Sanchia's mare led after them, Sanchia's voice screaming behind them.

They skirted the base of the cliffs for half a mile. Then Howard turned Sanchia's horse loose, driving the animal down into a dark ravine where there would be no finding it in the night-time.

'It's only a chance,' he said, 'but then that's better than just sitting and sucking our thumbs. We take the up-trail here.'

They came out upon the tablelands above Bear Valley. There was better light here; the trail was less narrow and steep; they could look down and see the light in the cabin.

Later they were to know just what had been Sanchia Murray's quick reply to their move. And then they were to know, too, where Jim Courtot's hang-out had been during these last weeks in which he had seemed to vanish. Sanchia, with a golden labour before her, had promptly turned to her 'right hand.' On foot, since there was no other way, and running until she was breathless and spent, she hurried across the narrow valley, climbed the low hills at its eastern edge, and plunged down into the ravine which was the head of Dry Gulch. Up the farther side she clambered, again running, panting and sobbing with the exertion she put upon herself, until she came to another broken cliff-ridge. There she had stood calling. And, from a hidden hole in the rocks, giving entrance to a cave, like a wolf from its lair, there had come at her calling Jim Courtot.

CHAPTER XXVI

WHEN DAY DAWNED

Upon the flat top of Red Dirt Hill, Howard and Helen drove their stakes. Thereafter they made a little fire in the shelter of a tumble of boulders and camped throughout the night under the blazing desert stars. Were they right? Were they wrong? They did not know. In the darkness they could make out little of the face of the earth about them. Alan thought himself certain of one thing: that only near here could it be likely that Longstreet should have broken off fragments of stone with so plain a marking of red dirt on them. Helen merely knew that her father had more than once climbed up here, though she had laughed at him for seeking gold upon the exalted heights. To know anything beyond this meagre and unsatisfying data, they must await the dawn.

The hours passed and Sanchia Murray did not come. Before now, they estimated, she could have hurried here even though she came on foot; before now, had she thought of it and had the patience, she might have found Longstreet's horse. Yet she did not come. The fact made their uncertainty the greater. They had ample opportunity to ask themselves a hundred times if they had done the foolish thing in racing off here. Should they have held by Sanchia?

Toward morning it grew chill and they came closer together over their little brush fire. They spoke in lowered voices, and not always of Helen's father and of his gold. At times they spoke of themselves. To-morrow Helen might be mistress of a bonanza; to-morrow she might be, as she was to-night, a girl but briefly removed from pennilessness. As the stars waxed and began at last to wane and the sky brightened, as the still thin air grew colder at the first promises of another day, they discussed the matter quietly. And it seemed that this was not the only consideration in the world, nor yet even the chiefest. But—

'I can't come to you like a beggar-girl,' she whispered.

'If I lost everything I had—and I could not lose everything since I would go on loving you—would that make any difference, Helen?'

She hesitated. 'You know,' she said quietly at last.

So, when the pallid sky gave way to the rosy tints of the new day, they knew everything, being richly wise in the wisdom of youth. Even it was granted them to see the red earth about them and to know that Alan's surmise had led them aright. Just yonder in a little hollow to which the shadows clung longest, were the marks left by Longstreet's pick; there was a tiny pit in which he had toiled exposing a vein of rock from which he had chipped his samples; near the spot his location stake and notice. Promptly they removed their own stakes, taking claims on both sides of his.

'We were right!' called Alan triumphantly. 'But how about Sanchia? He told her and—'

'Look!' Helen caught his arm and pointed.

Upon a neighbouring hill, by air-line not over half a mile from their own, but almost twice that distance by the trail one must follow down and up the rugged slopes, were two figures. Clearly limned against the sky, they were like black outlines against a pink curtain.

'That is Sanchia!' Helen was positive. 'There is a man with her. It—Do you think—'

He did not know why she should think what he knew she did think; what he himself was thinking. It was altogether too far to distinguish one man from another. It might even be Longstreet himself. But he knew that she feared it was Jim Courtot, to whom naturally Sanchia would turn at a moment like this; and never from the first did he doubt that it was Courtot.

'It's some one of Sanchia's crowd,' he said with high assumption of carelessness. 'But here is what I can't understand! Your father told Sanchia; she has raced off and staked; and as sure as fate, they are on the wrong hill! Sanchia wouldn't make a blunder like that!'

Helen was frowning meditatively. She understood what Howard had in mind, and she, too, was perplexed.

'Do you know,' she cried suddenly, 'I think we have failed to do papa justice!'

'What do you mean?'

'He never said outright that he had told her; he merely let us think that he had. He never once said positively that he had faith in Sanchia; he just said, over and over, that one accused should be given a chance to prove his innocence! Now, supposing that he had led Sanchia to think that his mine was over yonder on that other hill? He would be risking nothing; and at the same time he would be giving her that chance. No,' and it was a very thoughtful Helen who spoke, 'I don't know that we have ever done dear old pops justice.'

They stood, silent, watching the growing day and the two motionless figures upon the other hill. Those figures, as the day brightened, began to move about; plainly they were searching quite as Alan and Helen had searched just now.

They were making assurance doubly sure, or seeking to do so. They disappeared briefly. Again they stood, side by side, in relief against the sky.

'That is Jim Courtot, I know it.' Helen's hands were tight-pressed against her breast in which a sudden tumult was stirring. All of yesterday's premonition swept back over her. 'You two will meet this time. And then—'

'Listen, Helen. I no longer want to meet Jim Courtot. I would be content to let him pass by me and go on his own way now. But if he does come this way, if at last we must meet— Well, my dear,' he sought to make his smile utterly reassuring, 'I have met Jim Courtot before.'

But her sudden fear, after the way of fear when there is an unfounded dread at the bottom of it, gripped her as it had never done before; she felt a terrified certainty that if the two men met it would be Alan who died. She began to tremble.

Far down in the hollow lying between Red Dirt Hill and the eminence whereon stood Sanchia and Courtot, they saw a man riding. He came into a clearing; had they not from the beginning suspected who it must be they would have known Longstreet from that distance, from his characteristic carriage in the saddle. No man ever rode like James Edward Longstreet. And Courtot and Sanchia had seen him.

He jogged along placidly. They could fancy him smiling contentedly. Helen and Howard watched him; he was coming toward them. They glanced swiftly across the ravine; there the two figures stood close together, evidently conversing earnestly. The sun was not yet up. Longstreet rode into a thickness of shadow and disappeared. In five minutes he came into sight again. Courtot and Sanchia had not stirred. But now, as though galvanized, they moved. Courtot leaped from his boulder and began hurrying down into the canon, seeking to come up with the man on the horse. Sanchia followed. Even at the distance, however, she seemed slack-footed, like one who, having played out the game, knows that it is defeat.

'Papa is coming this way!—Jim Courtot is following him—in ten minutes more—'

She did not finish. Howard put his arms about her and felt her body shaking.

'You do love me,' he whispered.

She jerked away from him. A new look was in her eyes.

'Alan Howard,' she said steadily, 'I love you. With my whole heart and soul! But our love can never come to anything unless you love me just exactly as I love you!'

'Don't you know—'

'You do not know what it has meant to me, your shooting those two men in papa's quarrel. But they lived and I have tried to forget it all. If they had died, then what?' Her eyes widened. 'If you and Courtot meet, what will happen? If he kills you, there is an end. If—if you kill him, there is an end! Call it what you please, if it is not murder, it is a man killing a man. And it is horrible!'

Mystified, he stared at her.

'What can I do?' he muttered. 'You would not have me run from him, Helen? You do not want me to turn coward like that?'

'If you kill him,' she told him, her face dead-white, 'I will never marry you. I will go away to-morrow. If you would promise me not to shoot him, I would marry you this minute.'

He looked down into the ravine trail. Longstreet was appreciably nearer. So was Courtot. Behind Sanchia lagged spiritlessly, seeming of a mind to stop and turn back. He looked at Helen; she had had no sleep, she was unstrung, nervous, distraught. He gnawed at his lip and looked again toward Courtot.

'If you love me!' pleaded Helen wildly.

'I love you,' he said grimly. 'That is all that counts.'

He waited until she looked away from him. Then silently he drew his gun from its holster; the thing was madness, but just now there was no sanity in the universe. He could not run; he must not kill Courtot. He dropped the gun behind him and with the heel of his boot thrust it away from him so that it fell into a fissure in the rock. He turned again to watch Courtot coming on.

The eerie light of uncertainty which is neither day nor night lay across the hills. It was utterly silent. Then, the rattle of stones below; horse and rider were so close that they could see Longstreet's upturned face. Courtot was close behind him; Courtot looked up and they could see his face.

'You must go, now,' whispered Helen. 'You have promised me.'

'I am keeping my promise,' he said sternly. 'But I am not going to run from him. You would hate me for being a coward, Helen.'

She looked at him, puzzled. Then she saw that the holster at his hip was empty.

'Oh,' cried Helen wildly, 'not that! You must kill him, Alan. I was mad with fear. I—'

Stopping the flow of her words there swept over her the paralyzing certainty that it was useless to batter against fate; that a man's destiny was not to be thrust aside by a woman's love. For out of the silence there burst a sound which to her quivering nerves was fraught with word of death; that sound which in countless human hearts presages a death before the dawn—the long, lugubrious howling of a dog. It seemed to her to burst out of the nothingness of the sky, to arise in the void of an unseen ghostly world where spirit voices foretold the onrush of destruction.

Jim Courtot was hurrying up the slope. They saw him stop dead in his tracks. He, too, seemed turned to stone by the sound. It came again, the terrible howling of a dog, nearer as though the creature sped across the hills on the wings of the quickening morning wind. Sanchia stopped and began to draw back. Longstreet came on unconcernedly.

A third time, and again nearer, came the strange baying. Courtot held where he was, balancing briefly. Then they heard him cry out, his voice strange and hoarse; he whirled about and began to run. He was going down the trail now, running as a man runs only from his death, stumbling, cursing, rising and plunging on.

'Look!' Howard's fingers had locked upon Helen's arm. 'It is Kish Taka!'

She looked. Behind them, outlined against the sky, were a strange pair. A great beast, head down, howling as it ran, that was bigger than a desert wolf, and close behind it, gaunt body doubled, speeding like an arrow, a naked man. They flashed across the open space and sped down the steep slope of the ravine where, in the shadows, they became mere ghost figures.

'It is Kish Taka!' said Howard a second time. 'And again Kish Taka has saved my life.'

Dazed, the girl did not yet understand. She shivered and drew close to her lover, stepping into his arms. He held her tight, and they turned their fascinated eyes below. The speed of Jim Courtot in the grip of his terror was great; but it looked like lingering leisure compared to the speed of Kish Taka and his great hungering dog. And, now, behind Kish Taka came a second dog, like the first; and behind it a second man, like Kish Taka.

If Jim Courtot remembered his revolver, it must have been to know that not long would that stand between him and the two rushing, slavering beasts and the two avenging Indians behind him. His one hope was his hidden cave with its small orifice and concealed exit. And Jim Courtot must have realized how small was his chance of coming to it.

They saw him plunge on. The light slowly increased. They saw how the dogs and men gained upon him. They lost sight of all down in the ravine among the shadows. They saw Courtot again, still in the lead but losing ground. They lost sight of him again. They heard a wild scream, a gun fired, the howl of a dog. Another scream, tortured and terrified. Then, in the passes of the hills, it was as still as death.

Longstreet, alone, had not seen all of this; the dogs had swept on, but to him, deep in his own thoughts, they were but dogs barking as dogs have a way of doing. Sanchia sat in a crumpled heap, her face in her hands. Longstreet's face was smiling when he came to where his daughter stood with her lover's arms tight about her.

'I gave that woman her chance, and she was not innocent,' he announced equably. 'I wanted to make sure, but I had my doubts of her, my dear. Do you know,' he went on brightly, as though he were but now making a fresh discovery of tremendous importance to the world, 'I am inclined to believe that she is entirely untrustworthy! I first began to suspect her when she appeared to be in love with me!' He came closer and patted Helen's hand; his kindly eyes, passing over the stakes of his claim, were gentle as he peered reminiscently across the dead departed years. 'Why, no woman ever did that except your mother, my dear!'

Printed in Great Britain by Butler & Tanner Ltd., Frome and London

Choose from Thousands of 1stWorldLibrary Classics By

A. M. Barnard
Ada Leverson
Adolphus William Ward
Aesop
Agatha Christie
Alexander Aaronsohn
Alexander Kielland
Alexandre Dumas
Alfred Gatty
Alfred Ollivant
Alice Duer Miller
Alice Turner Curtis
Alice Dunbar
Allen Chapman
Alleyne Ireland
Ambrose Bierce
Amelia E. Barr
Amory H. Bradford
Andrew Lang
Andrew McFarland Davis
Andy Adams
Angela Brazil
Anna Alice Chapin
Anna Sewell
Annie Besant
Annie Hamilton Donnell
Annie Payson Call
Annie Roe Carr
Annonaymous
Anton Chekhov
Archibald Lee Fletcher
Arnold Bennett
Arthur C. Benson
Arthur Conan Doyle
Arthur M. Winfield
Arthur Ransome
Arthur Schnitzler
Arthur Train
Atticus
B.H. Baden-Powell
B. M. Bower
B. C. Chatterjee
Baroness Emmuska Orczy
Baroness Orczy
Basil King
Bayard Taylor
Ben Macomber
Bertha Muzzy Bower
Bjornstjerne Bjornson

Booth Tarkington
Boyd Cable
Bram Stoker
C. Collodi
C. E. Orr
C. M. Ingleby
Carolyn Wells
Catherine Parr Traill
Charles A. Eastman
Charles Amory Beach
Charles Dickens
Charles Dudley Warner
Charles Farrar Browne
Charles Ives
Charles Kingsley
Charles Klein
Charles Hanson Towne
Charles Lathrop Pack
Charles Romyn Dake
Charles Whibley
Charles Willing Beale
Charlotte M. Braeme
Charlotte M. Yonge
Charlotte Perkins Stetson
Clair W. Hayes
Clarence Day Jr.
Clarence E. Mulford
Clemence Housman
Confucius
Coningsby Dawson
Cornelis DeWitt Wilcox
Cyril Burleigh
D. H. Lawrence
Daniel Defoe
David Garnett
Dinah Craik
Don Carlos Janes
Donald Keyhoe
Dorothy Kilner
Dougan Clark
Douglas Fairbanks
E. Nesbit
E. P. Roe
E. Phillips Oppenheim
E. S. Brooks
Earl Barnes
Edgar Rice Burroughs
Edith Van Dyne
Edith Wharton

Edward Everett Hale
Edward J. O'Biren
Edward S. Ellis
Edwin L. Arnold
Eleanor Atkins
Eleanor Hallowell Abbott
Eliot Gregory
Elizabeth Gaskell
Elizabeth McCracken
Elizabeth Von Arnim
Ellem Key
Emerson Hough
Emilie F. Carlen
Emily Bronte
Emily Dickinson
Enid Bagnold
Enilor Macartney Lane
Erasmus W. Jones
Ernie Howard Pie
Ethel May Dell
Ethel Turner
Ethel Watts Mumford
Eugene Sue
Eugenie Foa
Eugene Wood
Eustace Hale Ball
Evelyn Everett-green
Everard Cotes
F. H. Cheley
F. J. Cross
F. Marion Crawford
Fannie E. Newberry
Federick Austin Ogg
Ferdinand Ossendowski
Fergus Hume
Florence A. Kilpatrick
Fremont B. Deering
Francis Bacon
Francis Darwin
Frances Hodgson Burnett
Frances Parkinson Keyes
Frank Gee Patchin
Frank Harris
Frank Jewett Mather
Frank L. Packard
Frank V. Webster
Frederic Stewart Isham
Frederick Trevor Hill
Frederick Winslow Taylor

Friedrich Kerst
Friedrich Nietzsche
Fyodor Dostoyevsky
G.A. Henty
G.K. Chesterton
Gabrielle E. Jackson
Garrett P. Serviss
Gaston Leroux
George A. Warren
George Ade
Geroge Bernard Shaw
George Cary Eggleston
George Durston
George Ebers
George Eliot
George Gissing
George MacDonald
George Meredith
George Orwell
George Sylvester Viereck
George Tucker
George W. Cable
George Wharton James
Gertrude Atherton
Gordon Casserly
Grace E. King
Grace Gallatin
Grace Greenwood
Grant Allen
Guillermo A. Sherwell
Gulielma Zollinger
Gustav Flaubert
H. A. Cody
H. B. Irving
H.C. Bailey
H. G. Wells
H. H. Munro
H. Irving Hancock
H. R. Naylor
H. Rider Haggard
H. W. C. Davis
Haldeman Julius
Hall Caine
Hamilton Wright Mabie
Hans Christian Andersen
Harold Avery
Harold McGrath
Harriet Beecher Stowe
Harry Castlemon
Harry Coghill
Harry Houidini

Hayden Carruth
Helent Hunt Jackson
Helen Nicolay
Hendrik Conscience
Hendy David Thoreau
Henri Barbusse
Henrik Ibsen
Henry Adams
Henry Ford
Henry Frost
Henry James
Henry Jones Ford
Henry Seton Merriman
Henry W Longfellow
Herbert A. Giles
Herbert Carter
Herbert N. Casson
Herman Hesse
Hildegard G. Frey
Homer
Honore De Balzac
Horace B. Day
Horace Walpole
Horatio Alger Jr.
Howard Pyle
Howard R. Garis
Hugh Lofting
Hugh Walpole
Humphry Ward
Ian Maclaren
Inez Haynes Gillmore
Irving Bacheller
Isabel Cecilia Williams
Isabel Hornibrook
Israel Abrahams
Ivan Turgenev
J.G.Austin
J. Henri Fabre
J. M. Barrie
J. M. Walsh
J. Macdonald Oxley
J. R. Miller
J. S. Fletcher
J. S. Knowles
J. Storer Clouston
J. W. Duffield
Jack London
Jacob Abbott
James Allen
James Andrews
James Baldwin

James Branch Cabell
James DeMille
James Joyce
James Lane Allen
James Lane Allen
James Oliver Curwood
James Oppenheim
James Otis
James R. Driscoll
Jane Abbott
Jane Austen
Jane L. Stewart
Janet Aldridge
Jens Peter Jacobsen
Jerome K. Jerome
Jessie Graham Flower
John Buchan
John Burroughs
John Cournos
John F. Kennedy
John Gay
John Glasworthy
John Habberton
John Joy Bell
John Kendrick Bangs
John Milton
John Philip Sousa
John Taintor Foote
Jonas Lauritz Idemil Lie
Jonathan Swift
Joseph A. Altsheler
Joseph Carey
Joseph Conrad
Joseph E. Badger Jr
Joseph Hergesheimer
Joseph Jacobs
Jules Vernes
Julian Hawthrone
Julie A Lippmann
Justin Huntly McCarthy
Kakuzo Okakura
Karle Wilson Baker
Kate Chopin
Kenneth Grahame
Kenneth McGaffey
Kate Langley Bosher
Kate Langley Bosher
Katherine Cecil Thurston
Katherine Stokes
L. A. Abbot
L. T. Meade

L. Frank Baum
Latta Griswold
Laura Dent Crane
Laura Lee Hope
Laurence Housman
Lawrence Beasley
Leo Tolstoy
Leonid Andreyev
Lewis Carroll
Lewis Sperry Chafer
Lilian Bell
Lloyd Osbourne
Louis Hughes
Louis Joseph Vance
Louis Tracy
Louisa May Alcott
Lucy Fitch Perkins
Lucy Maud Montgomery
Luther Benson
Lydia Miller Middleton
Lyndon Orr
M. Corvus
M. H. Adams
Margaret E. Sangster
Margret Howth
Margaret Vandercook
Margaret W. Hungerford
Margret Penrose
Maria Edgeworth
Maria Thompson Daviess
Mariano Azuela
Marion Polk Angellotti
Mark Overton
Mark Twain
Mary Austin
Mary Catherine Crowley
Mary Cole
Mary Hastings Bradley
Mary Roberts Rinehart
Mary Rowlandson
M. Wollstonecraft Shelley
Maud Lindsay
Max Beerbohm
Myra Kelly
Nathaniel Hawthrone
Nicolo Machiavelli
O. F. Walton
Oscar Wilde

Owen Johnson
P.G. Wodehouse
Paul and Mabel Thorne
Paul G. Tomlinson
Paul Severing
Percy Brebner
Percy Keese Fitzhugh
Peter B. Kyne
Plato
Quincy Allen
R. Derby Holmes
R. L. Stevenson
R. S. Ball
Rabindranath Tagore
Rahul Alvares
Ralph Bonehill
Ralph Henry Barbour
Ralph Victor
Ralph Waldo Emmerson
Rene Descartes
Ray Cummings
Rex Beach
Rex E. Beach
Richard Harding Davis
Richard Jefferies
Richard Le Gallienne
Robert Barr
Robert Frost
Robert Gordon Anderson
Robert L. Drake
Robert Lansing
Robert Lynd
Robert Michael Ballantyne
Robert W. Chambers
Rosa Nouchette Carey
Rudyard Kipling
Saint Augustine
Samuel B. Allison
Samuel Hopkins Adams
Sarah Bernhardt
Sarah C. Hallowell
Selma Lagerlof
Sherwood Anderson
Sigmund Freud
Standish O'Grady
Stanley Weyman
Stella Benson
Stella M. Francis

Stephen Crane
Stewart Edward White
Stijn Streuvels
Swami Abhedananda
Swami Parmananda
T. S. Ackland
T. S. Arthur
The Princess Der Ling
Thomas A. Janvier
Thomas A Kempis
Thomas Anderton
Thomas Bailey Aldrich
Thomas Bulfinch
Thomas De Quincey
Thomas Dixon
Thomas H. Huxley
Thomas Hardy
Thomas More
Thornton W. Burgess
U. S. Grant
Upton Sinclair
Valentine Williams
Various Authors
Vaughan Kester
Victor Appleton
Victor G. Durham
Victoria Cross
Virginia Woolf
Wadsworth Camp
Walter Camp
Walter Scott
Washington Irving
Wilbur Lawton
Wilkie Collins
Willa Cather
Willard F. Baker
William Dean Howells
William le Queux
W. Makepeace Thackeray
William W. Walter
William Shakespeare
Winston Churchill
Yei Theodora Ozaki
Yogi Ramacharaka
Young E. Allison
Zane Grey